Agape Means Love

Katherine Duke

In Honor of True Love: II John

Psalm 119:72

This book is a work of fiction and it is the product of the
authors imagination. It was written while the author lived
in Monteagle, TN and Tampa, FL.

Cover photo montage: Used by permission.

Bible quotations from King James 1611 version.

All references to literary works may be found on the World
Wide Web. Best efforts have been made to use only works in
the public domain.

Library of Congress Cataloging-in-Publication Data:
Requested.

Advice and consultation given by: Staff of Carrollwood Copy
Center and Printing, Inc. Tampa, FL.

ISBN: 9781438226620   (1438226620)

Published by: CreateSpace/Amazon.

Order from Amazon.com Cost:$20 plus tax.

Author contact information: 1006 West Bearss Avenue, Tampa,
FL 33613-1102 phone: 813-264-6736

e-mail:Donandkduke@verizon.net

Agape Means Love
Katherine Duke

Contents

Prologue

When TeJay came from lunch, the senior partner walked along the hallway and joined him in his office.

"You came here after college, TeJay, when you began law classes at night. Fifteen years and still not a partner brings us to a decision. Do you want a partnership or do you think about another law firm?"

"No thoughts about another firm, Rex, since I continue to bring in clients. What's on your mind?"

"We need assurance you stay and we keep these clients."

"You offer a partnership with a contract?"

"Maybe. You heard our unwritten requirement?"

"Yes, I know. Respectable family man with the right wife and does that mean a house in the suburbs?"

"Never seems like the right time to discuss our projections for the firm. We need some feed-back after you examine our partnership agreement."

The partner returned to the hallway and his office.

TeJay reached for his leather folder, and placed some working papers inside. Over lunch with a client, he used his lap-top with the back-up disk, which remained in the car. Computer off and lights out meant he left for the day. If needed, he carried his cell-phone.

After he entered the interstate ramp, he recognized his thirst. Tension demanded a candy bar and coke.

"Don't let anger cause you to take a swig of moonshine from a fruit jar," Claude advised. "Get some muscle work, even if you chop all the trees on the hillside."

Maude's response, "And, don't fill up with sugar either. It'll make you fat and ruin those teeth."

TeJay grew up with his grandparents, Claude and Maude, who lived up the hollow at the homestead house. His parents, Tip and Sarah Anna, reworked the big house over on the mail route. Sarah Anna taught school and Tip worked at the wind tunnel in Tullahoma, so the kids stayed with Claude and Maude while they worked.

At the next exit, he bought a pack of sugar-free gum and flavored bottled water. All five sticks went into his mouth before he understood his need to hit someone with words or a fist. "Control yourself old man," he self-talked and looked into the car mirror to see if he could smile. No smile. All the way home, he fussed and sang along with an AM station located on the brow of the mountain.

The interstate drive to his parents' farm in Cannon County took an hour. He drove his Porsche into the garage beneath the Loft, then went to the house to remove his tie and put on work clothes. The farm truck, parked beside the barn, started with a broken key left in the ignition. He drove the truck to the hill road, then turned off going up the hollow to the homestead. After opening a couple of livestock gates, he pulled up beside the limestone shelf rock with the spring flowing from underneath.

"Maude, Maude, I need you," he called aloud and in his imagination he saw his cataract blind grandmother open the screen door. Maude didn't speak, but the goats over the fence bleated an answer to his call that brought a shock of surprise.

He walked to the dark unpainted back porch and took the gourd dipper placed there for family use many years ago. First, he rinsed his hands in the cold water and splashed his face, before he swallowed.

From underneath the cabin he pulled out a push mower that Tip used for trimming. Exercise with sweat made the muscles of his torso ache and relaxed his emotions. Before he finished the mowing, he heard his Dad's truck on the hillside road. Like he thought, when Tip saw the gate open at the foot of the hill, he turned into the tractor ruts leading to the house.

"Hi, Dad, just finished some mowing and I'm putting your tools away."

TeJay moved to shake hands with his Dad.

"Thought it might be you when I noticed the gate unbuckled." Tip placed his arm across his son's shoulders and motioned to the swing on the porch. Long ago, Claude attached this swing to the rafters with heavy springs. Now with a steady to and fro movement, the swing bobbed to give emphasis to their talk.

"Guess, I need to tell you my situation. You encouraged my investment in the firm, when we discussed my becoming a partner. After lunch today, Rex came into my office. I brought in a new client this week, so I expected I might get a bonus with his thank you. Instead, he offered the partnership again with his threat that I need a wife."

Tip rubbed the stubble on his chin before he spoke. "If Claude asked you to stand on the chopping block and say your piece, what answer would you give?"

"One of his favorites because his words of wisdom kept me company when I pushed the mower. Your adoptive parents never gave up on your kids. Claude and Maude, never called grannie or poppa, yet the best grandparents for us four."

"Not a day goes by that I don't miss them. They left us this place and a heritage of memories. Your mother needs us for supper."

Often Tip seemed to change the subject, when he gave an answer. TeJay placed his hands to the back of his neck. Tip eased from the swing and walked to his truck. The warm motor spun when it started. He turned around crushing uncut yellow bittersweet weeds, then drove off toward home. TeJay understood Tip needed thinking time.

Before he finished the chore of putting the yard in order with the mower and tools in their places, he removed his undershirt. Again, he splashed his arms and face with the cold spring water, then wiped with the sweaty undershirt.

In the quiet eddy, he saw his reflection with no eyebrows. In first grade, the kid called Horse, called him pretty boy. When he ran, TeJay tripped him and rubbed his face in the dirt until he begged forgiveness. Horse and no others ever called him names.

Tip kept the edge of the spring clear with hauled-in gravel, even so TeJay searched for any movement by a copperhead. Bees hovered in the pink clover or landed on the wet silica clay before taking off to their hives placed near market-ready nursery stock. When he finished the put away, TeJay climbed into the farm truck and turned the broken key.

Quick and smooth, he thought as he drove to the hill road after he closed the cattle gates.

He parked the farm truck and climbed the back steps. The house seemed empty, so he went upstairs for a shower and clean clothes. When he returned to the kitchen, Sarah Anna asked him to set the table while she placed their food. Squash casserole, field peas, sliced tomatoes, cornbread, and sweet ice tea served with love she often said. Tip came from the deck and went to wash before they ate. TeJay felt the affirmation of his parents as they bowed their heads before he said thanks.

"Will you stay the night?"

"No, Mom, I work back-up for a fella in the hospital. I came home to get my bass fiddle. Dad, if you'll help me position it in the car. I planned this drive home, and in the process my emotions exploded."

"TeJay's bossman told him to get a wife. Our community question: Is that oldest boy of yours married yet? He still work down there in Nashville?"

"Mom, help me. Your eldest gets pushed to marriage."

"Your Mom's a jewel. I keep hoping you'll find a wife like her, and maybe that's your problem."

*   One   *

Hunched over the tall antique bass fiddle, TeJay stood
back in the shadows on the small carpet covered stage. When
the girl entered the side door of the Nashville Rodeo Steak
House, TeJay made eye contact. Even when he looked in
another direction, with his glance he kept seeking her face.

This girl chose a two person table edged to the wall.
No one joined her at the table, nor did she appear to be
waiting. Somehow, he felt drawn to her. TeJay never picked
up women. "Too many loose ends in this town and I'm a busy
man," he self-talked. His curiosity kept prodding and he
thought, Why? With this stranger, why this fascination?

"Who's Miss Magnolia Blossom?" he asked the guitar
player when their break came.

"She shares a room with Beatrice, the nurse and buddy of
Aubrey. They come often and he takes them home, I think."

TeJay moved behind a background screen away from the
walkway. His exercise included aerobic techniques to relax

the muscles in his arms. Do I speak to her or do I ignore
her? He moved his thumbs to his temples and smoothed the
wrinkles across his brow. With a quick movement, he thrust
away doubts.

"May I sit?" he asked and sat anyway without her
permission. Her look spoke no recognition except another
stranger. "I'm playing substitute for Aubrey tonight. I
guess you noticed. Heard you're his friend, so how is he?"

"Very weak. He might go live with his parents in
Atlanta."

"You come here often?"

"Most nights. Until I find a place to stay. I live
with Aubrey's buddy Beatrice who rents a studio apartment
equipped for one and my coming here or going to the mall
helps us share limited space with less stress. Either she
comes to pick me up or Aubrey gives me a lift home."

"How about my taking you home tonight?" TeJay talked
over the noise of the music makers who strummed with their
warm-up. Someone called from the stage, so he took his place
and continued his firm plunk of strings.

The dusky light enhanced her loveliness, and made him
want to see her beauty in daylight. She wore no jewels, but
her dress appeared like threads of black ribbon with a yoke
of jet-black beads extending to her neck like an attached

collar. He refused to stare, yet he observed her features
with intensity when he turned his eyes in her direction. The
phrase, she walks in beauty, seemed applicable.

By twelve, the crowd dispersed except for a few college
students. The owner locked the door and began his close out
for the night. TeJay held out his hand for the girl and
guided her toward the side door to his truck. Neither spoke
until he began his reverse from the parking slot near the
privacy fence.

"You need to tell me directions, Little One. Also,
what's your real name?"

"Cayrolynn. Cayrolynn Selaco, and I live out West End."

"My real name, Thomas Jr, gets shortened to TeJay, and I
play substitute for Aubrey until Saturday. How about my
bringing you home these nights and come Saturday night, I'll
buy you a real supper?"

"Really? You want to see me again?"

"Yes. All these traffic lights turn green, so we must
be near your corner."

"Two lights and I live the middle of the side street
after a right turn."

"Easy directions to follow."

TeJay parked parallel to the curb in front of the
restored house divided into apartments. The street light

gave brightness for safety, yet the quietness of mid-night led them to talk almost in a whisper.

"Are you from around here, Cayrolynn?"

"I came to Nashville about seven years ago after I finished high school. I grew up in a children's home in Alabama, but I call home my birthplace in Florida. And you, TeJay? Do you live here?"

"During the week, I'm here. My folks live in the country and that's where I grew up. I make my living in a law office, and often, I play substitute for some local band. Do you work, Cayrolynn?"

"Right now, I'm not working. I did work for an insurance company because my friend, Marthee from the children's home, worked there. She married Pitt and they moved to Gallatin."

Both watched a silver jeep inch down the street and park behind the truck. The person driving went into the house.

"That's my roommate, Beatrice, so maybe I should go inside now."

"Give me your number and I'll try to call you, otherwise, I'll see you tomorrow night."

TeJay wrote her number on the palm of his hand before he walked her to the door. He tousled her hair, said "Sweet Dreams, Miss Magnolia," then returned to his truck.

*   *   *

Thoughts of Cayrolynn drifted into and out of his thinking all day and this bothered him. He kept focused to each task and despised this nuisance to be thinking like a teenager with an intense emotion that didn't match his lifestyle. Before he left his office, he called her number, and received no answer.

Lack of sleep made him want to skip the substitute work. He ate a cheese sandwich, drank of glass of orange juice, and set the alarm for seven. In minutes, he slept. He fumbled for the alarm when it buzzed. His getting dressed followed the organized procedures taught by his Dad. Tip set methodical schedules for his sons to follow.

"Always, take the shower, even if only a rinse. Shave and wash off the facial shine. Use after shave. Remember clean underclothes, clean socks, and clean shirt." TeJay mumbled to himself and completed each task. He chose a black and white checked shirt with jeans worn last night. His getting ready took five minutes. He pulled on short boots, reached for his wallet and keys, before he straightened his wrinkled covers. "Dad would be proud of me," he self-talked.

His truck radio rendered news from NPR followed by a medley of music about September. He parked near the side door, entered the restaurant, and took the side table shared with Cayrolynn last night. These early minutes before the music, he drank coffee and tried to wake up.

Someone said remember everything, both the good and the bad. He remembered that before her marriage, Lexie, his sister, asked advice and questioned his love life.

"Will you ever marry, TeJay, because I never remember a girl friend for you except maybe, Mavis Davis?"

"When the right woman appears, I'll know. This old bachelor needs the right person and the right time."

"Andy became best friends with Glenda Rae-Ann in first grade, as for the rest of us, we never found a school mate steady. Marriage didn't happen awhile ago for us."

"I thought you held sweet crushes on William Robert Surles."

"Wildly Bert for me? Think again. Don't be surprised when you find the right one, TeJay. When Geeta became my roommate, she brought along her brother, the very best husband for me. Otherwise, I might be an unclaimed blessing, now hunting for a husband, or asking myself if I possess the gift of celibacy."

TeJay left his musing with the cold coffee and ice water, then took his place behind the tall double bass. Songs flowed from the Blue Ridge, Louisana, and Texas. He admired the woman vocalist who sang favorites called from the audience. Claude and Maude, his grandparents, sang these songs. Claude played a banjo, Maude a guitar, and he banged on a tin washtub with serving spoons.

*   *   *

Later, Cayrolynn took the chair where she sat last night, across from the place where he sat earlier. When their intermission came, he went to the table.

"I need a burger, well done, and a salad, how about you Cayrolynn? Same?" Cayrolynn nodded. A short break meant a fast supper.

"I thought about you, today. Tried to call you around six, but no answer. How's Aubrey?"

"No better, but Beatrice says, as soon as possible, his parents plan to move him home. I spent my day exploring for a place to live."

"Why did you move in with Beatrice?"

"I lived in a rented house with five other women. Each time someone moved, it left a space and we found another person. When we needed to sign a new lease, no one wanted legal responsibility. Beatrice suggested I stop over with her until something better showed up."

"So, you make plans?"

"Yes, I must find my own place. Beatrice puts no pressure. She understands my dilemma. The better classified ads come in the Sunday paper, so I try to follow each lead."

"Saturday night, I want to buy us dinner according to our plans, however we need some talking time to know each other better. Would you share a picnic with me and a ride down the Natchez Trace?"

"Sure. What time?"

"Nearer noon. I need a few minutes at the office, which I hope to cut short."

Cayrolynn watched TeJay step on stage. She felt intrigued by his keeping time with his feet. The fiddle player moved from his mike over to TeJay keeping identical pace and returned to play his lead, then back to TeJay with their identical foot measures.

Before close-up Beatrice came to eat, and collect Cayrolynn. TeJay watched and felt glad he made Saturday plans earlier because Cayrolynn left with Beatrice.

                    *   *   *

Saturday morning freedom, so Cayrolynn didn't move. She lay thinking about TeJay until Beatrice came home.

"I spent part of the night with Aubrey's parents at the hospital. All this anxiety and sorrow leaves me diminished. One day, someone will find a cure for HIV/AIDS, and I grieve it's not available now. What do you plan for today?"

"I'll depart so you can sleep. TeJay wants me to go

with him for a drive on the Natchez Trace. If our talk goes well, he plans dinner for us tonight. Otherwise, I think our friendship becomes a closed relationship."

"I pray mercy and grace for you, Cayrolynn. TeJay's one handsome man and he gives off good vibes. Blessings. You need to dress. Better hurry."

Beatrice went to sleep before Cayrolynn finished her shower and began her wait for TeJay.

*   *   *

Speed signs on the Trace caused slower travel and like a travelogue both talked with comments about the roadside and landscape. When their conversation reached a lull, TeJay put in a CD with bluegrass music and no vocals.

"You drive a car and a truck, TeJay?"

"The truck makes time at the farm easier. My commute in Nashville each day seems to go better with the car. Are you tired?"

"No, just interested."

After the state line, they continued to the Tennessee River where TeJay stopped at a wayside park with concrete picnic tables and attached benches.

"So, how far in miles did we travel to here?" Cayrolynn asked. "Maybe, a hundred or more?"

"About one hundred twenty-five, and did you become

bored?"

"Not really. You know, though, I'm ready for the deli provisions you brought along."

They sat eating in the warmth of early afternoon sunshine.

"I think we need to know more about each other, Cayrolynn. Unless you talked to someone who knows me, I'm a stranger. We take each other on trust, even so we need to know more. You, first, or me, doesn't matter."

"My Dad joined the Navy and came to Pensacola from Rhode Island. My Mother came from Alabama to get a job. My first memories come with living in a mobile home near East Bay in the Florida panhandle. At my age ten, my Mother asked a friend to take me to the children's home in Alabama because she fought cancer and faced death. Before that, she and my Dad separated and I can remember their screaming. She told my Dad to go back north and forget us."

"Was that fourth grade or fifth grade?"

"Fifth grade. In September, I went to the children's home."

"Did you know when your Mother died?"

"Yes. Lavender, a neighbor and friend, wrote me. My Mother liked to laugh. When I left that morning, she told me to find laughter, find joy, no sad songs."

"You said you don't work. Why?"

"Two reasons. My boss died. I felt so tired and sad. When I went to the doctor, she thought anemia or a fatigue factor. Now, I understand my problem is Fibromyalgia that appears as an intermittent muscle upheaval. I think I can avoid a day job, if I make enough money as a primitive artist. After my boss and mentor died, no one asked for my resignation. I went on disability because I felt so lost."

"I don't know Fibromyalgia."

"Beatrice works in my doctor's office that's a clinic. Her easy explanation says metabolic syndrome like diabetes that requires fresh air, exercise, and a healthy diet. Beatrice lacks beauty, yet she carries a tremendous soul and spirit. I'm thankful she offered to keep me until I'm ready to maneuver on my own again."

"I'm forty, Cayrolynn, and you seem very young."

"I'm twenty-five, TeJay, single and never married. Like most of my childhood playmates, I dreamed about a family and I loved to play dolls and make clothes for my Barbee. In the infinite plans and wisdom of a God I believe in, my life doesn't seem much. I trust my life means more than I can see or know."

Cayrolynn laughed. TeJay saw the laughter of her Mother and knew it wasn't foolishness. It became a way to fight evil when the way meant failure, and he recognized why he felt drawn to this girl. His Mother, Sarah Anna, lived her days taking care of little lost lambs. Now, he found himself following like his Mother's example with this woman.

"Interesting, you're forty."

"Yes, and you're twenty-five, but you look much younger, like a teenager. Your fresh beauty shines more than most women and I hope you'll be my friend."

When Cayrolynn laughed, again, he realized she thought he talked a line, so he continued.

"I grew up on a tree farm where we propagated nursery stock with trees and shrubs for landscape people. We still do. My Dad works at the wind tunnel or space center in Tullahoma and my Mother teaches first grade. I'm the oldest of four."

"How fortunate to have brothers and sisters. Sometimes, I would play like I had an identical twin."

"I began playing the guitar in seventh grade with my grandmother as my teacher. This man, who knew Uncle Dave Macon, started a local band and invited Claude, Maude, and me to join with him. My sister, Lexie, played the piano, and my brothers, Andy and Sam strummed along mostly on the ukulele. My playing made me money before I finished high school and continued during my college years at Murfreesboro."

"That's one of my inferiority feelings. No college," Cayrolynn said.

"Law school meant money and my brother, Andy, needed money for college and med school. With four of us and our college expenses, I recognized the financial load for my parents. So, I came to Nashville with my music and started law school part-time at the YMCA Law School."

"This means, you're a lawyer and play music, too."

"Yes. Many poor beginners come to Nashville; they grow with their music and become my clients, if they know me. I try to substitute back-up whenever I'm asked."

After they finished their meal and cleared the picnic table, TeJay brought two fold-away chairs from the back of his car. Rather than sit, they walked down to the boat ramp on the River and stood looking at the imperceptible movement of deep water.

*   *   *

In a bit, they walked back to the chairs and sought the shade beneath a hickory tree. Cayrolynn took a small book of sonnets from her purse. When her boss died, the contents of his desk went into the trash can. This treasured first edition, she retrieved. Right here, right now, she felt the joy of being beside TeJay. To ride in his Porsche, to eat lunch with this man she never knew; this present moment became a miracle because she seemed to know him, always.

The sun shifted so the ground became spotted with sunlight coming through the shade of the tree leaves. TeJay sat with closed eyes. Those darting all-seeing wise dark eyes caused her to look away across the wide expanse of the Tennessee River off to the left from this wayside park. Those odd eyebrows appeared like the bare brow of the no tree bluff across the river. His black hair, he pulled back into a short pony tail secured with a silver circle barrette not the usual elastic band.

"Stand still time," she thought. "Allow me to feel this moment, this indelible moment, forever."

Sun brown skin or even color from a sun lamp added to TeJay's appearance of authority. Cayrolynn remembered her Dad who turned scarlet in the Florida sun instead of brown and his face carried the red spider lines of an alcoholic made brighter with lack of the tanning sun.

Fear filled Cayrolynn that she couldn't be the person TeJay wanted her to be. He wanted a friend, but she lacked the family and education he possessed.

"Robert Browning found Elizabeth Barrett. Would God grant me such a blessing?" She thought and questioned as she watched TeJay.

She still held the book when a ground hog came sniffing.

She waved the book causing its flight and TeJay to sit straight.

"Two hours back to Nashville that means we arrive after dark. We should be ready for our dinner date by ten. Some friends of mine play good music at a supper club east of town tonight. So, fair maiden your knight and your chariot await your pleasure."

"And, fair maiden rejoins without a poetic response."

Both laughed.

*   Two   *

This Monday morning, TeJay dressed, made coffee, then went to collect his newspaper from the front door.

Shafe walked across from his condominium and called to TeJay when the door opened. "Mornin, ole man. Been lookin for you, so how's work and where do you keep yourself?"

"Come on in the house, and tell me what's happening, Shafe."

"Hope the smell of coffee means it's ready. We need to finish off our audit in Louisville, which keeps me busy until the first of the year, at least." Shafe became friends with TeJay when they shared a room during their college freshman year.

"I need to ask if I can stay in your condo while you work out of town. I met a girl, who looks for a place to stay, and if I offer her my guest room, then I need to ask a favor to occupy your guest room."

"Since you house sit for me, it's no problem. My

parents talk about Nashville and want to come with my aunt. When and for how long, they didn't say, but no matter. Plenty of space, as you know. Tell me about your friend."

"Young and pretty with a beauty more like Sarah Anna's than Lexie or Maude."

"Not from here?"

"From Alabama. Tell me about your parents and Vida."

"Sassy like always. How about yours?"

"Tip wants me home for a few days to help check the trees we plan to sell this year. He heard about a buyer from Denver, who collects for fall landscaping. This means we need to decide what takes the place of the rows we harvest."

"Spent my week-end with Vida and her folks. Vida starts a new job with the same company, but at a different location. Now, with her bonus, she makes more money than this CPA. She thinks an aunt from Delaware might move south to care for her parents. We spin a good plan and then, changes come and no wedding."

"She refuses to follow you around on your assignments, Shafe. No possibility for you to stay in one place or on a stable assignment, I guess."

"My assignments give me freedom, however if I married a wife, I wouldn't ask for the next slot in Switzerland."

"Does life pass us by without kids? I think about that.

We reach age forty. Do we choose our lifestyle, Shafe, or do
we allow circumstances to make the agenda?"

"Listen, TeJay, you talk serious too early in the
morning. You should take a plane and fly out to Hawaii for a
vacation and change of scenery. How do you say it, Lighten
Up, Ole Buddy."

"Correct, and I might just do that."

When he called Cayrolynn after lunch, no one answered.
At five, he left work early and went by her apartment.

"Hello, friend." Cayrolynn opened the door.

"Thought you might like some supper with me." TeJay
reached for her hand and they stood talking in the hallway
when Beatrice came home.

"Greetings, Beatrice. I came to ask Cayrolynn to eat
supper with me at a barbecue place out Belleview Road. Want
to join us?"

"You need to give us a few minutes, TeJay. Can you come
along, Beatrice?" Cayrolynn asked.

"Thanks and a good suggestion. My car needs some work,
so these days I borrow from Cayrolynn. When she moves out, I
hope I can buy from her, if she can manage without it."
Beatrice waited for TeJay's comment that he refrained from
giving. He walked out the door to his truck to wait because
studio apartments offered no room for stopping by.

"Ready now," Cayrolynn said when she climbed into the truck. She wore a tan cashmere sweater with khaki pants, so when she put on her navy jacket, TeJay recognized she dressed to look-a-like with him.

The truck stayed warm after his short drive from the office. Space for three people on the bench seat made for a tight squeeze, and TeJay felt the warmth of Cayrolynn beneath his arm when he shifted gears.

After work diners filled the restaurant, so they sat at a long middle table. However, with the brisk business, they waited for someone to bring silverware, water, and take their order.

"When did Aubrey's family take him home?" TeJay asked.

"We don't know because his sister came by yesterday to explain they rented a van so Aubrey could travel either lying down or sitting," Beatrice said.

"If his apartment becomes vacant, then can Cayrolynn live there?" TeJay asked.

"I shouldn't live there because of safety factors. Even with bars on the windows, lots of break-ins occur. Also, the apartment manager keeps a waiting list and Aubrey's apartment goes to the next person on the list."

"When the sister came," Beatrice said, "she asked me to close out the apartment. The family stayed there this past

week, so they took the furniture and possessions they wanted.
They paid the rent for one month and that completed the
lease. Aubrey left some items for friends. They can meet me
there for pick up, or I'll deliver."

                        *   *   *

    During their wait, TeJay looked around the restaurant to
see anyone he knew. Beatrice looked like his wife, a wife he
would've married in high school, and Cayrolynn with her
beauty and youth looked like his daughter. The thought "what
will people think" lacked maturity and he felt shattered that
it crossed his mind. He felt disgust with himself that his
thoughts included pride and selfishness because he went to
the apartment to invite Cayrolynn and circumstances developed
to include Beatrice.

    If classmates ostracized any child, Sarah Anna asked her
own children to bring that child home to play and eat. Now,
TeJay felt like his small child self who invited a playmate
home and heard his mother caution, "In our home, we include
and we affirm." TeJay's thought pattern reminded him that he
worked as an attorney-at-law and maybe counselor-at-law.
This thought made him think about personal faux pas, those
times when his remembrance gave him embarrassment. Maude
said if thoughts become painful, then seek forgiveness and a
contrite heart. Often people feel negative thoughts from

others, so he tried to think of some positive way to be the
good host.

"Sometimes, we come from the office to eat here, and I
wish someone would appear for me to introduce the two of
you." Easy conversation filled their waiting time.

One secretary came with her husband, and TeJay went to
invite them to join their table.

"Our son comes with his family. Thank you for the
invitation. Here, he comes now." Beatrice knew the
daughter-in-law and they talked about acquaintances. It's a
small world, TeJay thought. Even in the city, paths cross
and people know people who know each other.

Later, when TeJay thought about the evening, he felt
glad he reclaimed his best self and introduced these women.
Right brain and left brain, am I ashamed? Somehow, he knew
he followed his parent's teaching and his best self because
he felt no shame.

When they finished their meal, TeJay took them home and
asked Cayrolynn to join him for television. She refused with
an excuse to finish some art work. Beatrice went inside and
Cayrolynn tarried with TeJay in the truck. They sat
listening to a CD and Cayrolynn didn't move away from his
closeness. She smelled like the cleanness of lemon scented
laundry.

"Many people don't realize their illness, but I'm sick and I realize when I can operate I mustn't waste my hours."

"These precious days we can't lose, Cayrolynn. We must cement our friendship so that our life together leaves good memories. I need to go see my parents on Friday night. I'm busy with an investigative case this week, so no back-up music assignments. Plan for my seeing you on Saturday, if that's acceptable."

They sat for a few more minutes, then TeJay walked her to the door. He turned to hold her and her touch reminded him of a tiny hummingbird, so small and so fragile.

*   *   *

When Cayrolynn came into the apartment, she met the smell of soap, cologne, and tooth paste. She stood at the door for a moment, then Beatrice came from the bath and her tooth brushing.

"You make lazy conversation with TeJay, and tonight I felt like I took over our conversation with my topics and opinions. Tell me about your communication with him."

"Never thought about that. We talk, however we don't need to talk. We listen to music and tell each other what we think about. Time can't stand still, yet it evaporates when I'm with him. Look at the time now, and how did our leaving before seven turn those clock hands to ten?"

"Been looking for a feller like that all my life, Cayrolynn. Aubrey likes to laugh, but the last man I dated cracked his knuckles."

"Don't give up hope, Beatrice. Ask, seek, knock, and the right time, person, and situation occurs. It's true and it happens for you. Watch. So, Aubrey gave you his music system and library of records, cassettes, and CD's?"

"You know Aubrey kept his health problems secret from his family. I think he stayed in denial until the symptoms took over. His sister says returning home makes their responsibility for his estate easier. I tried to avoid taking anything from his apartment, but Aubrey insisted. When I asked his sister, she encouraged me to accept because most of his music neither she nor her parents like," Beatrice said.

"Like a vapor life slips away and we face eternal questions that involve relationships and people, yet with poor judgment we put material possessions, first. Me, too."

"Did TeJay say he would help you find a place to live?"

"Yes and no. Yesterday, he came for me to attend the church where he goes. He bought me the Sunday paper and I looked at the ads while he looked at some materials in the Law Library."

"Where does he live?"

"Somewhere rural with his parents, and he didn't tell me where in town."

"Cayrolynn, if I walked where you walk, I would know everything personal including his brand of deodorant. Maybe, our differences explain why this kind man found you and I'm still pining at the altar."

"All the trauma with Aubrey leaves you feeling blue and depressed. Hang tight, you say to me, so hang tight. We watch all those ego sexual lovey dovey advertisements on the television and we make unrealistic fiction."

"You're right. I found myself singing love and marriage and changed the words to sex and money. The frivolous and the pragmatic define a lifestyle of failure and success. Enough philosophy, so I pull down my bed and read myself to sleep. How about you?"

"I'll pull out my cot. Instead of a nap at noon, I took a long walk. I enjoy living here because you help me think through my ventures. I like living alone the way you do, and I like being here, but married people lose freedom when they gain their support system. Good-night, Beatrice. To everything there is a season, A time for every purpose under Heaven."

*   *   *

TeJay called at noon on Thursday.

"I kept remembering your car situation, Cayrolynn. If you need either my car or truck, I can lend you a vehicle."

"Oh, thank you, but I felt I should pay Beatrice some rent. We decided to exchange cars, and the value difference takes care of the problem. I need to get a new carburetor, otherwise except for thin tires the car comes in handy for local traffic or I can take a bus."

"You continue looking for a place to stay?"

"Yes, I continue to look. Even though Beatrice sees heartaches in her nursing job, when Aubrey moved to Atlanta she experienced loss. My being here helps, and I think she'll go see him next week. His family called and asked her to visit."

"Well, please tell me if I can help. I plan seeing you on Saturday."

"Sure."

Cayrolynn returned to the cross stitch sampler where she worked alphabet letters. Almost finished, and then a frame after she blocked the linen square. If someone purchases for two hundred dollars, I make money, she thought. Otherwise, the investment of time plus money for materials leaves me poorer.

*   Three   *

Tip finished the marinated sausages grilled over hot hickory brickets and opened the door from the deck to the screened porch. Stopped, listened, heard the sound of a familiar motor, then went to find Sarah Anna.

"Your eldest needs a plate, Beloved. When I'm hungry and ready to eat, here comes TeJay pushing the peddle of his little red wagon."

TeJay parked under the garage apartment called the Loft and came to the house.

"Friday night and we welcome you, TeJay," Sarah Anna said.

"Figured you came to show off a new car, but I see it's the same ole speedy."

"Now, Dad, can't a fella come for a free meal when you know my Mom wants me around?"

"Careful son or he'll awaken you at daybreak for farm chores." Sarah Anna laughed.

Food and family news took time. Sam lived in Branson, Andy in Memphis, and Lexie in Houston.

During the drive from Nashville to their family farm in Cannon County, TeJay thought about what to say to his parents about Cayrolynn. He quelled his hunger and waited for the right time to make his bid. After his mother's oatmeal cookies and ice cream, he became serious.

"Got a proposition for you both." He stalled. Even as a child, they noticed the tight lips and blinking eye with throat clearing when TeJay felt anxious. Now, they waited for his asking.

"I met a girl age twenty-five named Cayrolynn Selaco. She grew up in a children's home in Alabama and finished high school there. Then, she came to Nashville to join a friend from the home who helped Cayrolynn find a job working for an insurance company. She might still be working, but she decided to take a leave of absence. She needs a place to stay and I want to offer her my room in the Loft."

When TeJay stopped, Tip prodded. "And?" TeJay kept silent.

"You will marry her?" Sarah Anna asked and the thinking furrow on her brow deepened. TeJay never mentioned a serious relationship nor marriage, yet she always thought, Someday.

"Maybe, maybe I shall marry her."

"Does she live in your Nashville Condo?" Something didn't make sense and Tip needed the missing clue.

"No." TeJay answered with a negative nod.

"Explain, son."

"I know I ask a lot. I struck up a friendship with Cayrolynn who needs affirmation and parents like you two. She works on primitive art along with other hand-made crafts that she makes and sells through an artist consignment store south of town. If she lives in the Loft, she cuts her living expenses and obtains space to spread out."

"You want her to live in your place above the garage and you'll check on her?"

"Right, Dad."

"Of course, you may, however, we'll need your help. Loneliness haunts this place and you took off right out of high school." Tip didn't look at Sarah Anna and he didn't ask her permission nor seek her approval.

"How about you, Mom? Yes or No?"

Sarah Anna felt ambushed. Tip ignored her thoughts. She never saw this girl, and now, she would live with them. In her heart, she questioned whether she could trust the judgment of her son. TeJay became the five year old pleading with his mother, not his professional adult self.

"When will she come?"

"Tomorrow, if you approve." Already, TeJay made plans and Tip agreed.

"Saturday, in the morning, tomorrow, right?" Sarah Anna wanted to disagree and her eyes kept glancing to see the eyes of Tip, but saw nothing. TeJay avoided the words, nevertheless he made his request felt. Please Mom.

Talk comes easy in church with the good Samaritan story. To take this girl into the family meant an adoption that she didn't feel she could handle.

After TeJay left, Tip went to their bedroom. Sarah Anna cleaned the kitchen and watched one television program. She must face Tip's choice, so she moved down the hallway into their room. No lights. She turned on the bedside lamp, then saw Tip asleep. In their life together, Sarah Anna never remembered Tip crying. Sometimes, his eyes might tear and he blew his nose. Now, tissues from a box in the bath lay discarded on the floor.

Sarah Anna changed into a soft cotton gown, turned out the light, and slide in beside Tip without his awakening. When she awoke and heard Tip in the shower, her bedside clock said two.

"I think we should talk," Tip said. He came into the bedroom wearing boxers and continued to dry his dark hair with a large towel. "You don't want the girl, do you Sarah

Anna?"

"No, not really. TeJay makes a big request and I wish he didn't ask us."

"When Claude and Maude first took me in, Claude cautioned that my beginnings belonged to me. I guess I promised Claude to forget those things in the past and press forward. Before he died, he asked me if you understood the circumstances of my adoption. I told him no, and he said better that way.

"First, I didn't talk because I promised Claude. Later, we grew such a good family and home, it never seemed the right time to talk even though I think about my birth mother named Alyce, often. Then too, Maude might get her feelings hurt, if our kids said something about a real grandmother."

Tip returned the towel to its rack in the bath. He paused to think through his story and choice of words because he found the telling difficult.

"Horace, bed-ridden with emphysema, lived across the hall. Before she died, my Mom asked Horace to look after me, and he did.

"One day, Joey, a kid from upstairs sat with me on the front steps. Eight children and two parents made ten people to feed and Joey stayed hungry.

"Claude walked from the store with a bag of groceries

and Joey told him about our hunger. Joey asked Claude to share his food from the store. Instead, Claude took us to a diner two blocks down the street and bought us breakfast. Can you imagine food when we suffered with empty stomachs? The very best meal I ever ate, and Claude listened to our stories."

Tip moved to his mahogany chest for clean pajamas and that gave Sarah Anna a break. She doubled her pillow to elevate her head. You live with a man and you think you know him, but this doesn't mean you see inside his thinking process. She didn't know Tip when they married, however the marriage on faith proved successful; except for times of disagreement, when they worked things out.

"Soon after that Saturday morning, Claude came to see Horace. I sat with them during their talking, but I don't remember or know what occurred, except Claude asked for me. My mother gave Horace no legal papers for me and by that time, Horace needed the veterans hospital and full time care. Claude made arrangements for me to live with Maude and him and for Horace's moving."

"I know Maude said she didn't want children." Sarah Anna said. "According to Maude, she decided for you because she liked you. I guess they both wanted you."

"They took me in, spoiled me, and I became truly their

son, as you know. My Mom named me Thomas Jackson Partee and she told me the Partee came from her father's playing golf. Claude and Maude changed my birth certificate with my adoption to their name and I became Thomas Jackson Hillebee. Some of this you know, already. So, my mother called me, Little Tom, and Claude and Maude called me, Tip. I never knew any of my Mother's people nor anything about my Dad."

Sarah Anna noticed the puffy eyes of her husband.

"Tip did you cry when your Mother died?" She knew the answer before she questioned. Sarah Anna knew the time after the death of his mother brought Tip the silence of maturity. Maude talked about Tip's adoption and advised Sarah Anna, he'll tell you someday when the time comes right for Tip to review his memories.

She couldn't remember being sleepy, but she awoke released from some unconscious dream. Tip slept making easy snoring sounds. After going upstairs to the hall bath, she went into the kitchen and began coffee. The clock showed past eight before she heard Tip and went to check on him.

"Good thing we didn't ask men to harvest our tree crop this morning, with us, still in bed."

Tip pulled Sarah Anna down to his pillow and she felt a tinge of regretfulness that three little boys with hard heads didn't poach on their Dad's attention.

"I'm missing our sons. Lexie never came to burrow into our bed early mornings, but our sons liked to wake us up and tussle."

Neither Tip nor Sarah Anna went back to their conversation about Tip's adoption. After Maude's death, Sarah Anna brought a trunk of family photographs and culled these for scrapbooks and some for their backyard burning barrel. Snaps of Tip as a baby or his boyhood didn't show either Claude or Maude. In one, Tip leaned against a charming young girl labeled "Tip and Aunt Lil." Sarah Anna knew this photo showed Tip's mother.

All day Saturday, they waited and looked for TeJay, but he didn't come home as expected. Late afternoon, almost time for Sunday vespers, he drove a smaller moving truck into the backyard. Cayrolynn drove the red Porsche and parked in the garage under the Loft. Sarah Anna and Tip left the house and went to meet Cayrolynn. While they stood talking, Tip kept his truck keys jangling in his fingers.

"We'll be back in an hour, Son." Sarah Anna gave her usual first grade instructions. "If you feel hungry, then soup simmers on the stove."

"Be at home, TeJay," Tip said. "I need to stop for an errand, Miss Sarah Anna, so off we go and we wish you welcome, Cayrolynn."

Sarah Anna joined Tip on the high bench seat of his truck, before he started the quiet motor.

"Our errand allows TeJay space to tour our place with Cayrolynn and answer her questions without our presence. I hope you agree, Beloved."

"Sure. It's a good idea."

Before Tip turned off the hill climb gravel road, she knew they would stop at the spring near the Ole Lonesome Place. Tip turned and pulled up before the gate where Sarah Anna got out and unhooked the chain, then pushed the swinging panel open for Tip to drive across the grate constructed with pipes to deter the cattle. She pulled the gate closed, then she returned to the truck. Country people know this exercise, where the gate gets opened and the driver or passenger drives the car, tractor, or truck through, but stops for the closing of the gate before continuing their journey.

Tonight, they startled no deer drinking at the spring nor birds swift in flight. After he made the turn around, Tip parked vertical to the viewing rock and turned off the motor. Lights gleamed from homes across the valley. Prayer came easily to Tip and Sarah Anna. Before they drove up the hill to Brush Arbor Church, they sought blessings and guidance for TeJay and Cayrolynn.

Ten people showed for the testimony and praise service, so they tarried with their neighbors.

"Tell that big city lawyer of yours we would like to see his face more often. He might like to bring his fiddle to a tractor pull." Friends often sent messages to TeJay or one of their other children.

Tip placed his work chapped hand on Sarah Anna's shoulder to guide her to the door.

"Well, we must go home to see if we can help move stuff upstairs, Sarah Anna."

"Strange, I think Maude felt as I feel now, when you brought me to the hollow. I remember Claude filled their yard with stacked cut wood getting ready for winter, about this time of the year."

"You think what goes around, comes around."

When they returned home, TeJay sat at the table eating soup. Cayrolynn munched on a cracker with peanut butter.

"Come join us here, parents. Cayrolynn eats but she needs encouragement since we didn't stop for supper on the way over."

Tip set out apples, cheese, crackers, while Sarah Anna made de-caf.

"Most times, we munch when we don't need a meal, Cayrolynn," Sarah Anna said. "However, you won't go hungry here."

TeJay talked about their plans while Cayrolynn watched and acquiesced because she found no other place to live.

"Tell us your story, Cayrolynn," Tip requested and Sarah Anna felt uncomfortable because Cayrolynn appeared nervous.

"TeJay told you that I work at crafts and primitive art. Right now, I maintain a 'scrape by existence' with my savings ad small earnings. Also, I took a leave of absence from my job because my doctor says my tests show fibromyalgia. At first, I felt tired, that meant a fatigue syndrome and maybe Barr-Epstein factor. My body seems to say hypochondriac when I know I suffer from anemia."

"Our son didn't tell us much, Cayrolynn, but if you can abide the loneliness of this place, then it becomes a haven of rest for you and a place of healing. Tip's adopted mother named Maude found health here when they moved from Detroit," Sarah Anna said.

"I wish Maude could take footsteps with you over the hollow to see her healing plants, Cayrolynn," Tip said.

"What about transportation, TeJay? Did you think about a car for Cayrolynn if she gets cabin fever?" Sarah Anna asked.

"Andy says, when Glenda Rae-Ann's parents go into an assisted living residence, they want to sell their big car.

Sometimes, I need a better car for use with clients, so I agreed to buy their extra car. Right now, I'll leave little red for Cayrolynn and keep my truck in town. I need to buy another car soon. If necessary, I can lease like the smaller moving truck outside with Cayrolynn's belongings."

"Sounds like good planning." Tip stood. "We can help with unloading."

"In case, she needs to travel for an errand, I marked a map for her. She shouldn't be wandering over unknown hill roads." TeJay stood and gave a hand to Cayrolynn, who stood.

"No, Cayrolynn," Sarah Anna said, "the logging roads and gravel county roads become unsafe after storms and rain run-off. Any road without the regular school bus route gets no immediate repair even if it's a mail route. On the paved asphalt roads, the sparse traffic means no help if your car breaks down or slips off the road in wet or icy weather."

"No one lives near, no near neighbors," Tip added, "and it may seem too quiet for you. At the end of the Loft, we keep a farm truck that needs no key. Turn the switch and it runs. Out in the barn, we keep Claude's old army jeep that travels anywhere in any weather and we keep the key on the nail above the door. You can reach it from the ladder going to the hayloft. Not often, only sometimes, cars or trucks go by over on the main road. Those you can see and hear because noise carries a long way, also talking does, too."

"Did you get moved upstairs, TeJay, or do you need our help?" Sarah Anna asked.

"We need help."

The Loft contained the furnishings left by TeJay and Sam. While Tip and TeJay unloaded, Sarah Anna and Cayrolynn made the bed and placed clothes in Cayrolynn's closet.

"Be at home here, Cayrolynn," Sarah Anna advised. "Feeling misplaced, homesick, or rejected will make you most unhappy. You must tell us if you experience nightmares, or fears or become unhappy." Cayrolynn made no answer, so Sarah Anna went around the bed and hugged her.

When they completed the unpacking, Tip and Sarah Anna went to the house and TeJay followed. He chose to sleep in the bedroom they labeled Lexie's room.

"Shafe needs his apartment for his family and if Cayrolynn stays in my Condo I might be in the way at Shafe's. This way, Cayrolynn sleeps in the Loft and she gets affirmation from me and my family."

"Will she acclimate to the quiet loneliness, do you think?" Sarah Anna asked.

"We'll see. If she appears desolate and homesick, then I need advice from you both. She says the idea of being here appeals, but time will tell."

"You commute everyday, and will you continue the substitute part-time musician role?" Tip asked.

"Most nights, I plan to come home with exceptions when my work piles up. Some work I'll finish here, but Saturday presents problems for my work and my music."

After they went to bed, Sarah Anna felt sleep coming but said to Tip, "I hope this means one of our children will decide to keep the homeplace and live here in our hollow."

"Let's see how this scenario plays out," Tip said before he turned over and heard Sarah Anna with her deep breathing of relaxed sleep.

*   Four   *

By six o'clock on Monday morning, TeJay traveled I-24 on his way to his downtown law office driving the empty rental truck that he would return by noon. He arrived at his desk about seven-thirty according to his usual planned schedule.

Before beginning work, TeJay called Sam.

"How did the folks respond?"

"Very well, I think." TeJay felt hedged with Sam's personal inquires. "Dad seemed open and helpful, and Mom hid behind her professional facade."

"TeJay, my brother, you expand with a teen age crush and with as much love as you attach to a new car. I fear for you and I fear for the girl. You come on strong and then you zero out. Before, I watch you give the rush. I'm right and you agree. Are you Amnon chasing Tamar?"

"Sam, I need help. Yes, you know my history with women. Please don't place any curse or self-fulling prophecy on me.

Please don't. I want to help this woman. I agree it's an emotion, an emotion of storm."

Sam heard the tension in his brother's voice that lowered at least two octaves and became the base tone of an attorney presenting before a court.

"TeJay, you make our parents pick up the slack. They'll retire soon. They need grandchildren not another child."

"I promise you, Sam, until Cayrolynn moves on, she holds first place priority in my life."

"Does she know that?"

"No. Any legal or financial commitments might sink me. I can give her a place to stay."

"What about our family? Is it a one man show when our parents become involved?"

"All, I can say Sam, to your analysis of this situation, thanks for your understanding and help. You ask the hard questions."

Sam felt his early morning grumpy harshness. If TeJay made this call at nine p.m., when he relaxed before the television or with the kids, the keenness of response might show more kindness and be gentler. He reached for his near-by coffee mug and took a drink while TeJay waited.

"You caught me with my wake-up coffee, TeJay. Be assured, older brother, you can count on me."

*   *   *

After the conversation, after he hung up the telephone, Sam stood thinking. He felt the same tight heart he experienced the day he and Max pulled into Branson and he realized he must make his own decision whether to commit himself and his hard earned truck to the wishes of what he supposed to be a cult and a cult leader. He allowed Max to talk him into this venture and then, he felt unsure. Also, the cold weather seeped into the truck and the drizzle of icy snow made driving difficult. Sam spoke aloud to himself, "TeJay, may God give you wisdom. You need it."

*   *   *

When TeJay finished his conversation, he placed the telephone further over on his desk, reached for his calendar, and for the nearest working file. This file concerned an IRS tax rebuttal and research for the case would take all day.

An empty page filled the calendar except for the usual Monday morning conference at eight with the partners of the firm and their breakfast. If he left the firm and took his clients, they would suffer. He delayed his decision, but not the pressure. Now, he must consider Cayrolynn, too.

"If I become a partner, it means less time for her. Commute time plus the work day leaves no extra time," TeJay self-talked. No negative nor depressing thoughts and even his conversation with Sam left no tinges of disturbed remorse. Within himself, he knew he made the right decision about Cayrolynn. "I know, I know," he sang to himself.

*   *   *

After they came from work, both Tip and Sarah Anna began to stop by the Loft. Cayrolynn never joined them for their supper nor cooked for them, however if Sarah Anna cooked pot roast or a meat loaf, she would bring a sampling to Cayrolynn. Her thanks assured them, she felt at home.

"My, you look busy tonight," Sarah Anna said when she stopped by.

"We learned many crafts at the children's home because they felt it would keep us out of trouble. Their conclusions paid off. I gain such peace and patience when I listen to music and work counted cross stitch."

Spread across the table lay elementary coloring books and squared copy paper. For this pattern, Cayrolynn, with painstaking care, drew her pattern and numbered the colors on her diagram according to the numbers on her skeins of thread.

"Show me your project, Cayrolynn."

From a wooden artist case, she took completed work stapled to cardboard, ready to be matted, then framed. Tip came during their conversation.

"She's an artist, forsure," Tip said.

"I agree, Cayrolynn." Sarah Anna admired the precision of the work and the beauty of blended colors.

"Do you show in a gallery?" Tip asked.

"No, not yet. TeJay asked me that question. I belong to an artist cooperative near Nashville."

"Cayrolynn," Tip offered, "I could help you mat and frame your work to sell. Across the years, I helped Sarah Anna frame our children's work and it's a task I enjoy."

Around eight, when TeJay came home, he found them engrossed with Cayrolynn's patterns.

"So, what goes on here?" TeJay showed his delight in being home. He pulled Cayrolynn's hair and kept his hand on her shoulder. Cayrolynn mentioned her work to TeJay, and now he saw examples.

"You did this Cayrolynn?" In his mind, TeJay seemed to see a rose bud, tight, with only the outer fringe of pink petals showing, and encased in the extended greenery of the stem. However, as it blossomed, it became a remarkable beauty with numerous shades. Cayrolynn became the rose beginning to blossom.

*   *   *

Sarah Anna saw the Loft as the hideaway possession of her sons, TeJay and Sam. For her, it remained off limits, but not for Cayrolynn, it became her new home. Spasmodic cleaning filled her time when she needed a break from needle work. Record collections from the teen age years of Sam and TeJay yielded music unknown to Cayrolynn. Happy sound filled the Loft keeping her company whatever her task.

In the corners, in the cabinets, and closets, she found disheveled and unorganized clothes of denim, khaki, flannel, plus other fabrics with many colors and in various states of repair. Some garments went to the washer downstairs, others in a basket for mending, and some she hung in the closets. In the process, she found wearable clothes for herself. Jeans, shirts, and baggy sweat shirts added variety to her meager stay-at-home wardrobe.

"Cayrolynn, you make this place liveable." Sarah Anna looked around the Loft and noticed the changes. "Books dusted, arranged, and returned to the bookcases that Tip and Claude built for our sons."

"Words of encouragement, Sarah Anna. This basket holds old magazines, some comics and sheets of music culled and stacked waiting for TeJay's approval to keep or throw away."

"So, these books or materials, you wrapped in white paper and labeled?"

"I saw that idea in a decorator magazine and it helps avoid a mis-matched clutter look. At Christmas, rewrap might add decorating color for the season."

"When both Tip and I take a day off, I can ask him to position the ladder and help me wash the windows. It became our big project one year to build a clubhouse for the boys. The plans for a treehouse, den, hide away, became this apartment, which made me glad. Sometimes, I would leave home to get away from the sounds of good music according to TeJay. After we built the Loft, I thought we might not see so much of our sons. Didn't happen that way. Often, at midnight, I would hear them creeping upstairs to bed. At least the decibels were banned from the house."

"I work along, Sarah Anna, and I enjoy being here because it's my home and I thank you," Cayrolynn said.

"I'm glad, Cayrolynn." Sarah Anna left and Cayrolynn remembered her conversation with TeJay.

"This place is yours," TeJay told her. "Sam will never return except for a visit, maybe. My parents travel to see them because Sam works and when he takes time off, he goes boating with his family on the lake. So, it all belongs to you. Don't be shy with your new home."

"You sleep over in Lexie's room, TeJay, so you won't mind if I clean your old room here?"

TeJay laughed.

"My secrets, if I kept secrets, I took them to my Condo long ago. Yes, include my room in your domain."

Cayrolynn did find secrets in TeJay's room, at least, they seemed like secrets to her. TeJay kept a careful collection of songs and music he created. Some poems carried tunes, while others lacked cohesion. She tried to put thought patterns together in some organized way to construct a file of materials. After her clean-up foray, she asked TeJay to look at this file of his work that she gathered and arranged.

"The commute takes my time," TeJay told Cayrolynn one Saturday afternoon when he felt the fatigue of the drive home after a morning of work. "I'm not complaining. I just feel the pressure for more hours everyday."

"Can you think of ways, I can help, TeJay? Would you like for me to move back to Nashville?" Cayrolynn asked with pain and fear. She loved this Loft with the views of the hollow shaped like a mountain fold surrounded by hills.

"The answer's no because I want you here. I do miss both the creativity and the therapy of odd jobs with my music. I try to write, but the task gets postponed with the demands of my work. I guess I don't really miss the substitute band work, but I would like time to work on musical compositions." TeJay became thoughtful. "I shouldn't say that. Erase. I don't want you feeling guilty or thinking that you infringe in any way. You don't."

His touch of affirmation gave her assurance.

*   *   *

One week or so later, TeJay and Tip watched football. Cayrolynn went for a walk down the property fence line, then she stopped before the basketball goal and pitched baskets with a ball that needed air. When she returned, Tip left and TeJay clicked off the television before he turned for talk.

"About our conversation, Cayrolynn, if we could work together at odd times like now. We might try our efforts at song writing, just to see if we can spark creativity."

Cayrolynn brought the materials she gathered. These pages along with her navy rhyming dictionary, she placed on the coffee table.

"This file contains your work in progress that I put together during my cleaning of the Loft. Some pages contain scribbles or doodles, but I thought you might like to look instead of my throwing all away."

He turned on music to hear himself playing the guitar. After Cayrolynn took her place across from him, he picked up his guitar and began strumming.

"You write poetry?" he asked when he noticed the book.

"Sure, sometimes." Cayrolynn didn't want her life interest to block the originality of TeJay. "Most poetry written today doesn't rhyme."

"Show me your work." Cayrolynn handed him the green unlocked five year diary. Every entry included a verse she wrote. Never did she share with others her poems copied into the diary.

He opened the book and began to read. TeJay read making no comments. These heart poems became her life pegs written from the anguish and change she knew. When her situations changed poetry became her emotional release.

"You think inventive ideas, Cayrolynn. Please, I need your help with my writing. Will you?"

"Of course, yes."

Before supper, Sarah Anna called to ask them to drive over to the interstate to a steak house. TeJay relayed the request and Cayrolynn nodded yes.

"Sure, we'll follow you two because I want to shop at the superstore Wal-Mart. Cayrolynn needs fresh fruit."

During the supper conversation, TeJay told about their plan to create some musical material and try for publication and sales.

"Your parents lend their listening ears, if you need our suggestions," Tip said.

"Sure Dad, and you too Mom."

"You said Sam worked with you in the past, so you must seek his input." Cayrolynn added.

*   *   *

The next Saturday morning, TeJay needed to go for lunch in town, so he called Cayrolynn to ask for a couple of hours working on songs before he left.

"How about your creativity quotient this morning, Cayrolynn?"

"Just made coffee, so come along for a cup and I'll get out the guitar with all your notes."

This professional person Cayrolynn saw gave her a different view of this man who left early and came home late each day. She questioned, if with charcoal, she could draw his profile on newsprint.

Nose straight and wide from his forehead, small narrow upper lip with wide bottom, defined chin with no extra flesh, and smooth white teeth making his eye teeth appear missing. Across his forehead, a few extended parallel lines like wrinkles of thought and wisdom. Why the mono eyebrows? Sometime, maybe he would say or she would have courage to ask. Today, he combed his hair into shape like Andrew Jackson. No silver barrette nor musician look, instead dark eyes focused while he read. She liked this man.

His long sleeve white shirt, the collar button-down, came crisp from a Nashville laundry. He wore a navy and white stripped tie that matched his four button blazer.

No cuff links and no smell of after shave, but the cleanness of early morning soap. "Only God could give me this Blessing," she reminded herself. The telephone rang and TeJay answered.

"Look, Andy," TeJay nodded as he spoke to his brother. "If you get a divorce, or if you get a legal separation, if your heart's knit with Glenda Rae-Ann's, you'll never be free. Only you can decide, whether your soul's knit together with her soul?"

While TeJay talked, he watched Cayrolynn. In his heart he knew his heart bonded with hers. If marriages are made in heaven, he was bonded with this woman with angels as witnesses.

Cayrolynn turned to look at TeJay. Both knew that TeJay talked about the two of them. What a revelation she thought. Then, he gathered his briefcase for his departure.

"Take care. I'll call you, Cayrolynn. Agape." Before his departure, she waited as he read. Now, she poured herself coffee, and began to peel an orange for breakfast.

Sometimes, TeJay might pinch her arm or pull her hair, or twist her ear lobe, and sometimes she wanted to share his touch. Her reservations came when she remembered her medical prognosis that she compared to those people living in the Carvile leprosarium waiting for the miracle of healing.

In her heart, Cayrolynn prayed spontaneously and constantly for herself. "Please may I have the miracle of wholeness. Please heal body, soul, and spirit, please Sir."

She didn't move the pages where TeJay worked on his music. She left her navy rhyming book and the green diary with his scrap paper notes. When Sarah Anna came with Tip to the Loft, she noticed the unlocked diary that lay on the table.

"So, you try some song writing with work in progress?" Tip asked. He picked up the rhyming dictionary and Sarah Anna chose the diary hidden beneath the pages.

"Please, may I read your poems?"

"Of course."

*   *   *

Most Saturday's when a break from chores and errands permitted, Sarah Anna browsed through recent magazines. Eye fatigue meant rest. Today, she changed her modus operandi and pulled her stainless from the cabinet. She cleaned each piece and rinsed. Tip came and helped her dry and put away.

"Most women polish and dry the silver. Where did you find the idea to clean stainless?"

"From a box on the shelf at the hardware when I looked for copper cleanser. You know, Tip, Carolynn's beauty amazes me because she's beautiful. When we meet people, often they remind us of another person. Someone we know now, or someone we knew before, comes to our mind. I don't think I ever knew anyone like Cayrolynn."

"She reminds me of Lexie at age eight. It's like she put herself into deep freeze when she went to the children's home and only now does she begin to thaw."

"I feel such gratitude in her generosity. When she allowed me to read her poems, I felt like she gave me a badge of approval."

"We seem to need to give things and it's part of our culture and lifestyle, I think. She never possessed things to give, so she learned to give of herself. In that way, she resembles you, Sarah Anna. First graders respond to your smile and touch, so you continue the practice with everyone you meet."

When Tip gave her a compliment, it filled her heart with joy more than a baker's dozen of long stemmed roses brought from the florist.

*   Five   *

"This day," Cayrolynn quoted to herself because each day brought some extra chore like washing the clothes found in the Loft.

Around lunch this day, Cayrolynn took the basketball outside and in the warm sunshine tried for baskets.

"Bounce. Bounce. Backboard hit. Bounce." The sound echoed up the hollow. No birds chattered at this mid-day hour, however further up the hollow buzzards circled showing life and death in the quietness of these hills still untouched by developers or paved roads. Most of the hardwood trees replanted themselves, some wild cedar gave a touch of greenery, but no pine for the Florida paper mill at Port St. Joe or for the mill on the Alabama River. She thought about those overloaded trucks that allowed no passing with massive logs balanced near the cab and thin tops behind swinging along two lane roads.

Autumn colors exploded like fireworks or sparklers in a

progression from green to muted fall, to brown, then to
leafless branches. In the fence row, loggers left a mixture
of unwanteds like persimmon, sassafras, frayed cedar, and
others injured with attached barbed wire. The briskness of
the blowing wind caused brown unshed leaves to flutter from
their perches and shower around her.

Need some lanolin cream for my face she thought when
gusts brought glow to her cheeks and a feeling of chapness,
so she returned to the laundry room. The exercise gave
pounding to her heart and a weakness to her knees. Her sinus
began to drain.

She left the washed clothes in stacked order and then
completed the ritual of checking the locked doors.

"I'm like Lavender who lived at the end of the lane with
all the mobile homes strung out down the sandy road called
Boat Ramp Landing near East Bay. If she hung clothes on the
line or worked in her garden, she locked her house, and tied
her key with a knot in the corner of a handkerchief."
Cayrolynn self talked on the way upstairs.

Before she closed the blinds to the west cutting off the
afternoon sun, she removed her pharmacy bottles from the
kitchen cabinet. The allergy medicine caused immediate and
deep sleep. She stood there undecided, then took the tablet
and knew dizziness would come in moments. Time to take the

other tablets at supper with food and milk. With blinds
closed, she lay across her bed and went to sleep. In her
doze between sleep and wakefulness, she heard voices. Men
talking.

"Hello, the house."

"Ain't nobody here, Hank. They all work. We take the
truck and be gone."

"We need to switch our clothes. Maybe, they might keep
some farm clothes. Try that door."

Cayrolynn heard the laundry room door shoved open and
exclamations about all the clothes. She felt fear, and like
herself as a child she looked for a place to hide.

"Maybe, they won't look in the closet."

She took a pillow from the bed and lay on the closet
floor. This walk-in room locked with a push catch that
secured the door on the inside. Those men pushed open the
locked door downstairs, so it wasn't a sheltered protection,
only a hiding place. She could hear nothing. She covered
herself with a blanket from the shelf and shivered with
remembrances of her childhood. The blanket gave warmth in
the cold dark closet. Fear made her stiff. With regrets,
she remembered she failed to call 911 or Sarah Anna at
school, however the medicine she took earlier caused her to
go back to sleep.

She awoke when she heard Sarah Anna screaming for her.

"I'm here, I'm here, Sarah Anna." Sarah Anna ran back down the stairs and Cayrolynn's voice brought surprise.

"What happened? what happened, Cayrolynn?"

"I don't know. I took my allergy meds and I heard voices, so I hid in the closet and dozed again, I guess."

Tip came and they looked at the disheveled laundry room with the adjoining bath built for clean-up after farm work. He called the sheriff while Sarah Anna and Cayrolynn returned to the Loft.

"When the law comes, we won't go downstairs because I taught school and you slept, that's, unless you saw them or you want to answer questions."

"No, I didn't see them."

"Tip will show the sheriff the vandalism and report the truck gone."

The telephone rang and Sarah Anna answered.

"If you will, TeJay, stop in Murfreesboro and bring us those ready to serve barbecue plates. We'll eat here in the Loft. Here's Cayrolynn."

"Strangers came calling, TeJay. I was asleep, however they used the bath downstairs, changed into clean clothes from those in the laundry room, and took the farm truck."

"Are you hurt?"

"No. I didn't see them."

Tip called Sarah Anna to come down to talk with the sheriff. Cayrolynn turned on the television and began working on her cross stitch. The sheriff and the detectives stayed talking. They pulled out to the road, as TeJay pulled into the yard.

"Not a very happy meal, after all the excitement of this episode," TeJay said.

"It's a happy meal because we eat good food and no one got hurt," Tip answered.

"I feel guilty," Cayrolynn said, "that I didn't call Sarah Anna or the sheriff. I hid. When my Dad came home drinking or if he boozed it up at home, he would cry and then go to sleep. Not my Mom, she would sing, then get mad. She would hit us, my Dad and me, break dishes, and move furniture. I learned to hide at Lavender's or sometimes under the bed."

"People learn to fight or flee, Cayrolynn. Most women learn techniques to get their way without fighting. It's not lack of courage, just easier for most women to flee. Men flee, too." TeJay said without criticism.

"A soft answer turneth away wrath," Sarah Anna added.

"Cayrolynn, sometimes, I think God gives us a sixth sense," Tip said. "I guess it's what Sarah Anna calls her premonition."

"Like the thought to take a different way home and miss an accident or shop at one store and find a bargain, or see someone who needs help or a kind word," Sarah Anna said.

"When I joined the army and went to Korea, I guess with the immaturity of my youth, I thought a fight would cure everything. Men with no back bone might run away, but real men knew how to fight. I was so naive."

"We would ask you about the war, yet you told us very little, Dad," TeJay said.

"It's not easy for me to talk about, TeJay. Cayrolynn took her pillow and slept in the closet reminds me of my war experience."

"What, Tip?" Sarah Anna hoped Tip would tell because so often he would seem to want to talk, then turn away.

"Things happen in war, not like the planned out strategy. Sometimes, I think about those days on the DMZ. These heavy thoughts bite. Somehow, no matter the reason, my unit was lost. Because of the sound of big guns, off there, far away, we thought we stayed near our own people and would be found or find our way back."

Tip seemed to be sweating, so Sarah Anna went into the kitchen and brought back a glass of ice water, a roll of paper towels, plus a kitchen towel. She felt like she might make Tip feel embarrassed, so she sat beside him so that he touched her and didn't look into her eyes. He took the water and drank. With the telling of the story, he continued to sip the water.

"When dusk closed around us, we posted sentries. We each took our turn and we felt protected from surprises. I took my turn with sentry duty and no happenings. After I turned over my spot to another, I returned to my gear under the overhanging branches of a large cedar-type evergreen. The wind moaned, a moaning wind in the tree tops, and a brushing of branches against the ground where I positioned myself for a nap against the trunk of the tree. Thinking back, it seems as though I only dozed."

TeJay moved to sit beside Cayrolynn.

"I awoke, completely awake, and my mother, Alyce, seemed to say, "Need you to go to Horace's room, now.""

Tip stopped and coughed.

"My mother made our expenses with men. I'm ashamed. They would come at all hours, so she worked it out with Horace for me to stay across the hall with him. Together, we took my quilt and pillow, knocked on Horace's door, placed the pallet on the floor, and at once, I went to sleep again."

Tip stopped to breathe and drink water.

"I remember, I said, yes, Mom, before I remembered I was

behind the enemy line in frigid winter time under the evergreen with branches that brushed the earth near my head. The echo of the winds muffled sounds around me."

"Climb the tree," she commanded.

"When I was about six feet up, I could feel the sway of the top of the tree. With my sixth sense, or my third ear, I realized the enemy crawled into camp. Someone was crawling into my space below. At any moment, I feared I would feel a foreign hand on my bare ankle."

Cayrolynn listened and nodded encouragement.

"The wind in the trees covered the sounds of small noises. Movement of the tree top kept me from climbing higher. My dry socks placed in my pockets earlier needed to be on my cold feet. With caution, I eased on my socks. Branches crackle, but these didn't. One sock on, and then the other. Fear would strike me later, but at this point my wary thoughts heeded carefulness.

"I never lived in the country during my childhood, but I knew dawn brings a twitter of birds. I realized I heard birds, even though it remained dark. The density of the branches kept me in the dark, yet I knew the blackness was turning gray. Some gibberish of a foreign whisper seemed to waft upward, although about this I'm not sure.

"With touch and feel, I lodged myself into the crook of

the tree. Now, I knew I mustn't go to sleep until I could
determine the circumstance below. I guess I feared most
daylight coming. It seemed like hours passed before I heard
any noises except for the intermittent big guns far in the
distance sounding more like a vague echo answering the
rumbles in my empty stomach. I felt my words, 'I thirst, I
thirst.' Thirst bothered me more than hunger."

Sarah Anna moved and returned with another ice water for
Tip, and soda for herself, Cayrolynn, and TeJay.

"I heard the trucks or vehicles moving with caution as
though in neutral gear through the brush. I heard no doors
open nor any language. Except for the muted motors, all
stayed silent. I kept moving my head trying to see, not
moving the branches that blocked my view and kept me in the
dark. Then, one of the brown army trucks moved into my
vision with a big red cross painted on the top and side.
Even the red cross might be cover for the enemy, so I
waited."

TeJay sat with his arm on the couch behind Cayrolynn.
He felt the prickles of no movement and stood, before going
to the bath.

"Wait a minute, Dad. I want to hear this."

Sarah Anna thought of the times she heard her sons ask
Tip to tell about his war experiences. Often he would tell

about some man he met or where someone came from. He became a sharp-shooter in service and liked to explain about guns. During the time he studied engineering at TN Tech, he went to see Sergeant York at Jamestown.

Claude kept a collection of guns with some from his family and some from Maude's family who lived in West Virginia. With Claude along, Tip taught his sons to hunt.

TeJay returned and sat next to Cayrolynn, so that he clasped and unclasped her hand.

"The wind still blew, but the sound lessened and I knew if I moved I would be heard. I thought I heard the crank of a motor and a truck begin to move away. My caution became the fear to be left behind. Still feeling my way, I moved down the branches. When I reached the ground I noticed my shoes and pack missing. I thought I heard someone say, 'Captain, can you help me here?' I crawled to the nearest truck. I pulled myself into the empty cab and onto the middle of the bench seat. With unspeakable joy, I saw a strip of white adhesive tape on which someone wrote in English, Made in Detroit City. Me, I thought, me, I was made in Detroit."

Sarah Anna changed her place and moved her chair to give herself full view of Tip while he talked.

"I must have fainted or hallucinated because I can

remember asking about the city limit sign. It seemed like
the tape on the dash became the city limit sign. I know
there were four trucks, parked, being loaded with my unit.
When the hospital corpsmen returned, they found me sitting
there like a drunk man mumbling about Detroit.

"I wanted to ask about my buddies, but instead I kept
complaining about my feet and my lack of boots. The driver
told me he would check my feet as soon as we passed into our
own territory and behind our lines.

"To my knowledge, no one ever asked me what happened.
I either fainted or blacked out for some reason because
my next memory concerns my being on a gurney in a large
makeshift hospital tent barrack. They adjusted my arm for an
intravenous type injection with several bottles hanging
around. I remember saying, it's my feet and someone
answered, we know, your feet.

"War isn't like paper shuffling, even though that
occurs. Things happen. When the doctor came, he told me,
'Soldier, we decided to send you stateside on a hospital ship
leaving soon.' In my confusion, I remember I said, Detroit?
He said, yes, Detroit. This was not a question, but an order
with fast delivery. So with others, I was put into an
ambulance bus. I remember my bandaged feet, the trip to the
port, and being carried to the hospital ship.

"If I had remained in Korea in the hospital or if I had received reassignment, I might know what happened to my unit. Sometimes, I'm curious and have questions.

"I experienced sea sickness going over, and more sea sickness coming home. I was a mess. One day before arrival, one of the medics by mistake left his clip board on my bed. I read, 'Frost bitten toes and exposure when enemy over ran his unit position. Recommend Medical Discharge.' By reading those comments, I understood what happened when we came to shore.

"Once I thought about twenty years and retirement from service, but now, I wanted the discharge. When we reached Seattle, I knew I wanted to go home."

"My Dad lost his toes and got a Purple Heart, Cayrolynn," TeJay said.

"Time for some pecan pie and ice cream, I think." Sarah Anna felt the tension drain from Tip when he arose and went with her downstairs to the deep freeze. Pie defrosted in the microwave and vanilla ice cream gave them a reason to sit at the table.

The telephone rang and TeJay told Andy about the men stopping by during the afternoon and stealing the farm truck. After a few minutes, TeJay hung up with the comment that Andy might talk to the parents later.

"Come on downstairs and look at my frames for Cayrolynn's cross stitch." On the way down, Tip continued his words to Cayrolynn.

"I'm sorry I became so strung out with my story, Cayrolynn, like the "Rime of the Ancient Mariner." Your break-in causes me fear. We'll check our country security, again, because sometimes farm families get a few criminal types wandering around."

"We want you safe, Cayrolynn. We never experience vandalism and this exception causes us concern." TeJay said.

"Why don't you get your guitar and play us some tunes that we know and allow us to sing along." Sarah Anna said.

"Better start with Suwanee River or she will nag and nag, huh, Dad?"

"Cayrolynn, you need to suggest some songs you know, otherwise, we'll flood you with our favorites. Sarah Anna likes Stephen Foster melodies, TeJay likes the lonesome songs of the old Appalachians, and I like them all," Tip said.

"Tip likes southern gospel from the forties," TeJay said.

Cayrolynn joined in the singing making a family quartet. Somehow, she could think of no favorites for suggestions.

*   *   *

Over-night the weather changed from windy sunshine to a misty cloud that filled the hollow. Cayrolynn liked to feel and see and hear each day begin and here she lived among the tree tops. With blinds raised, she watched the dawn. On bright days the dust motes, shimmered in the peek of sun-rays.

Before she took up her needle work, she watched the clouds shift, which gave an opening to see farther up the hollow. By lunch, she knew this weather pattern would move off and the dull grayness of fall-time moisture would permeate the hollow like an overcast shadow.

Sometimes, on the coast, hurricanes would move on shore and other times rain fell in torrents. Her Mom would turn on all the lights and play loud music.

Rainy days for Cayrolynn meant looking for a time out place like the 'cubby' that preschool teachers used. No need for time out, today, so she remembered and turned on all the lights before she began the long playing Cajun music.

When she heard some noises, Cayrolynn moved to the windows. She felt safe, but didn't forget yesterday. Across the field, she saw two men climbing through the barbed wire fence. In a moment, they disappeared in the hillside woods that extended to the road going toward the interstate. The shed near the acre of young dogwood held supplies, mulch, and offered shelter. She questioned if these two spent the night there and if they would return or travel to safer places. Today's weather offered no comfort to hitch-hikers, but by dark they could blend with the homeless people in Nashville shelters.

*   Six   *

Early morning rain pushed by wind gusts beat against her windows and the noise helped her awake. Cold falling rain, and Cayrolynn awoke feeling healthy. Toes stretched to the foot of the bed touched the rungs of the antique mahogany four poster. This bed belonged to Claude and Maude, however she didn't know TeJay's grandparents. Arms placed under her pillow elevated her head with sleep tousled hair. She murmured to herself, I must get up, but not yet.

The telephone rang before she finished her dozing.

"Good morning, Cayrolynn. I'll be home by four and I want us to go shopping in Tullahoma. Did you sleep well, and is the sky falling down this morning?"

"Good morning, TeJay and yes, I'm awake, and we have rain beating against my windows like white water rapids. I haven't looked out, but we must to losing all our oak leaves. Yes, the sky is falling down."

"Are you feeling creative enough for a shopping

venture?"

"Sure. I'll be ready when you come. Was your commute
to work easy this morning?"

"Overcast and a dark dawn, without rain like you
describe. Keep yourself dry and I'll be there before supper.
Bye, Adios."

"Bye, friend."

Before moving from Nashville, Cayrolynn went for an easy
care hair-cut that she could manage. Often, she used a dark
red color shampoo that gave her hair high-lights. After she
finished her bath, she dressed in a black skirt with a blue
cotton sweater.

"You-hoo, Cayrolynn."

"Just a minute, and I'll let you inside."

"My, it smells so good in here."

"TeJay called from work and wants us to go shopping in
Tullahoma when he gets here. I'm getting ready. Help me
open my blinds. I forgot it's Saturday and you're home
today."

"Tip suffers from cabin fever with all the rain, so
we'll drive over to McMinnville to talk to a man about our
nursery stock. Tip wants to sell more dogwood because some
of his trees grow too mature, he says."

"Sarah Anna, thank you for coming to check on me. I

keep thinking about Tip's stolen truck. It bothers me."

"Cayrolynn, they'll find it. You did the right thing.
If you called the sheriff and he came while those men were
here, maybe someone might be dead. Tip fixed the door where
they entered. That's our scare, to have some wanderer
prowling around. Vandals do damage without burglary."

"Oh, banana bread for my breakfast, what a treat."

"Can I make you a cup of coffee?"

"No, I prefer milk. How about you? Is Tip waiting?"

"Hot tea, and I'll heat the water. He said he would
come knocking when he's ready. I think he plans to telephone
Sam, then read the mail and pay our bills."

"TeJay said shopping in Tullahoma and I question why not
the mall at Murfreesboro or at Hickory Hollow. Please, Sarah
Anna you must taste this hot bread you brought me."

"My grandmother loved a cup of green tea on a rainy day.
She bought me a tea set and she enjoyed playing tea party."

"You said you lived in Memphis. How did you meet Tip?"

"My grandparents lived on a farm in northern Mississippi
near the state line, but yes, I'm from Memphis. My kids like
our meeting story so much that I'm surprised TeJay didn't
tell you the details, already."

"Often, I wish for more time with TeJay."

"Well, I went to Dauphin Island with a youth group from

my church. Tip went there with a friend from work."

"Sounds like a party week-end."

"My semester ended and this week before summer school gave me a short holiday. My mother, who worked as a nurse, encouraged me to go."

"Summer and a beach party," Cayrolynn said.

"I took a small over-nite bag on the bus with me, and placed my big bag with the other luggage near the bus. Somehow, my suitcase got left in the rec room at church."

"Which meant you went to the beach with no clothes."

"Right, and so traumatic for me. I was so upset. We went to a bonfire that first night and Tip with his friend joined our group and others at the bonfire. He saw me shivering and gave me his heavy jacket. He wore a sweat shirt and a toboggan, I remember. We sat on blankets and sang choruses with the fire burning low to red coals.   Tip left and I gave his friend the jacket before I returned to the motel."

"Did you get his name or was it a chance hello?"

"Nothing, really. The next afternoon, I took the flimsy motel bedspread to the beach and weighted the ends with wet sand against the blowing breeze. The afternoon tide turned seaward leaving a wet rind of sand. Often, one stray wave almost touched the spread, then lapsed into a flush outward.

I watched translucent crabs move in disjointed fashion scrambling into various tunnels and they kept my attention."

"I spent days on the beach near Pensacola and I watched those, too."

"The glare of noon sun moved westward and I kept a personal vigil with the sea and sky, then felt annoyed when Tip approached. Since my luggage didn't come with the bus, I purchased a repulsive brief two piece swim suit from the gift shop.

"Young people become enticed by clothes and lack the wisdom to see their own youthful beauty. Once, when I fumed about my lifestyle here in the hollow, Maude corrected me with her compliment, but I couldn't see my beauty."

"Somehow, I find it difficult to see you fume."

"I came here to a different life. True, I stayed busy, but TeJay came in nine months at the end of my first school teaching year. No one warned me about the weeps some women encounter after the birth of a child. Tears flowed. My Mother sent me vitamins that I should have taken from the beginning."

"Was it depression?"

"Poor health, I think. Anyway, back to the beach. Tip came across the sand to find me. He made some trite statement about my luggage, while he stood looking at me and at the Gulf. Somehow, I became furious with anger. The emotion I felt dissipated and I felt the buoyancy of his care. He did care because he shared his jacket. Before he spoke, I noticed the crisp texture of his brown suntan and the white evenness of his teeth. Handsome man and no boy, I told myself."

"Tip is still handsome and you are beautiful, too, Sarah Anna. I hope you know that. You, both, make me feel so special with your kindness to me."

"The lost luggage subject showed Tip's tension. Everyone exhausted that topic, so I made no comment. When I remained silent, Tip started back to the motel walking in the deep soft sand. My rudeness with no greeting and no answer gave Tip a lost feeling, he said later.

"Anyway, I realized my offensive manners gave the appearance of rejection. Some life decisions get made in a moment, so I sat up and called."

"Did you know love at first sight or later?"

"Later, I think. The morning the tornado invaded the hollow caused me to know I never wanted to lose him.

"There on the beach I tried to stand on the uneven dry sand beneath the spread. He gave me his hand and pulled me up to stand beside him. When two people try to find each other, often they lack needed communication. Words seem disconnected. The luggage subject was passe and Tip felt his inadequacy to open a conversation or for a greeting, I guess."

"But, you didn't know him, then."

"Correct, but I knew enough to answer him with a smile and charm filled words."

"Funny, I think, and your kids know all this?"

"Of course, and lots more, too."

"Your description sounds like a movie in the making or words by an art major."

"He asked me to go for food and how much time and I told him I would meet him in the lobby in thirty minutes."

"Were you dating someone in Memphis?"

"No. I wasn't a good-time girl with lots of dates. There on the beach, I think, I almost lost him. I questioned myself, Why am I like this? At once, I'm full of come hither and the next moment I experience extreme repulsion. I still ask myself, when I look inward, why? I have no answers except lack of experience in the ways of love and less knowledge of my emotions.

"You asked me to tell you how I met Tip, Cayrolynn, and I don't know why I'm loading you with all these thoughts. We told our children about our meeting, but no emotional introspection."

"It's interesting how people meet, I think. I wanted
you to tell me."

"You're a good listener. Tip's buddy, went with my
friends on the bus to a place near Bellingrath Gardens for
supper. Neither of us joined them, so Tip took me to the
causeway and the diner that belonged to a Greek couple.

"My friends handed over extra items, so I wore borrowed
clothes. Dinner dates remain in our memory by what we wear,
not what we eat, I think. I wore a double sized red checked
shirt, with the bottoms of my white pajamas. I remember I
showered and used a headband belonging to my roommate to pull
back my wet hair. Then, dressed, I put on white tennis shoes
to make myself shorter than Tip. I creamed my sun and wind
burned freckled face, used lip gloss, and cologne from the
over-nite case and felt date ready."

"You stand taller than Tip."

"Yes, because my growth in heigth came during my early
twenties."

"Don't let me stop your thoughts. I do want to hear."

"When I came to the motel lobby, Tip placed an out-dated
magazine back on the table. Well read by many and by himself
at least ten times, he said later. When we went out to the
truck, I needed a small push to gain the bench seat, and I
still do. Do I sound like a record?" Sarah Anna asked.

"I find it funny because it sounds like rote memory. Does that mean you recited so often to your kids it comes all packaged?"

"Exactly."

"So, how does the story end?"

"I need to think about what to skip. Tip came to see me in Memphis on the fourth of July and we married on Labor Day and I came here to be his wife and teach school."

Tip called from down stairs looking for Sarah Anna.

"Cayrolynn asked me to tell her about our first meeting, so she heard a lot."

"Did Sarah Anna tell you that I tried to chase her home and she wouldn't allow it. Took me three months to persuade her to marry me and bring her here to live."

"I think we knew from the beginning, but I wanted to finish my summer school with my already paid fees," Sarah Anna said.

"I came home to see if she could teach in our Wayside School with two years of college. Our school board member asked for her to teach first grade and she kept her job all these years."

"Tip, Claude, and Maude kept the children, along with Rose, a neighbor we hired. I worked and took classes in Murfreesboro until I graduated," Sarah Anna said.

"Do you really enjoy being a teacher, Sarah Anna?" Cayrolynn asked.

"I do, Cayrolynn. I told you my Mother worked as a nurse and my brother became a doctor. I felt pleased when I married because it became easier for my Mother to meet tuition payments for my brother. Our son, Andy, lives with my brother in my Mother's house."

"When Andy went to Medical School in Memphis, his wife went to Medical School in Birmingham. Maybe, TeJay told you," Tip said.

"Seems like I have known TeJay all my life, but no, he says very little about his family," Cayrolynn said.

"Well, Sarah Anna and I spent one summer in Memphis helping restore her Mother's house. It happens to be in a good historical area with cherished old houses."

"On another day, we'll tell you about the restoration of our homeplace here. That first winter, we knew TeJay needed a home and work on the house made life difficult," Sarah Anna said.

"Sarah Anna's right. Life became difficult for both of us, and now, we think and plan for our retirement."

Sarah Anna and Tip started toward the door and Cayrolynn followed them downstairs. Sarah Anna continued the conversation.

"We know we must begin plans for retirement, nevertheless we aren't there yet."

"Tell TeJay, if he can spare the time, he might find us some football tickets."

Sarah Anna and Tip walked toward their truck while Cayrolynn turned to the clothes rack where she untangled hangers. Last week, she placed clean clothes on these racks after she subtracted them from the dryer. Those marauders came and took clothes leaving spaces and disorder. She picked up some hangers that lay jumbled on the floor and returned them to the rack, then turned to shut the door.

In a way, she felt like a peeping Tom watching Tip help Sarah Anna into the truck, so she turned back to the rack until the truck moved out of the yard. For a minute, she stood catching her breath and realized never in her life could she remember any couple who loved until retirement age. This touch and kiss between Tip and Sarah Anna showed private people who stayed in love for forty years.

She closed and locked the door, then returned to upstairs where all the windows sweated moisture. With paper towels, she began to wipe them clean and found it a chore, so she closed the blinds and turned on the lights. The video movie seemed like a good way to spend time until TeJay came. Boring, she thought, and clicked it off. Her cross stitch

lay on her work basket, which she picked up, then pushed
start for TeJay's guitar music before threading a needle.

She heard TeJay's truck and knew he parked behind the
house, then in a few minutes, he would call. Sometimes,
going out the door took time, so she found her purse and
jacket, then turned out the lights except for one in the
hall. The telephone rang.

"Are you ready? I think we'll take little red."

"I'll meet you at the car."

The escapee jailbirds took the farm truck and left the
unseen car parked in the garage under the Loft.

"Didn't they see this car, TeJay?"

"I think not. The farm truck fits the environment and
not so noticeable as the car. I don't think they looked
around the place at all. They saw the truck, found the
clothes, and took off. Did you save your hunger for our meal
or did you sneak a snack?"

"Your Mom's banana bread earlier, but no lunch and I'm
hungry."

When they left their driveway, TeJay turned east and
took the gravel hillside road over Slingshot Ridge.

"If you starve, we'll eat at the interstate. Or,
otherwise, we'll shop at the mall in the valley, then eat at
the buffet house on Monteagle mountain. Which?"

"The mountain, please."

Cayrolynn saw the Porsche as a small car, but it wasn't small. After they reached the mall, TeJay noticed the gasoline gauge.

"Remind me, Cayrolynn, I don't want to walk for gasoline tonight, or should you walk?" Both laughed. Cayrolynn recognized the tease. During the trip, she glanced at TeJay, but he seemed lost in some thought pattern and forgot her presence.

Seven

"Why do you go shopping, TeJay?"

"We need walking shoes. My farm boots don't feel comfortable for hill climbing and my good boots serve for city life. Both of us need ankle protection against copperheads."

"You plan for us to go hiking on the farm?"

"Yes, and other places like Old Fort or picnics in one of the state parks. Each winter, Tip burns a section of our land to clear the weeds and flush out the snakes, so we all take a gun or hoe for protection."

"Do you find many snakes?"

"Yes. The best protection means be on guard and don't surprise them. More appear around the spring at Maude and Claude's place, but they are prevalent everywhere and dangerous. Someone suggested a snake fence to divert their path. We never tried the suggestion, but we might."

Cayrolynn watched the way TeJay purchased. He took her

to several stores, until he found the precise item he wanted.

"You must be fortunate, TeJay. Seldom do stores
carry particular items any person plans to buy."

From a kiosk, TeJay bought both a small coffee. For a
few minutes they stood, then moved to an empty demonstration
table left from a sales promotion earlier in the day.

"Cayrolynn, if you don't agree, you must say no. I want
to purchase friendship rings for us. I think a gold wedding
band unless the jewelry store owner makes a better
suggestion. When you work on your needle craft, my ring will
help you think of me. When I struggle with legal paper work,
a gold band will remind me of you and your work at home in
the Loft."

"Rings show a covenant relationship. You want the rings
to show friendship?"

"Marriage is a covenant relationship and I think being
friends can be covenant, too."

"So, you want us to look, now?"

"Yes, can we? It's your decision."

"I think you saddle yourself with me and I'm not sure,
I'm worth it."

"Yes or no?"

"Yes."

In the jewelry store, TeJay saw the circle of diamonds.

His eyes' question. Did she like it? Yes, she liked it.

"We need this ring in Cayrolynn's size or altered to fit, if possible, and the plain gold in my size," TeJay said.

Cayrolynn watched this professional jeweler, who seemed alone in his shop, until his wife came from the back. Glitzsy sales didn't fit his merchandise. She understood TeJay came here because he either knew this shop or someone told him. Maybe, Sarah Anna or Lexie shopped here. The ring TeJay sought for Cayrolynn didn't exist alone.

"Sir," the jeweler said and placed other items on the counter, "this circle of diamonds includes another ring to make a matching set. The gold ring in design opens like a window and the diamonds make panes with four in the masculine ring and six in the feminine."

"The 14K gold rings set with stones in white gold?"

"The 18K gold rings set with stones in platinum." Mr. David, the jeweler took the pair of rings from a tray in the glass counter and handed both to TeJay.

"Cayrolynn, do you like these rings?"

"You see their beauty, TeJay."

Both took the rings and placed them on their fingers.

"If you notice, these rings differ from my other sets. They come by consignment from a man whose son works in California. The boss of the son gave him the rings as

partial payment for work completed according to the papers
the Dad showed me. One of those cash hungry business deals
where the owner scrambles to make payroll. These rings came
from a personal design shop by a jewelry artist."

They left the rings on the glass counter when TeJay took
her hand and guided her to the front of the store.

"Cayrolynn, I need to talk prices. Please, could you
wait for me on one of those benches somewhere down the mall
concourse."

"Sure. It's not a Nashville mall, TeJay."

Both laughed. The tension and the ornate mall
description that TeJay worded brought laughter.

Cayrolynn returned to the bleachers placed in the
central corridor of the mall. She sat watching the Saturday
evening strollers, who came to see and be seen, to purchase
and window shop, and to enjoy weather protection at no cost.
TeJay moved to the back of the store with the jeweler for
their negotiations.

She thought about their hands and the rings on their
fingers. Before, she noticed TeJay's short stubby hands with
strong fingers to play string instruments. Now, she thought
about his inverted dome circle fingernails. Every person
differs like their fingerprint. She thought about his
flexible wrists and sturdy hands that she knew with touch and

appearance.

In a few minutes, TeJay returned with the comment that their rings would be sized and picked up by Tip. Outside the night turned cold, but before they entered the car, TeJay stopped to ask if she remembered other needed shopping.

"No." She wanted new make-up, but avoided the stress with TeJay waiting and watching.

The trip up the mountain stayed slow because they followed a tractor trailer with a driver who knew about accidents on these short curves. Cayrolynn understood TeJay tagged along behind trying to avoid any head-on with someone who lacked judgment about speed and the passing lanes.

"We eat late. I didn't realize the time, Cayrolynn."

"The shopping kept us busy and I didn't notice the time either. Anyway, we'll eat too much and get tight tummies."

TeJay heard some tears and a teensy hiccup. The stone gates of the Sewanee Domain indicated a lay-by with parking at the overlook. After TeJay stopped, he turned to Cayrolynn.

"Why the emotion?"

"Sorry. Two words I grapple with and circulate in my thinking. Appreciation and Forgiveness. The forgiveness I seek means I forgive being me. Your Mother gives me time in affirmation, but more in value. She gives me appreciation.

Now, you give me appreciation with this friendship ring. My insecurity and inferiority rises to strike me and I cry."

"I think you show need for food. Your tears release tension and show fatigue. Be at peace with yourself and know your thinking must change when you care for yourself with food and rest," TeJay said.

At the mountain cabin restaurant, they sat on the glass protected porch and shared space with a group of college students partying after a play. Cayrolynn thought about Sarah Anna's words, "All young people are beautiful." In the dimmed overhead light and the table candles, she couldn't know how TeJay saw her. The shopping left her a little high with excitement.

"I need to drink water and de-caf or I'll never sleep tonight. Sarah Anna asked me to church and I said yes," Cayrolynn said.

"My Mother teaches a good class and you'll like it. Did she tell news about Lexie or the others?"

"She came over to wait until Tip came for her, and she didn't mention the family. She told me about meeting Tip on the beach."

"She tells that story like a poetic chant. We asked so many times. I think many people would like to retire to the beach including my Mother. She enjoyed her grandparents farm in northern Mississippi, yet she felt at home in Memphis, and her impossible change to life in the hollow became possible with her remembrances and daydreams."

"You must recall many stores told during your childhood by your Mother and Maude?"

"Claude, too. He told stories and taught me to whistle. I hope you enjoyed my Mother's recitation because she takes a long time to drawl it out. Did she finish with the part about going to the Greek fish house?"

"No. Tip came for her. Tip said to remind you about a football game, if you could purchase tickets."

"When you finish your salad, Cayrolynn, try the veggies cooked with the pot roast. Tip and I like the vegetables. Sweet potatoes without the ham, fried okra without the fish and hush puppies, carrots and potatoes without the roast, which gives a vegetable meal with country taste."

"I noticed rhubarb deep dish pie. My Dad liked rhubarb pie, but I never remember my Mom trying to make it. She called it a Yankee dish."

"My Mother likes buttermilk and cornbread with sweet onion, which my Dad doesn't understand. Corn flakes with milk suit him better, he says."

After they left the restaurant, TeJay continued his talk about family.

"I like my sister and my brothers. We each live different lives and lifestyles. Sam seems to be in my thoughts tonight, and I'll tell you about him. It's not my intention to bore you with tales about my family, Cayrolynn. Since you live amongst us, you'll understand us better, I think. It's inclusion in our family."

"No brothers or sisters for me, TeJay, nor to my knowledge, any cousins. Neither did I keep up with other kids at the children's home except for Marthee."

"My parents go to see Sam at Thanksgiving and to Lexie's house at Christmas. We'll figure out something for us, too. We might go see where you grew up."

"Gas, TeJay." Cayrolynn felt glad she remembered before they entered the four lane.

"Thought forsure, you wanted to try out those new boots and hike back up the mountain for gasoline."

The cloud that smothered the gas station showed bright lights like gas lamps on picture postcards. For a moment, Cayrolynn left the car with the thought she would wash the windshield, but TeJay stabilized the gas nozzle and took the sponge with handle from her. The penetrating cold left chill bumps, so she reached for her jacket before she slide into the car again.

TeJay watched his driving going down the mountain 70%

grade, then began to talk about Sam.

"My brother, Dad's second son, favors him most. He went to Tech to become another engineer like my Dad, then dropped out after Christmas his second year. That's the story. He became friends with someone at Tech, who had a cousin in Branson. This main-line church in Chicago owns a retreat and trains missionaries for their church and other mission groups. When Sam left Tech, he thought he might be going to join a cult."

"Sounds frightening."

"Yes. He thought better about the plans and didn't spend the night at the retreat. He found a garage open and applied for a job fixing cars and farm tractors. The owner, Bubba Jones, prefers to work on big diesel trucks. He helped Sam find a place to live and gave him a work set-up."

"Except for college, he never lived away from home before?" Cayrolynn asked.

"Never. The whole painful episode hit him hard and us, too. He went to church with Bubba and Eloise, Bubba's wife. Bubba taught the Bible study class for the men in the church. Sam saw this interesting girl in the choir, then she disappeared for about three months. When she returned, he met her and asked her to go to lunch. She worked down in Arkansas in a hospital as a nurse, but went on a mission trip with one of the groups from the Retreat."

"This sounds like the girl Sam married."

"Yes, Toney, but I need to back up here and tell about when Sam left home."

"I can see a difficult experience for all of you."

"Yes. At first, Tip and Sarah Anna didn't hear from Sam. Sam wrote me a letter and we began to write and talk on the telephone. Then, at Easter, Tip and Sarah Anna went to see Sam. They didn't wait for the prodigal son to come home, but went to fetch him."

TeJay left the interstate and drove along the barrens following the ridge line before going down into their hollow. He eased into the parking before a closed store, opened his door, and stood to remove his jacket. Cayrolynn felt the car warmth, but didn't bother to remove her jacket because she understood they would soon reach the cross roads and pass down the incline to home.

"Sam decided not to come home. While my parents visited, they helped Sam buy five acres on the lake and the double wide mobile home he rented from a long distance truck driver named Speed Ketchum. So, you hear a very abbreviated account of what took place."

"This means Sam chose to stay in Branson to live and work, rather than come home."

"Right. This means when Sam dated Toney, he held a job and owned a home."

"At what age, about twenty?"

"About. After church, Sam asked Toney to lunch and they drove from the crossroads where they live into Branson and spent the afternoon together. They went back to Sam's and made popcorn, you know, just a good conversation and time spent together. Sam said he knew he loved Toney, then."

"So, when did they get married?"

"Sam told me he didn't see Toney for about two weeks, however he knew her work schedule varied. Then, she came into the shop where he helped Bubba and told him she needed to see him about something. She asked if she could see him that night."

"What a surprise for Sam."

"Bubba heard Toney. Sam said she couldn't keep back the tears. So, Bubba stopped, early. He told Sam to go on home and see what Toney wanted."

"You say, this crossroads or small community allows everyone to know each other?"

"I believe so because it's located several miles out of Branson. Sam went home and ate a bowl of soup for supper, he told me. He called Toney. She said not to come to her house, but she would come right over. Never could Sam realize Toney's problem. At Christmas, much to her sorrow and horror, she made a baby with someone almost a stranger. While on the mission trip in Peru, she considered abortion and suicide. Now, she came to ask Sam to marry her. They talked until after midnight with no decision. You can imagine the emotion. I think they both cried."

"How old is Toney?"

"Five years older than Sam."

"And, the real father doesn't know."

"Toney never told the real father, at least, that's what she told Sam."

"Leaving home and then this problem seems traumatic."

"When Sam got to work the next morning, Bubba asked him what Toney wanted. So, Sam told Bubba. Then, Bubba asked Sam what decision he made. When Sam shook his shoulders and made no response, Bubba told Sam that Toney would make him a good wife. In great forgiveness, there is great love, Bubba said. Otherwise, maybe you should follow your parents home."

"That sounds very blunt, TeJay."

"Well, when people say it's a hard world out there, it's true. Sam expected Bubba to take up for Toney because he knew her from birth. Also, Sam knew he preferred going home, if Toney refused to be part of his life in Missouri."

"What happened next?"

"They finished the mechanics on the truck and Bubba told Sam to take the remainder of the day off. Sam went home and sat pouring over his Bible, which Tip and Sarah Anna taught us as the way to make decisions. Moseman Eldridge, Toney's Dad, opened the door and came inside. Sam didn't lock the door, nor hear Mose when he entered. Sam told me, that Mose pointed the gun ready to kill him. Sam knew Mose thought he made Toney pregnant."

TeJay paused, but Cayrolynn spoke no comment.

"Sam explained to Mose that he met Toney the previous Sunday two weeks before and the child didn't belong to him. Mose, filled with anger, asked Sam the name of the father. Sam didn't know, but he told Mose that he thought he would marry Toney. He asked Mose for his help, if he and Toney married."

"Did Sam think Mose would really kill him?"

"From what Sam said, it wasn't play like. Mose heard about Toney from Connie, his wife, and the news gave him hysteria."

"My Dad might be disturbed if not drunk. How fortunate for Toney to have a concerned Dad and parents that care."

"Sam called a number Toney gave him for her work at the hospital. When she came to the telephone, Sam told her about Mose being there. Sam took the leadership and suggested she make the arrangements for their marriage. Since she worked, they couldn't talk. Sam handed the phone to Mose, who needed some assurance."

"Did you and your family go to the wedding?"

"Toney suggested the two of them go to Eureka Springs over the line in Arkansas and not include relatives nor friends. She moved into the double wide with Sam. So, Tip and Sarah Anna became grandparents five times."

"Grandparents for Lexie's two and that makes seven."

"The first boy, they named for Moseman and called Maney. Number two named Tom for Tip and me because I'm a junior. Number three for Andy and Uncle Andrew and called Drew, then four for Sam and called Samuel or Little Samuel."

"Did they give their daughter a family name, too?"

"Yes. You might say so with the names of two grandmothers and her mother, named Sarah Constance and called Saycee. I think the reason this fills my thoughts, concerns Sam's proposition. He tells us about a large house on the lake where the owner will sell at a loss. This native stone estate holds space for Sam's family with a guest house large enough for Tip and Sarah Anna, also for Andy and me, too. Sam needs Andy and me to help him buy the place."

"You think about a vacation place and will your parents live there when they retire?"

"My parents can't be sure. They want to live near Lexie
and her brood, too. Maybe, spend part of the year with Sam,
and then some time in Mississippi. That is, if their
retirement monies cover this lifestyle."

"Am I a problem to their plans, TeJay?"

"I wouldn't be telling you, if you presented a problem,
Cayrolynn. Of course, not. When they retire, they talk
about selling the place and moving. Not yet, though. This
homestead means home for all of us, including Sam even when
he can't take time to come home."

When they parked under the Loft, TeJay reached for her
and held her like a Saturday night date at the drive-in movie
before being forced to take her home. After they left the
car, she climbed the stairs and TeJay went to the house.

She found all the lights turned on with Tip watching a
movie and fiddlin with some frames for art work. Sarah Anna
heard the car and arrived with packages of popcorn for the
microwave.

Later, before Cayrolynn slept, she rethought their
conversation. All her life she prayed for a family and God
answered better than any wishes she ever dreamed. Fears like
sweet dreams pushed out reality until she remembered the two
men climbing through the barbed wire fence.

*   Eight   *

"I want us to make some holiday plans, Cayrolynn. Thanksgiving, Christmas, and a vacation week at New Year's will give us time together and time with the family."

This Saturday morning, TeJay came for coffee with Cayrolynn and sat waiting for Tip to go to the fields.

"If we make no plans, we experience a flat day or negative celebration."

"Do you work a substitute band assignment over the holidays, TeJay?"

"No. However, it's not a time of traveling for us. I thought we might take a trip at Thanksgiving, but plans change, and Lexie will come home. I think it best for us to be here."

"Um-m, Lexie comes home and I didn't know that. What did you do to make a memory day as a child, maybe at age six or seven?"

"We liked to climb the hills and look for black walnuts

and hick-a-nuts. I still know the place of those trees."

"With acceptable weather, you think we might explore?" Cayrolynn asked.

"Maybe."

"At the children's home in Alabama, we planned because Maybelle, my cottage parent, along with those people in charge, wanted happy children, not discipline problems. Most of my Florida holidays passed with my hiding out because kids with parents, who celebrate with a bottle, miss out on big days."

"Tip liked a jig-saw puzzle, so he bought three or four and we gathered around to put in pieces. Good weather meant our being outside; otherwise, we found inside projects."

"You gathered around to sing and did you read the Thanksgiving poem?"

"Sure. Claude liked a story called <u>Acres</u> <u>of</u> <u>Diamonds</u> that he read at Thanksgiving. We passed the book around and took turns reading one paragraph or one page each. The lesson he tried to implant came from the experiences of his own life. He wanted us to live in the hollow, not wander off to find work and live up north as he did with his job. He felt he redeemed his life by moving back at retirement."

"Many folks, who retired, lived near us in Florida. Men spent their time fishing, and often, wives tagged along on the boat," Cayrolynn said.

"Sarah Anna liked for us to dramatize Plymouth Rock and the Pilgrims. We dressed up and either read the script or spoke it. Claude and Maude became our clapping audience. Tip gave us good reviews."

"You memorized the Bible Christmas story and did you know the poem about Santa coming the night before Christmas?"

"Christmas involved our school and church programs."

"How about food, lots of food?"

"Maude cooked. Sarah Anna didn't cook up stuff, but Maude did. One Christmas, a large family lived up on the crest of our ridge. Tip went there after lunch and asked for the kids to come down and play. Tip and Claude planned because they gave us broom stick horses, wooden double barrel shot guns, and a choice of hats from an array ready for throw away. Maude took our pictures and I'll show you those. What a rowdy bunch, and I looked like a mountaineer. By the next Christmas, the family moved on."

"I guess it's never possible to explain the joy of a fun day," Cayrolynn said.

"Probably not. Maude brought sandwiches to the yard, and water to drink, I remember. We were too sweaty for hot cocoa and Mom frowned on sodas. Then, Maude's special cakes, both coconut and white fruit cake, ended our feast. One of the boys said the cake was better than store bought. Maude liked to repeat that remark when she baked us a cake."

"If Lexie comes here for Thanksgiving and your parents go to Galveston for Christmas, then Sam and his family won't come either holiday?"

The telephone rang and TeJay answered. Cayrolynn heard the greeting of a client, so she went downstairs to the garage hobby room.

"Oh, Tip, TeJay waited for you, but now he talks on the telephone."

"I heard the phone ring when I came inside, and I wanted to check the glue on these frames."

"Thank you for these handsome frames because they insure the sale of my work," Cayrolynn said.

"My pleasure, and here's my son ready for some real work. Sarah Anna works on papers and class plans, but she'll come over soon for coffee, Cayrolynn."

The needle craft took her complete attention, so she lost her sense of time. When she heard TeJay and Tip, she glanced at the clock to see past noon and no lunch.

"Want to go to the house for a sandwich, Cayrolynn?"

"No. I stayed busy and I think Sarah Anna must be busy, too, because I didn't hear from her all morning."

"Did you eat?"

"No, but now, I'll use the juicer. See you later, TeJay. I'm not in the mood for soup or a sandwich, today."

Her emotions seemed to play tricks. Too much togetherness meant she wore her welcome out. She questioned herself with a queasiness about joining the family or staying with her work.

*   *   *

Magazines printed helpful suggestions for the holidays. Gifts created for Sarah Anna, Tip, and TeJay needed thought. She decided to make a sampler for Sarah Anna with the names of her seven grandchildren. For Tip, a candy jar filled with wrapped nuts or peppermints to keep on his workshop cabinet. What for TeJay? It remained a question.

"TeJay, do you think Sarah Anna would like a grandmother sampler including the names of her grandchildren?"

"Do you plan to include the three stillborns buried in the cemetery?"

"You mean the babies of Rae-Ann and Andy?"

"Yes."

"I didn't think of them, so I need to rethink my gift for Sarah Anna. Remembrances should show thoughtfulness and I'm not sure I want to include grief."

"What do you plan for Tip?"

"Candy, but not home-made."

"What do you plan for TeJay?"

She threw a pillow and missed. Laughter.

"You plan gifts and my family will appreciate your creativity. I want to tell you some impressions about Andy and Glenda Rae-Ann. Maybe, Sarah Anna told you, did she?"

"No. Tip mentioned it."

"Rae's parents moved here when she began first grade. Her Dad worked as principal for Wayside School where my Mom taught first and her Mother taught fifth grade. Andy and Rae became like identical twins, inseparable. Tip and Mom wouldn't allow any sleep overs nor long trips, otherwise Andy got included on all the field trips Rae's parents took. I think Rae's I.Q. measures higher than Andy, although both made all A's. Rae smiles, but seems self-conscious and practical. Andy appears like a happy-go-lucky fella, not a prankster or jokester, but not serious either."

"She became a sister in your family?"

"Some yes, and some no, because she never left the influence of her parents. They wanted her to go to college down in Alabama, however she chose to go to Tennessee with Andy. I think she decided for those babies; all little girls, all stillbirths, one, two, and three."

"She took classes, that meant being a student, a wife, and soon a mother?"

"Yes. After number three, she made sure, no more with tubes tied or some such. Andy finished the university in June and she fell behind, but finished in December. She looked terrible. Andy worked summers in Memphis at the hospital, so he applied for Med School and became a student there. Rae didn't get accepted, but she received acceptance at the Med School in Birmingham. Her parents moved with her to Alabama. So, Andy and Rae with intense studies and distance seldom saw each other."

"She lived with her parents. What did Tip and Sarah Anna say to this arrangement?"

"Mother told Andy and Rae, when Andy first talked his ambition to be like our doctor uncle, to expect difficulties. She saw her mother, the nurse, and her brother, the doctor. My Mom tried to dissuade Andy, then Rae followed Andy. All the time, my Mother asked negative questions about their choice of life work."

"You think Rae followed Andy with no choice of her own?"

"Well, Rae wanted to be a baby doctor and Andy didn't want pediatrics. Andy wanted to study cells and cancer which Rae didn't like. Both seem right for the study they chose."

"Did she live with her parents in Alabama?"

"Their retirement hit during those years, and I think they bought a house. Her Dad found some work at a college in

Birmingham. Andy filled the place of son for them, so they
expected him to visit. Andy went there, but I don't think
Rae made visits to Memphis. My Mom says, Rae anguished with
hurt over her non-acceptance to the Med school in Memphis and
over the lost babies. She stopped the babies to keep pace
with Andy."

"Now Rae and her parents live in Mobile. Andy lives in
Memphis and never the twain shall meet."

"Tip and Sarah Anna find the situation traumatic. Rae's
parents own a house on the beach and she keeps a condo in
town. Andy goes to the beach, however Rae gets medical calls
or finds herself scheduled for hospital duty. Rae lost all
interest in sex after she lost the last baby. Andy calls her
Frigid Frieda."

"With all the medical help available, Rae won't seek a
specialist to help with her problem?"

"You don't seek help when you won't admit your problem.
Andy says it's like she blocked out a whole healthy part of
her personhood. She refuses to discuss it with him."

"They make no plans to practice near each other nor live
together?"

"Not yet. My Mother thinks Andy feels beholden to our
uncle. Rae feels responsibility for her parents.
Significant adults in our lives become mentors, but parents

can impose and assume dominate roles, unwise and unhealthy."

"I know, TeJay, when I left the children's home, the
housemother, Maybelle, asked me to remember all the girls at
Christmas and on their birthdays. She complained about her
own children all the time. When she retired, she moved to
Mississippi where her children live. She lives with a
sister, now. I know she didn't mean to impose, but it kept
me beholden to her and to the home."

"So, what do you do for these girls?"

"I send a card for each girl at Christmas with five
dollars enclosed for each, and I send a card to Maybelle."

"You keep a list of girls with birthdays?" TeJay asked.

"Most times, I send a card and a gift. I remember my
unhappy days and I feel it serves like repayment or giving a
tithe. Give and it shall be given to you, pressed down and
running over."

"Do you remember other people? How about the woman who
lived at the end of the road where you lived in Florida?"

"You mean Lavender, no. If you decide for us to make a
trip there, maybe someone will know if they buried her in the
church cemetery over on the main road where she attended."

"If you hold reservations or hesitations, we won't go
where you grew up, Cayrolynn."

"I feel my own hurt, and I hurt for Andy and Rae. All

those school years together and now, nothing.   How sad."

"Where did your Mother meet your Dad?"

"In Pensacola, before he retired from service.   He came from New Jersey and my Mother's from South Alabama.   My Mother finished high school and came looking for a job.   She worked at a five and dime, then started singing at a club out on the beach."

"She played the guitar, you said."

"Yes, and she taught me, too.   She wanted me to go along and sing with her, but I felt too shy, afraid and withdrawn. By the time she knew about the cancer, she didn't work because of her drinking problem.   Lavender kept me, took me to church, and made sure I caught the bus for school. Sometimes, when I think about those times, I get depressed. When the sun shines, I count my blessings, and walk on the sunny side of the street.   When it rains, I call it the early rain and the latter rain, which means blessings, too."

"It's my joy that you find happiness, Cayrolynn.   I want to help you with your Christmas cards."

"Finished those already, want to see a sample?"

Cayrolynn brought out cards with a cross stitch bookmark enclosed and a personal poem composed for each girl.

"Do you know any of these girls?" TeJay asked.

"No, but they send me their school pictures."

"It's like closet prayer, Cayrolynn, and agape means love. Come, we need exercise and Tip will join us for a few baskets, forsure."

When Cayrolynn first came, she lacked energy for the rough basketball, now she held her own. TeJay saw her strength and marveled in her health.

"Don't play toss-up with TeJay, Cayrolynn, he plays rough." Most times, Sarah Anna didn't come out to play. Today, she came from the house with Tip. Time-out came when some friends driving by saw them outside. After they drove into the backyard, throwing baskets ceased. TeJay took Cayrolynn by the hand and walked her down the lane beside the growing orchard of young trees ready for winter with brown branches and no leaves.

"Tip mows walkways around the farm using his tractor and bush-hog. He likes to walk and look at the stock he plans to sell. His mowing makes it easier to take a walk anytime we come home."

Cayrolynn didn't remove her hand from the strength of TeJay's grip. At the end of the field, they came to the old rock fence held in place by steel stakes and edges of barbed-wire. In the fence row stood a persimmon tree and along the path sassafras bushes.

"Maude kept sassafras roots for tea. Do you remember

sassafras tea made with lots of sugar?"

"Yes. Maybelle made sassafras tea and I like it."

They noticed Tip and Sarah Anna climb their steps to the deck and enter the house with their friends.

After a long walk around the orchard, they walked up the lane with TeJay swinging her hand in cadence to their steps.

"Would you like to come Christmas shopping one day after Thanksgiving and allow me to treat you to lunch?" TeJay asked.

"I would like that TeJay, but the people at the gallery called and asked me to bring in more items. They sold all my art and I forgot to tell you. Tip finished the frames before I blocked and pressed my work. He plans to help me put everything together, so I can take it when I go. I would like to come for lunch with you, but I don't want the time limits of a schedule."

"So, you come to town and I feel very left out. Tell me whenever you can come meet me."

"If I'm looking for my Christmas gifts, I won't allow you to snoop. Don't feel rejection. Besides, what will you buy your parents?"

"They both like cheese. I buy a basket and fill it, or I find one already packed. The extras like crackers or jam don't suit their taste, so it's wasteful and unwanted.

I prefer to make my own choices. Last Christmas, I bought a
round hoop cheese, but they like samples or variety better."

"Do you know the basket-maker north of Woodbury? Can we
go there to look at their inventory of handmade baskets?"

"You mean now? Sure. I need to tell my parents about
this expedition, so if you wait for a moment, I'll return.
We'll take my truck, in case it's off the paved road."

"I think it's a good Saturday afternoon activity and
their wood strips smell so clean."

                    *   *   *

On the return trip after they bought baskets from an
older couple who sold apples and sweet potatoes at a roadside
shed, TeJay asked about her health.

"Will you see your doctor while you're in town?"

"My next appointment is in January, so I don't plan to
see my doctor until then. I feel good except for fatigue
sometimes."

"When your boss died, did you feel anger?"

"Anger? No. I felt fear. I knew my boss needed
medical help. Often he would come in the morning and give me
instructions, then disappear for the day."

"Why did your feel fear?"

"I didn't know he had the virus, but I suspected and
after his death we were all tested. My test showed anemia

and I told the doctor about my fatigue. My fear that I had HIV, too, proved wrong, but the doctor saw my fears and suggested my stopping out of work for awhile. I couldn't work and maybe that doesn't make sense, TeJay."

"Yes, it makes sense, Cayrolynn. Before I met you, my boss or the firm chief partner talked to me about becoming a partner and the pressure made me very angry. My motivation evaporated and it made working difficult."

"You choose not to become a partner, TeJay?"

"My anger and the pressure concerned the requirements for partnership. I met you and I'm not so angry any more, but I feel like I pushed it down inside and eventually I must deal with it. How about you?"

"My fibromyalgia is better, but fear haunts me like a shadow and often I experience nightmares. At least, I know, I'm not dying with something incurable. Most people who fill medical offices are women and I hate being sick. Every tomorrow means another day with no energy."

"Well, we're home and I hope Tip remembered to cook hamburgers for us when he fired up the grill for my Mother. Don't hide out in the Loft, Cayrolynn, come along with me and make my parents happy you're here."

*   Nine   *

Thanksgiving came, and Lexie came home.

Cayrolynn looked at the photograph of this daughter Tip and Sarah Anna adored. Surface friendship, so hypocritical and shallow, or genuine heart response, Cayrolynn questioned and felt apprehension.

"I plan to pick up Lexie, Matt, and Sann at the airport, then be home early tonight." TeJay called Cayrolynn from the office. "It's difficult to work any day before a holiday. Around here, people take off Friday at noon every week."

"What does this mean, TeJay? You're into a mood to flee the coop as Maybelle would say?"

"Tip liked to talk about self-discipline. He still does. I'm not a bug-out person, what ever that means. However, today, like any proud uncle, I'll meet the plane."

"Don't let me be a problem this week-end, TeJay. If you think it best, you could take me to your condominium until Monday."

"Why would I do that?"

"I'm feeling like an imposition to your family. These few hours, Sarah Anna needs undivided attention for her family."

"Cayrolynn, your sense of displacement or self inflicted inferiority gives you a left out feeling. Please, don't."

                    *   *   *

Earlier, pre-dawn she listened for TeJay to leave in the Porsche, but he took his truck. Curiosity thwarted her tears. Later she listened for Tip's truck to leave and before eight, Sarah Anna's car. Both came home at noon, and afterwards, Sarah Anna called to say they cleaned and made preparations for the family.

Almost five, TeJay came home in a rented van. The rented van meant TeJay made excellent plans, as usual. Lexie came to the Loft with TeJay and the children into the arms of their grandparents to be carried into the house.

"Welcome to the homestead, Cayrolynn. You look different from the photographs TeJay sent us," Lexie said.

"You look different, too, and I didn't know about the pictures," Cayrolynn added.

"My babies may cause havoc, even so, we all go to church tonight. We miss Rae, Andy, and Sam when we get together, but we'll talk with them this week-end. Do you sing,

Cayrolynn?"

"A little."

"Please bring a guitar and sing a small chorus for us. It's a family time for our community, so friends and neighbors will pack us out. We want them to know you."

Cayrolynn knew TeJay saw her hesitate, yet both Lexie and TeJay ignored her pause. She remembered gossip from her youth. She could hear women say, that's TeJay's friend who lives with Tip and Sarah Anna. Lexie smelled sweet and her words spoke courage for this Thanksgiving service.

When Lexie went to the house, TeJay followed his sister, then he returned with a bag from the deli.

"Chicken wings to reheat, and fresh baked bread for our supper. Not coffee, Cayrolynn, but some de-caf, okay?"

TeJay helped place their food on the table before he moved to her chair like Prince Charming. Neither showed surprise when Cayrolynn turned to receive his touch. They finished their meal, loaded the dishwasher, and checked the thermostat after both commented on too much heat.

"You make your choice, Cayrolynn. Will you go to church to hear Lexie and join the sing-a-long?"

"My preference means I stay home, TeJay. If we go, will we stand out like strangers?"

"I wish I could tell you we can sit in the back. You'll

see every seat filled and the pews mushroomed. I'll go first and see where we can sit, maybe near an exit door by the choir."

"It's your family party, so please try to put me in some unobtrusive place."

*   *   *

No place to park, so TeJay drove into the cemetery and others followed him. The stars felt close and sparkled like signal lights in the clear coldness of winter twilight.

"Is God in the heavens?" Cayrolynn questioned. "The black hole to the north according to scientists and near the throne room, if the earth becomes the footstool."

Cayrolynn felt her feet shift on uneven soil and TeJay almost tripped. They reached for each other at the same time and walked together, linked, giving support to each other on the dark pathway. Others behind them, almost stumbled and chorused alarm at the grassed path.

They went into the chapel through a side entrance as TeJay suggested earlier, and already, Tip led the singing. When the place held no more room nor chairs, Tip asked Lexie to give a devotional. She stood in front among teenagers seated cross-legged on the carpet, not behind the lectern. She talked about thanks living with thanks giving. Cayrolynn expected testimony time, but Lexie led in prayer, then several others stood and led in prayer. Tip asked for requests from the hymnal and began the singing again. Lexie took her children by their hands and came out the side door. TeJay felt for Cayrolynn's hand and they followed.

"My children squirm too much for a country service, so off to bed for you two."

"May we skip our bath this time, Mom?" Matt asked.

"We'll see." Lexie answered.

Lexie introduced her children as they walked along to the van. She rode to church with her parents, now she joined TeJay and Cayrolynn for their ride home. Cayrolynn felt a shyness toward these grand-children, so she made no conversation except to speak. Children respond to voice and facial expressions. In the darkness, they couldn't see. Tomorrow, she might secure their friendship. When she lived at the children's home, she liked to keep preschoolers interested with stories and songs including made-up verses with their names. Most became friends.

TeJay drove down the ridge line road, now bright in the autumn moonlight. Cedar mixed with leaf-less hardwood blocked the view of the hollow. When the road curved west down into the pocket of the hollow, they could see across the valley.

"I love this view," Cayrolynn said.

"Me, too, and it becomes a homesick remembrance, sometimes, because near the ocean, we lack these hills. Often, I watch cloud formations that seem to block my view of these hills, but like a mirage no hills appear. Tomorrow, I'll show you my favorite places, Cayrolynn. From the church, we can hear a tremendous echo. It's the same place where I decided about my calling. I'll show you."

"You make a good suggestion, Lexie," TeJay said. "Cayrolynn works for her Christmas sales and she needs a different day."

"Yes, I would like that," Cayrolynn said.

"My Mom feeds us breakfast whenever we awake on Thanksgiving with soup for lunch. Our turkey meal comes around four or five. After a busy day outside, we all feel starved. It depends, if the weather stays acceptable."

When they parked behind the house, Matt and Sann clamored for hot chocolate.

"I know your Grand-Dad's promise, so I'll warm your cocoa, but not his story tonight. I'll read you a book and we, all three, will go to sleep. Too much excitement this day for us."

TeJay helped Lexie into the house, then followed Cayrolynn to the Loft. He stood looking at her work before he sat beside her and offered suggestions.

"Your sister doesn't look like either of your parents."

"My sister's her own person, forsure. My Mother never knew her Dad's people, so she thinks Lexie must favor the family she never knew," TeJay said.

"Soft thin hair that curls like a wind-blown thistle brush, with a smile that shows her upper teeth and gum, and a voice soft and penetrating that makes her a unique person. She's so small and energetic."

"And genuine, Cayrolynn. Get her to tell you about William Robert called Wildy Bert. He carried this crush on Lexie and it's our family tease."

"Where did she find her husband?"

"He's the brother of her college roommate. Tales about roommates led Lexie to ask for a single room. When she moved to campus, some mix-up gave Lexie a roommate. With over crowding during the freshman year, Lexie understood she would not live alone.

"My parents drove her over there and found Lexie scheduled to live with Rosetia Sanchez, called Geeta, from Brownsville, Texas. For some reason, Rosetia came one week late. So, my parents helped Lexie unpack and be ready for classes. One week later, they went to meet the roommate and her parents. My parents and Lexie liked Roseita and her family. Geeta's the life-of-the-party kind of girl. She wore flamboyant western clothes and made straight A's without studying. Lexie expected she wouldn't stay the year, but she did, then married the following summer. This wedding in Texas gave Lexie time with the older brother who works as an oil geologist."

"When did Lexie marry?"

"After she finished college. Tip warned Lexie about finishing. Sam didn't finish and now, Sam says, he wishes for the lost degree."

"You chose MTSU and Sam chose Tech?"

"Sam liked to walk in Tip's footsteps. The student who lured him to the church encampment in Branson came from Kentucky and lived down the hall."

"Shafe became your roommate?"

"At the beginning, I joined with some guys from Nashville, but they liked to party. I met Shafe in one of my classes."

"Does he live around here?"

"Down on the Tennessee-Alabama line between Huntsville and Fayetteville. Shafe found a job and wanted to move to an apartment. Tip approved, so we scrounged furniture from our relatives and moved off campus. I worked country music jobs in high school and decided to continue. Sarah Anna feared for my grades, but no problem.

"When Shafe and I finished at Murfreesboro, we found an apartment in Nashville. By the time I finished law school, Shafe wanted us to buy a condo and divide the cost with expenses. This worked well for us, then Shafe began plans to marry and bought his own condominium.

"Cayrolynn, you know all about my family. Your time, so fess up. Did you find the girls in your cottage like family?"

"Yes and no."

TeJay leaned his head back to rest on the couch. When knock-out sleep hits, not until wake-up moments come, does anyone understand they lost being awake. Cayrolynn knew TeJay would have a crick and a sore shoulder if he stayed in this odd position. When she tried to help him reposition, TeJay awoke. He left for the house and Cayrolynn wasted no time in her lock-up of the Loft and going to bed.

Thursday morning, she slept late and awoke with the ringing of the telephone.

"Cayrolynn, your breakfast will be brunch and then Lexie wants to go exploring with you," Sarah Anna said.

"Tell Lexie I need some time to be awake and dress for our excursion."

"Doesn't feel like Thanksgiving. I fear this won't be a day for hunger, even with my baked turkey breast. Lexie brought us a spiral honey ham. My grandchildren like peanut butter and jelly with soup. So much, for this grandmother's big holiday meal."

    "Never fear, Sarah Anna, because by Sunday your refrigerator will be empty."

    Cayrolynn felt some need in Sarah Anna, something that caused her to stay on the telephone. Maybe, she missed prior times with her own grandparents, or times with Claude and Maude, or not seeing Andy and Rae, or the empty place for Sam and his family.

    "Sarah Anna with your school teaching, I see you as a Mother who is accustomed to 'being all things.' Does this cliche, which seems to apply, bother you?"

    "At present, no, Cayrolynn. Yes, back awhile ago, when I felt the tired fatigue of family, home, and job. I guess I miss Maude the most at Thanksgiving. She wouldn't cook a meal because she wanted me to begin my own family traditions.

    "Remember the song, over the river and through the woods to grandmother's house, we go? Maude loved that melody, but she would pack my frig on Wednesday before the holiday with everything ready. Even talking about her, gives me painful nostalgia. 'Nope.' Her word. She refused my family any food or chair at her table when she said they needed to eat at home. She understood my fatigue, because she worked until she and Claude came to the hollow."

"TeJay says Lexie looks like Maude. So, you have reason to be homesick for days past. Women remember. I miss my Mother, Lavender, and Maybelle, because I learned from each of them. So, I understand your early morning recollections. Are your children awake?"

"Can't you hear them? Tip keeps them happy until Lexie gets downstairs. See you in a bit, Cayrolynn."

Cayrolynn replaced the telephone, then hurried to finish her bath before the children appeared with Tip to look at their grandfather's shop.

"Did I hear you on the phone with my Mother earlier?" TeJay asked when he came over.

"Yes. She misses bygone days."

"Hill traditions say everybody comes home to the old homeplace. Maude and Claude wanted that tradition for our family. Wealthy families own enclaves big enough for three or four generations. I blend into whatever my family plans, but it's nice this year to have you participate with me, so I'm not the ole bachelor hanging around."

"Today, I feel energetic."

"Yes, you're pretty with clean hair and a pretty smile."

"If my fibromyalgia draws me up and winces away my energy, I hope I'll not be a burden to you and your family."

"Poor thought pattern because we live each day with no regrets for tomorrow. I bought you a couple new books about beating the odds."

"From the do it yourself bookstore shelves. Thank you, TeJay."

Cayrolynn didn't mean to flinch or move away. Subconscious movement away. Now, conscious holding tight, to give the assurance that she craved security.

*   Ten   *

"My children enjoy my parents, so they bubble with happiness and I feel at peace leaving them."

Cayrolynn watched Lexie guide Sarah Anna's car with an expertise that showed practice in Houston traffic.

"Children plus a job and family, Lexie, I know you stay busy." Cayrolynn pulled on her hair in a way that seemed to say when she was younger she put either a straight tress or a bundled switch into her mouth to chew like sucking on her thumb.

"Whenever Lance goes away for oil exploration or on a geology field trip, my life stays quiet. When he comes home, I try to limit my work. This schedule gives us quality time together and time for us to enjoy our family. Neither of us appreciate much social life because our jobs stay too demanding."

This gravel road with its short jack knife curves upward and around the hill took Lexie's attention, even though she

met no other cars nor trucks. At the church, she drove to
the back of the cemetery. The cemetery spread out along a
series of terraces escaping from the ridge top plateau.
Crushed rock dumped and smoothed at intervals like jutting
elbows extended the walking paths and opened spaces to make
hillside parking possible.

Brush Arbor Cemetery stretched to a jump-off tree line
curbed with rejected railroad cross ties. Along the ridge
chrysanthemums blossomed yellow in the fall and that yellow
of sunshine reappeared with daffodils in the spring. The
cemetery looked like a museum of sculpture made with granite
and marble, then with chiselled calligraphy.

"Claude died the year of my birth, so I never knew him.
See here these gravestones for Claude with Maude beside him."

Lexie stopped to tie her shoe. Cayrolynn secured her
brown watch cap, pulled it tight, and found a tissue to blow
her nose. The crispness of the wind brought tears to her
eyes.

"Claude helped Maude keep the boys and they appreciated
him. Or, should I say they loved him? My Dad's a good
teacher like my Mom, but I think Claude spent more time
teaching the boys about farm tools, plants, and animals.
TeJay tells about Claude showing him property lines and legal
land rights. If the deed says a tree marks the boundary,

then cut down the tree, and drive a steel stake, Claude advised. Trees grow, trees die, storms take trees out, and erosion moves rocks, if they mark a property line. You drive a stake for property protection. According to Maude, Claude was a miser and if you watch, TeJay counts his pennies, too."

They walked to the church and sat on the back steps protected from the wind and warmed by the sun.

"Most years our church stays unpainted, but this year she wears a new white coat. Summer foliage hides it from view across the valley. When the leaves from the hardwoods join the mulch of past seasons, it shines like a beacon!"

"Tell me about your call to ministry." Again, Cayrolynn pulled tissues from her pocket and blew her nose. "Sorry, Lexie, the mountain breeze causes my allergy to act up."

"I never wanted to be a pastor-preacher. The first summer Andy worked at the hospital in Memphis, when he came home he told me about the chaplain. I thought women might be accepted at a government hospital because of affirmative action. Then, before I began seminary, chaplain positions working with children opened. So, I knew where I belonged. God gives us a calling and then He places us."

"So, how did you know?"

"Come, I'll show you." Together they walked down a pathway marked by weathered gray concrete boundaries

outlining the grave plots. Most of these graves belong to
Claude's people. These gravestones belong to us with our
plot here. You see these dual graves for Claude and Maude
and the three babies belong to Andy and Rae."

"Someone keeps this plot because it shows care."

"My Mom. Her prized grand-children because she seldom
sees Sam and his five. I make double efforts for her to play
with Matt and Sann. During my months in seminary, my parents
came and brought the children back here, whenever possible.
Often, they took time from their jobs. It gave me time to
prepare for tests and write my papers."

"You were thankful and grateful."

"Very thankful and very grateful." Lexie didn't watch
for her feet and stumbled on a fallen branch. She reached
down to retrieve the decayed limb, then threw it down the
hill.

"One Sunday, I waited for my family here, by walking
around these terraces. Like the distant roar of ocean waters
or a whisper that I repeated, the words came 'I am going to
be a preacher when I grow up.' And, in my heart I knew truth.
When I felt the truth and bigness of my words, I screamed
them across the hollow. One great gust seemed to gather my
words and write them on the wind so that I heard the echo of
reverberations across the hollow."

"You told your family?"

"Yes. Tip liked for us to sing. He would call one of my brothers to the front almost every service. He began to ask me to read the scripture and if no preacher came for the day, we would sing a lot, and he would ask me to give a devotional. Most of those first years, I read from a devotional book belonging to my Mother. Later, I began to compose my own talks."

They sat on the rock wall stacked when Brush Arbor Church lacked a building and restacked before homecoming each summer. Land grant settlers came here after the war of 1812. Cayrolynn sat in her own thoughts, and blew her nose in cadence with the gusts. Lexie watched Cayrolynn who looked like a small cocoon wrapped in brown paper.

"Tell me, Cayrolynn, does your health problem seem like a death warrant to you?"

Lexie realized she seemed intrusive and rude.

"No, and here's a good place to tell you. These graves mean victory for these people. If they loved, then someone mourned. I didn't understand that death offers more than living. I do now. I learn to live with fibromyalgia and a lifestyle acceptable to the pain."

"Do you take special medicines?"

"Mild sleeping tablets, muscle relaxers, and vitamins.

I try to follow the doctor's instructions. Everyday, I try
for outside exercise and my living here without work tension
and office demands allows healing, I think."

"Miracles happen, Cayrolynn. Failure to seek medical
help seems like tempting God, which is wrong."

"Sometimes, I think about snake handlers and question
'how read ye?' when stories appear in the newspaper. Why
would anyone make God prove Himself?"

"Prayers do get answered," Lexie said, "answers come in
many ways. Joy comes in the morning. Please promise me,
Cayrolynn, you'll seek new medicines and therapies that come
available."

They stood and looked across the hollow. Cayrolynn
watched while Lexie went to the back of each head stone and
placed her hands like a mother caresses a bassinet. From her
pocket she took a bag of stones and placed several near the
edge of each granite slab. Cayrolynn saw other stones,
crushed white marble and water washed geology finds, all
placed with prayers of remembrances. "And I will give you a
white stone, and on the stone a new name written, which no
man knoweth saving you that receiveth it," she quoted to
herself.

"My Mother doesn't like plastic flowers, Cayrolynn. She
watched Rae choose a gray rock from the edge of the graves to

take back to campus after the first funeral. Sometime
thereafter, she suggested the prayer pebbles of remembrance.
On our back porch, you'll notice a basket of small stones.
Even my Dad will take a few for his pocket when he thinks he
might be coming here."

"Your stones seem to be clear green and blue marbles,
Lexie, like those bought from a florist who adds pebbles to
green oasis to make plants and flowers stand tall."

"And, a few white polished marble chips that I found
yesterday at the airport when I bought my Mother some flowers
for her table."

"Interesting. TeJay brings some cut flowers to divide
between the Loft and the house, and I like to mix mine with
greenery from the yard. Here, wild flowers flaunt their
blossoms and all fall we enjoyed leaves with their change of
color," Cayrolynn said.

"Sometimes, I see a color and with nostalgia I see my
remembrances of unbelievable changing landscapes of color
with purple and orange and yellow. Often, I remember a sweet
gum or a maple and a leaf half green and half color. Beauty
indescribable."

Cayrolynn felt the peace of this place. People value
their country church and talk about it. Today, no sounds
came from the hollow below, and no bees, nor yellow jackets,

nor hornets, nor waspers, buzzed with random flight and subversive landings. They walked past the cemetery arbor built by one of Claude's grandfathers, who was a blacksmith. The copper roof turned chalky blue green and the iron grill work showed some green paint with some black from the primer used to curb rust.

Cayrolynn stopped before she opened the car door and looked back to the graveyard. Eventual resting places become the last memories of life on earth. Questions. Would she be planted here one day beside TeJay and near his family?

"I want us to stop by the place where Claude and Maude lived. They lived in a double-wide mobile home that Tip sold after Maude died. The old cabin built by Claude's ancestors on the shelf rock deteriorated to a nonlivable status. With no way to add plumbing, it couldn't be redeemed."

The field gate creaked open and Lexie didn't close it after she drove through. They followed the gray sand wagon tracks tracing the hollow branch toward the old house site. When they pulled into the yard, each noticed the grass mowed, weeds pulled, and debris moved into a pile ready for burning.

"Your Dad knows you come here, so he mows it for you."

"Dad likes this place. We thought Sam would live here when he finished college. Claude and Maude bought the place from relatives after my Dad shipped out for Korea. Part of the land, they secured by paying back taxes."

They sat on the gray rock extending from a shelf rock
outcropping with a spring running from underneath.

"Our family loves this place that Maude called the
pocket, but it's not a mountain pocket, rather the head of
the hollow with the spring. Pocket means a mineral deposit
back in the mountains or a basin in the hills hidden away.
In our mountain ridge further north the cliff hides a fold
over in the strata. Instead of a cove or hollow, we would be
called Claude's fold. Maybe, you heard all this before,
Cayrolynn. Sorry, if I'm repetitious."

Lexie tasted a piece of watercress before she asked
Cayrolynn about her family. Cayrolynn saw the genuineness of
the questions Lexie asked. She answered with openness
allowing the pent up sadness of her life to flow like
festering pus from a boil that needs to be cauterized.

Once Maude told Sarah Anna that Lexie held a sixth sense
because discernment seemed to be one of her gifts. When
others flounder in lack of wisdom, Maude thought, Lexie sees
far beyond the current conversation. She sees meanings and
nuances that belong to a sixth sense.

"Children who keep bad memories try to forget, Lexie.
Lavender, an old woman and my friend, lived at the end of the
dirt road where we rented a trailer in Florida. Up where the

dirt road entered the paved road stood a church much like
your Brush Arbor Church. Lavender took me there and any
other children whose parents allowed them to go.

"When my parents boozed, it meant I escaped to her
house. I remember one night, my Mother kept a singing
contract at a club near the beach at Fort Walton and I stayed
home. When I heard the truck pull-up, I hid under the bed.
How can I describe a bad night? My Mother kept screaming.
My Dad passed out drunk and slept in his stupor. When my
Mother screamed, she threw things. She hit my Dad with the
lamp that broke and I thought my Dad would beat her. He
didn't; instead he left. After all became quiet, I listened
to be sure my Mother went to sleep. I took off lickety-split
to Lavender's trailer.

"Lavender told me about sex. Teachers talk about sex in
home economics class, but not about the emotions women have.
I'm glad Lavender told me because she understood my Mother.
When girls on my school bus giggled and told secrets, I went
to Lavender to discuss what I heard.

"Before my Mother sent me to the children's home,
Lavender led me in discussions about her beliefs. She was an
old timey Christian who would say I know, that I know, I know
that. I became a member of her church, Victory Tabernacle,
and then, baptized in the river at East Bay. I tell you all

this, Lexie, and it appears I possessed bad parents which isn't true. Except for drinking, they cared for me. Then, my Mother got cancer and she didn't want me there during her last days. I'm not afraid of dying, but I hate to think about the last days of the dying process because those days of pain I fear."

"Cayrolynn, did you never have a boy friend?"

"No. I know it sounds strange. Some boys my age lived at the home, but they seemed not right for me. In Nashville, I joined up with people who brought their guitars to the house where we lived. We crowded folks into our space for Friday and Saturday night music. Sometimes, we charcoaled hamburgers or hot dogs, but no drinking, because we knew better. I thought, a couple of times, some man might be acceptable to date, but I never got serious about anyone. At work I saw my boss as my mentor. I guess I see most men like father figures or brothers to me."

"I understand, Cayrolynn. In high school, I liked William Robert Surles. Tip thinks Wildly Bert came in the jail group who stole our truck. Someone in the group knew where we kept our burning barrel for yard trash. They burned their jail clothes in the barrel."

"This homeplace brings memories for you, I think."

"TeJay says I look like Maude with my blow-away hair and

my dimpled smile."

"She became your best friend?"

"Yes. When I made my decision about preaching, she didn't think it parallel to the Bible teachings. She took her big print and showed me the verses. Then, she suggested I buy a notebook so she could tell me secrets. When my Mother went to professional meetings and Tip needed to work or couldn't be home, she would dictate verses to me from her big Bible. I thought I would keep her Bible when she died, however it became lost in the shuffle of her things."

"I know where it is, Lexie. I found it with my cleaning of the Loft and I read her markings of promises. What kinds of verses did she tell you?"

"She said she never heard a sermon about Satan and I needed to see him in the Bible."

"I never heard a sermon about Satan, either."

"It's easier to preach about the love of God and spiritual warfare gets included somewhere."

"So, where did she begin?"

"With the lying spirit."

"You mean, that comes first?" Cayrolynn asked.

"I hate little slips of the tongue, when I tell a lie with no aforethought. Like did you eat dessert for supper? No. But, I did and I question myself, why would I lie?

Absolutely, no reason. Then, I question, do I take it back and say that's a lie or do I let it slide. Either, I lose face with my lie, or get into confusion. Is it my selfish sin or is the devil knocking at my door?"

"So, Satan comes first as the lying spirit?"

"According to Maude, he comes first. Then, others follow and Maude wrote them all out for me."

"Lexie, I think God does tell some people special secrets, like my friend Lavender. I know she had the gift of prayer or intercession, and a double portion of the Holy Spirit."

"Cayrolynn, whatever God gives becomes a journey to spiritual maturity. I try to use all my Bible knowledge in my work. I pray for the children and their parents who touch my life. Who knows if God will turn and leave a blessing?"

"In the harshness of secular life, we see God off separated from our existence. Why did my Mother die with cancer? Why does this spirit of infirmity attach itself to me? Why? Why?"

"Cayrolynn, who knows? Nobody. My only answer is that I'm so glad God brought you into our family. I'm glad you'll join our family in our cemetery plot on the hillside."

"I'm glad my name is written in heaven and I'll see you

there. A-men and Selah. There's your Dad. Like days of your childhood, he comes looking for you."

Lexie stood and waved to her Dad. Tip walked up the road to them.

"Did you notice, I cut the yellow bittersweet from the center strip, including bushes along the roadway, and scared away the snakes? Your Mother says I keep it clean so the deer will come drink from the spring. Water flows better when the spring is clean," Tip said.

"We noticed and found it easy to sit on the rock. Were my kids giving you trouble? Do you need me?"

"They went to sleep. Sarah Anna sent me out to find you two. She thinks you need a cup of tea. She wants me to begin a bed of charcoal embers to turn red and season until we come for our bonfire and toasting of marshmallows. Memories for our babies, she says."

"I know my Mom. She'll pad us up with warm clothes, otherwise, it'll be too chilly."

* Eleven *

When Lexie and Cayrolynn drove into the yard after their visit to the cemetery, they saw a rental car parked behind the house.

"Someone in the family decided to surprise my Mother. I guess my uncle or Andy."

"I'll see you after supper, Lexie. I don't think I should be outside with my allergy plus the coldness of this bothersome wind," Cayrolynn said.

Lexie nodded agreement and Cayrolynn went to the Loft instead of following her up the steps into the house. In a few minutes, TeJay came to check on her.

"Won't you join us for supper or do you want us to take a drive and eat at whatever we find open?"

"I prefer to stay here and listen to music with no food except for fruit. I want you to eat with your family, enjoy the bonfire with the kids, and make my excuses. This afternoon with Lexie gave joy, but took my energy."

"My Uncle Andrew came and he'll wander over to meet you
before he departs. When he visits, he keeps no schedule, so
he might leave tomorrow, or Sunday, or Monday. Whenever.
With indecision, he tries to avoid the trauma of good-byes
because when we were younger, Andy would beg him to stay."

"What should I call your uncle?"

"Doctor or Andrew. Before he became a doctor, we called
him Uncle Doctor. Sometimes, my Dad calls him Professor, but
my Mother calls him, Brother."

"I hope Sarah Anna won't feel negative toward me because
I withdraw. Sometimes, when a person doesn't understand,
they hold a grudge."

"No worry. My parents include not exclude. She would
worry more if she thought you burdened yourself either
physically or emotionally. I'm concerned you chilled while
outside with Lexie this afternoon. Your runny nose seems
better. Did you take your allergy medicine?"

"Yes, and I'm better. You go join your family and
forget me because I want to read and maybe, take a nap at
dusk, even if I awaken early tomorrow."

TeJay turned on the television, clicked across the
channels, and left it programed to a western movie that he
stood watching for a few minutes. Cayrolynn went into her
bedroom and closed the door. She changed from the warm

sweater and pants into a softer pull-on paisley blouse and a matching long skirt. Sometimes, when she shopped, she bought clothes she never expected to wear. Eventually, she gave unwanted clothes away or placed them in Goodwill at the shopping center. This outfit, she kept. Tonight seemed the right time for the at home clothes that looked like a magazine advertisement. Allergy pollen settles on the face or hair, so she creamed her face to take away pollutants and put on new make-up. When she returned to the television and the movie, she changed the channel and began to eat a mellow apple. The core she threw away, before she stretched out on the couch with a pillow. Sleep came quickly.

Sarah found her there, covered her with a quilt, and turned off the loud bright screen. To quiet any extraneous noises, she started a long playing CD of blue grass. Then, she locked upstairs before going to Tip's shop where the family enjoyed story swapping.

Daylight edged the blinds before Cayrolynn felt the need to go to the bath. She changed into pants and a sweater for a new day. She stretched to feel for any cricks or soreness from her night of sleep. After she opened the blinds, she watched TeJay come from the house. At the bottom of the stairs, he called to her. When he came into the room, he brought a draft of cold air from the stairwell.

"How about breakfast in Murfreesboro, Cayrolynn? I need
to pick up some papers at the office, so we'll drive into
Nashville and then return here."

"If you need to work today, please don't include me,
TeJay."

"I don't need to work, but to take off all week-end
doesn't fit my work demands, either. I thought I might go
into work, but now I want to stay here. We should return
before lunch. Wanta come?"

"Sure, but I need a few minutes. I'll meet you at the
car."

"You must dress for this nippy weather."

"Did you tell your Mother?"

"No one stirs at the house, but I told Tip last night I
planned to ask you to come along."

They ate breakfast at the Waffle House before they took
the interstate. Deep inside Cayrolynn knew her thinking
became skewed. Meditation of my heart she kept saying to
herself, then she couldn't keep back the tears. Feelings of
insecurity and inferiority swamped her. At first, TeJay
thought her allergy must be bothersome, then he realized the
tears. At Hickory Hollow, he exited and drove into a service
station with drink machines. He chose a soda for himself and
water for Cayrolynn. When he returned to the car, he watched

her when she took the water, drank, and made an effort to
stop the tears.

"Tell me."

"Pity party.   Inferiority."

"Listen to me, Cayrolynn.   My bosses want to meet you
and it must be a casual affair.   Not a party or dinner, but
the meeting must be comfortable for us.   I never told you
because I didn't want you all up tight.   Only the
professionals will work this after Thanksgiving Friday
because the staff takes time off to hit the pre-Christmas
sales.   Then, I take you with me without explanation and you
get disturbed and make your eyes all red and nose blue."

"My nose isn't blue."

"Look."

Cayrolynn pulled down the car visor with the attached
mirror.   No blue nose, but red eyes, no lipstick, and blurred
make-up.

"Can you repair the damages?"

Cayrolynn drank from the water bottle and dug in her
purse for tidy-up make-up.   With his long arm stretch, TeJay
reached for a roll of paper towels in the back seat.

"Now, do I look better?"

"Better than any early morning wife.   They'll feel envy
because I find a beautiful woman.   Beautiful on the inside

and outside. Can you take a real compliment or do you think
it flattery?"

"Oh, TeJay, I'll cry again."

"No fair. In time, you'll meet everyone in my office,
but today I want a simple occasion."

Neither talked and after thirty minutes, TeJay pulled
into parking behind his office building. He used his key for
entrance into the building. Cayrolynn felt vulnerable along
with the realization she never came here before.

In his office, on the wall facing him, TeJay hung no art
nor diplomas, rather he mounted one frame put together by
Tip. Separated by a cream mat, a photograph of Sarah Anna,
another of Lexie and her children, and a photo of Cayrolynn
that Tip took one Saturday when she worked in his shop.
TeJay kept a spotless desk.

"If a client comes here, I don't want attention diverted
from our conference with my personal business spread around.
Files, we keep down the hallway in a fireproof closet and in
the bookshelves behind these sliding doors."

Cayrolynn showed her surprise when two owner partners
appeared with their wives. She didn't know what they knew
about her, but both seemed to think them married. Since they
received no gifts from these people, she refrained from any
explanation.

"We want you to come to lunch with us, TeJay. Will
you?" The partner who asked smiled not with big teeth but
with thoughtful eyes wrinkled at the corners.

"My Mom expects us back there because her house fills
with relatives. Cayrolynn and I escaped, but soon we need to
be in the middle of the fray again. Please no hurt feelings
about our refusal."

"We must make some plans for dinner and we want you
included, Cayrolynn." He watched her as he spoke.

"Thank you, I hope we can come."

On their way out of the building, Cayrolynn entered the
door marked Ladies. Now, she understood the earlier tears.
Some premonition stole her peace because she entered an
unknown situation. Her premonition continued and plagued her
with bothersome tears. She reached into a stall and gathered
paper to blow her nose. The door opened and the petite wife,
Pearl, entered to speak with her.

"We wanted to meet you, Cayrolynn. TeJay didn't tell us
about your wedding, however you chose beautiful rings. Let
me see." She reached for Cayrolynn's hand and the withheld
tears flowed.

"I'm sorry, Pearl, this is allergy." Between sniffles,
Cayrolynn, spoke, wiped her eyes, and her nose.

"My husband told TeJay he would never be a partner, if

he couldn't find a wife. So, he got busy in a hurry, and we feel so happy he found you."

Cayrolynn spewed tears. She gushed tears.

"Sorry. I took an allergy tablet. So, sorry."

"I understand," Pearl said. Cayrolynn knew she didn't. Wynell came in the door, and Cayrolynn departed. TeJay stood talking to the partners.

"So, sorry, TeJay," Cayrolynn said and saw alarm on the face of Rex, the senior partner and husband of Pearl.

"Cayrolynn suffers from allergies. She stayed out too long yesterday in the cold wind with my sister, Lexie."

"Maybe, she should see a doctor or go to emergency," Rex said.

"She will," TeJay said. "We left one doctor at home, my uncle Andrew from Memphis. My brother Andy, and his wife Glenda Rae-Ann, both doctors, may come today. They'll dry her nose and eyes with antihistamine and cause her to sleep all week-end. See you fellers on Monday," TeJay said. He placed his arm around her shoulder and ushered her out the door to the parking lot. The step off the landscaped curb made it convenient to kiss her on her cheek, which he did, and tugged her closer. The CD began playing when TeJay started the car. He drove with one hand and Cayrolynn closed her eyes trying to relax and stop the tears.

Later, TeJay voiced his admiration for her responses.
He discounted her embarrassment over the tears. The barbed
words of Pearl inflicted pain to her heart. She felt chills.
She couldn't bring herself to tell TeJay.

"It's natural to say, 'Y'all come,' but you refrained.
So, this command performance you passed a-o-kay. These
people I consider friends not snoops, however on a Sunday
drive they might like to drop by. I admire your discretion."

TeJay drove with a fierce determination to get them
home. She closed her eyes, again, and weighed words. TeJay
didn't hear Pearl. Real or not real? "What in this world?"
rang in her ears. Like a wreck on the highway and bystanders
questioned "What in this world?" She couldn't broadside him
now. Questions must wait.

"In the process of living, TeJay, I think everyone comes
to happenings or events where they must pass muster. I'm
glad if you feel pleased."

"We need to make a decision, my family and I, if we'll
help Sam buy the big house near Branson. Right now, I tarry
to go into partnership with the firm. I don't know if I need
a new abode in Nashville or if I'll find clients in Branson
and go there to live. Often, the commute from home to
Nashville gets bothersome, but I like having you at the farm
rather than in town. Decisions. Decisions."

"Like pulling the petals from a daisy. Yes, he loves me, or no he doesn't."

"Do you love me, Cayrolynn?"

"Yes sir, three bags full, a bushel and a peck and a hug around the neck."

"I'm serious and you put me off with a nursery rhyme."

"Otherwise, you might stop here beside the interstate and we would never get home."

"And, don't you know it."

In her heart, Cayrolynn listened to the easy tease TeJay gave with his repartee. Sometimes, she questioned about a child for TeJay and herself even though the thought showed her impossible life. Any thoughts of her chronic pain reminded her of poverty, loneliness, and feebleness. These dark thoughts brought her back to count her blessings. Once she saw a news interview with a Swiss banker and she made comparisons to Tip. Sarah Anna seemed more like the wife of the international banker than a first grade teacher in a rural school. In personal ways, their children resembled the unique appearance of their parents. The thought of no baby making with TeJay hurt.

"If you continue to speed, Speedy, you'll land us in the hoosegow."

"That's an interesting word. Wonder where it

originated? Will you pay my fine?"

"Sorry. No cash. No check. So you'll need to stay
until your Poppa comes for you."

"Cayrolynn, be a sweetie pie and find us another CD or
some radio. Don't be surprised to find Sam and his family at
home or Andy and Rae."

At the Beechgrove exit, they left the interstate and
angled around the hills on the bleak asphalt road past
rural looking homes. Now, TeJay drove slowly and reached for
her hand, which he held as he drove. When they reached home,
another rental car took parking space behind the house.

"I hope Andy didn't come alone. I hope he brought
Glenda Rae-Ann. Come with me Cayrolynn and help me discover
who's here."

Before they left the car, Andy came bounding into the
garage.

"Tip says it's too cold for a walk over the fields, but
I wanted to get a view of the land, if you aren't too tired,
big Brother."

"Hi, Andy. This is my Cayrolynn. Be kind to her
because I took her in to meet the big bosses, today. She
passed the test, but it left her all tired out, I think."

"Hi, little Sister. Come inside and meet my wife. Did
you meet our uncle?"

154

Cayrolynn didn't speak.

"She needs to meet our family and I'll go inside with
her. Lexie may want to join us on your hike."

Only Lexie and Rae sat on the couch talking. Others
scattered out of sight in the big house. Rae-Ann felt drawn
to Cayrolynn and followed her to the Loft. Lexie went off
with her brothers.

"My medicine lacks power today, I think. Most days I
feel at peace. Please give me your impressions of these
prescriptions, Rae-Ann," Cayrolynn said. Rae-Ann took the
cosmetic bag and began to sort through the array of brown
pill containers.

"Andy and I met at the airport in Nashville this
morning. I spent yesterday with my parents who live near
Mobile. Most of the time, Andy and I live apart and I miss
him. I'm sure the family tells you about us. Our coming
here makes me feel like age six and at home again."

"You understand, Rae, about my fibromyalgia. This
morning when TeJay took me to his office I couldn't stop my
tears and I didn't understand. I seldom cry. Maybe, I need
some vitamin or mineral I'm not taking."

"When I cry, Cayrolynn, I look at the calendar and count
the days. About day twenty-five to day twenty-eight, those
pre days may bring floods of tears for no reason. Did the

wives make comments? I doubt symptoms of either fibromyalgia or even depression."

"Yes and no. I said allergy, and it might be. They seemed all wrapped up in my marriage to TeJay, but we never discussed marriage. He gave me this covenant ring of friendship."

"Tip and Sarah Anna love you and so does TeJay. Andy loves me, but our lives changed with my miscarriages. The responsibility for birth control belonged to me and I tried. I tried, but not with success, as you know."

"I admire your gumption, Rae-Ann, and your strong faith. I don't know you, but I hope your marriage will blend with your lifestyle."

"Lexie suggested I look at your work. I'm searching for four framed creative art forms of some type to encourage and make children happy. Can you give a suggestion?"

"Come downstairs, and look at the frames Tip made for me. If you could find some example to help me see your space with a child's eyes, it might help determine a design. My work comes alive with the mats and frames Tip creates."

Tip and his brother-in-law, Andrew, sat on the stools around the work table. Cayrolynn felt included with the introductions to Andrew and she questioned how Rae-Ann felt about this august man. Andrew sat in repose with his arms

folded across his chest. On the tragus of his left ear a
large clear mole protruded. Cayrolynn couldn't understand
why a man of medicine didn't take time to secure its removal.
Neither gushed over her work, however they both wanted to
buy.

"If Tip will sell, then you may take either work you
choose," Cayrolynn said.

Tip watched Cayrolynn and saw she couldn't name a price
for her work.

"You must allow Cayrolynn's gift of your choice. Then,
if you want other pieces, she will accept those by commission
and charge like her gallery charges its customers. Is that
fair?"

"Yes. Andrew you go first because I can't decide.
She's going to make four designs for my office, so I think I
won't choose any of these. Tip will you help us with frames?
I feel artistic ignorance. I see such beauty and charm in
your work, Cayrolynn."

"Rae, you remember the mirror in our front hall put
there by the decorator?" Andrew asked. "I never liked that
mirror, so I believe I will take the two needlepoint designs
of the ships. My Dad worked as a river pilot. These will
remind me of my Mother who liked handiwork of all kinds and
my Dad who loved boats."

"Here's blue tissue paper for wrapping, Andrew," Cayrolynn said. "Tip help me please, and I'll use this masking tape for sealing."

"You make our Cayrolynn very happy, Andrew," Tip said.

"When you come to visit with us in Memphis, Rae-Ann, you can enjoy the work of Cayrolynn instead of that tacky mirror."

Cayrolynn understood Andrew gave Rae-Ann his approval. Whatever the problems between Andy and Rae-Ann, she enjoyed the respect and love of Andrew. One old bachelor uncle with a namesake nephew, his best friend, who felt cut off from his nephew's wife, and he loved her like a daughter. Cayrolynn felt no surprise in this discovery. She understood the women in this family were beloved.

"I like the colors in this needlepoint, Cayrolynn. If you can show me some illustrations, then we can decide on designs with these colors."

"If we return upstairs, I can show you my patterns and my current work. I call my self a primitive artist and the consignment shop that sells my work, also sells primitive antiques."

"So, you work as a small business woman?"

"You ask difficult questions, Rae-Ann. Sure, my work keeps me busy and builds self confidence, but my beliefs

and this family keeps me going on and on, too. I don't know
doctoring, but the smile of a child, a surprise kiss from a
grateful little one, and the joy of watching healing take
place must be rewards of high value."

"I need you around, Cayrolynn, when my spirit droops.
So, when you make these fabric paintings or quilted
tapestries for me, I'll look at them and remember your
encouragement."

Tip watched the reactions of Cayrolynn and remembered
her insecurities. She seemed poised and at peace with Rae,
Andrew, and this family. Was it her mental stability and
early life, or maybe, these days of illness and lack of
healing? Who would know? Maybe, he should suggest to TeJay
to talk with the nurse and the doctor at the clinic again.

159

*   Twelve   *

"Where's the family?" Tip asked Rae-Ann and Cayrolynn.

"Andy and TeJay bundled themselves in layers to go
tramping with Lexie across the hills. Sarah Anna keeps her
grand-children and they either read or go to sleep, I think."

Rae-Ann answered and raked her hand through her dark
heavy hair with an unconscious motion that seemed to be a
common practice when she talked. Cayrolynn remembered that
hair carries the most germs and she marveled at this gesture.

"Maybe, I should make a pot of coffee," Cayrolynn
suggested.

"Not for me, Cayrolynn," Andrew answered. "I'll join my
sister in her grandmother role."

"I think I'll take my gun out for some practice
shooting, maybe meet up with my kids, that is, if they look
for black walnuts," Tip said.

"How about you, Rae-Ann?"

"No coffee, however hot apple cider or a cuppa tea, if

you offer such," Rae-Ann said.

"Come with me, we must check the downstairs larder."

Before they settled on the opposite couches with their cinnamon spiced hot cider, Cayrolynn clicked on music with a soft sound and Rae-Ann checked the thermostat to add another degree of warmth.

"I read about fibromyalgia, Cayrolynn. I guess everyone questions you about your health. Do you see ultimate healing?"

"I try to adhere to the advice of my doctor. I seem to be either in remission or the medicine works, so I guess I'm learning to cope."

"Do you enjoy your quiet life here at the farm?"

"I'm never bored. Without the demands of an office, I sleep and eat according to my schedule. When I came here I slept long hours, and awoke stiff. Now, I get normal hours of sleep and good exercise. Often, I feel like one of Jeremiah's clay pots with cracks where my energy seeps out, so I need the potter's wheel to fix the cracks and keep my energy intact. My art keeps me busy and my mind interested in accomplishments."

"Patients think doctors can't understand. After my three miscarriages and we decided to tie my tubes, when I say I understand, I do understand."

"I appreciate your talking with me. Most people can't
talk or listen to me because it's so self-centered. Me, too,
I dislike being regaled with tales about aches and pains.
Will you ever have babies?"

"I'll never be a baby maker, so this gives Andy and me
lots of problems. The loss of my babies, then not being
accepted with Andy in medical school, and not working near
him seems very unjust."

"Rae, no one can keep you from bitterness or emotional
trauma or pity parties," Cayrolynn said. "It seems like if
you experience failure in life, emotional vibes stick out
like thorns, which gives bullies permission to strike. Not
only bullies, people react to me in unforeseen ways and their
response seems negative."

"You react from happenings in your childhood,
Cayrolynn?" Rae-Ann asked.

"When TeJay came over that first night at the steak-
house to talk to me, I feared he would walk away if I refused
to flirt and promise sexual favors. My Mother sang in beach
clubs or honkey-tonks and I knew pick-ups. My Dad stopped
putting me on stage and left me at home when I reacted with
fright. People scare me, so I stay quiet," Cayrolynn said.

"Patients carry thoughts that influence their medical
problems. One person might experience a virus while another

skips it or it causes little discomfort," Rae said.

"Before I learned to cope with the pain of fibromyalgia, or took prescribed medicine, I thought about people in jail, being accused of some crime. Me, being fatigued with pain like a hypochondriac. Seeking, but not finding a clue. I think about prisoners of war, or people in car accidents, or some catastrophic news item in the paper. Thoughts concern generalized people, people with trauma, and no help nor hope at all, so I gave up. When TeJay spoke to me, my personal question was, when do I die. Do I wait for reasons for my pain or make my life shorter?"

"You came to some conclusions or did circumstances and happenings make the decisions for you?"

"I think before TeJay, I nagged myself with self-talk about whether really great people experience more selfhood. Now, that I know TeJay and this family, I find Lexie's sermon delivered for me. I can't wrap myself in bitterness because bitterness shares hate. I must be wrapped in agape love, inside and outside. Agape is a matchless life-mender."

"At the time, I experienced the still births, we say miscarriages, but they were still births, I never slowed with my studies. However, now when my parents need me and they become more feeble and Andy doesn't live with me, life seems meaningless," Rae-Ann said.

"Thank you for coming here for these holidays. Everyone goes away for Christmas and maybe you should consider bringing Andy here again to this house of quietness and peace, a place to be lonesome and renewed, yet you may find it a place of comfort and togetherness."

"I think you talk me into it, Cayrolynn."

"Rae-Ann, I guess every girl dreams the Cinderella dream. I don't know why God gave me TeJay and this family. Sometimes, I fear to awaken and think I'll find myself a homeless woman on the street."

"We moved here when I was six when my Dad worked the job of principal of our school and my Mother taught fifth grade. Sarah Anna taught my first grade and I became best friend with classmate, Andy."

"Do you ever think of another man who might take your interest?" Cayrolynn asked.

"I know many men. Now that I'm older, my only interest remains the same, Andy. If we divorce, then I doubt I'll ever find another that I can trust. Andy's a little boy and a tease, yet he's very professional and brilliant. My Andy's the type to travel on edge, however never did he buy any car except a very traditional black four door. He grins a-lot, yet never as a hypocrite. Since he lives away from me, maybe women think he's up for grabs," Rae-Ann said.

"No one here said that. Is baby-making involved in the male ego, do you think?" Cayrolynn asked. "My Dad was a strutter, sometimes with a beer in his hand, and sometimes with a cigar or a pipe. I think he saw my Mom like an ornament he put on with pride because she sang for easy money. Me, I saw no real love and no care for her except when he showed her off and with that same behavior towards me. He would brag about being a Navy man which meant a generalization for his masculinity."

"Do your memories cause you to fear the men in this family?" Rae-Ann asked.

"TeJay's so different and Tip, too, because toys for them means tools, trucks, and maybe work. Even when he makes music with his guitar, TeJay thinks. He's a thinking man. I watch and listen to him speak, keeping time, as he touches his fingers to the strings. I recognized his sensitiveness the first night when I met him. He played a big bass fiddle with more than the rhythmic plonk."

"Since I didn't have a sister or a sibling, I grew up knowing Tip and Sarah Anna and their sons. Lexie came later, and she's certainly different. My Mother talked about imprinting in the womb because Lexie favors Maude. TeJay and Andy differ from Sam. Sam looks like Tip, however the male ego prevails in this family, forsure."

"Did you play dolls and wear little girl clothes or did your parents dress you like your playmates in jeans and kid shirts?" Cayrolynn asked.

"I watched the boys and matched them in 'follow the leader' style, how-some-ever with a few frilly pinafores and lacey trimmed socks. The boys all began shaving before they could shave and used Tip's aftershave and mousse on their hair with a hair dryer. Claude and Tip allowed me to learn carpentry skills with the hammer and the saw. Sarah Anna saw my interest in science during first grade. She would buy a whole chicken, or two whole chickens for her family, so Andy and I could divide them with kitchen shears and help cook. We watched the birth process and delivered our first piglets when we were first graders," Rae-Ann explained.

"Were other girls in your class included?" Cayrolynn asked.

"No, there were few girls in my class, yet the constant experiments like planting and growing trees or building something like the Loft, didn't interest most girls. I made very few friends in school, in grade school, high school, or college. When my parents went to Alabama to check on things, I would stay with Maude or with Andy's family. You would have liked Maude. She punctuated her conversation with 'what a pity.' What a pity, she would say."

The telephone rang.

"Cayrolynn, Andrew and I are pulling out the family photograph albums. Would you and Rae-Ann like to come over?"

"This is Sarah Anna calling, Rae-Ann, and she wants to know if we'll join her and Uncle Andrew in looking at family albums?"

"Say, yes."

Later, when Cayrolynn thought about her conversation with Rae-Ann, she questioned with second thoughts if her words gave assurance.

*   *   *

"TeJay," Cayrolynn said, "she included me like a sister, not like a doctor patient. She loves Andy, but she doubts his love for her."

"My brothers and I, we didn't push each other for our parents attention. Maybe, Sarah Anna added Lexie because she loved Glenda Rae-Ann. Sometimes, it seems as though parents achieve or fulfill a sibling relationship equal with their children. Claude and Maude included Tip like an equal, still in our family, chores became learning tasks and Sarah Anna coined the phrase, 'What can you learn, today?' With four adults around, teaching these kids kept everyone busy."

"Do you think Andy loves Rae-Ann?" Cayrolynn asked.

"Yes, and I think someday, they will be partners in

work, too. Not now, not yet, sometime in the future."

"Two busy days, Thursday-Thanksgiving and Friday with our trip to town and conversations here. What for Saturday and Sunday?" Cayrolynn asked.

"Uncle Andrew cooks us pancakes. Lexie goes to her college and seminary on the mountain. Andy and Rae might go to the football game in Nashville. The grandparents drive the tractor or the truck with the babies and what would you like to do?"

"Play monopoly. I love to play monopoly and keep the game in process for a day or two," Cayrolynn answered.

"We need to play here, otherwise, we may find little helping fingers demanding constant attention."

*   *   *

Cayrolynn felt with anticipation this pancake ritual. First, she felt the need to hibernate, then Tip called from his workshop downstairs to hurry her up for the pancakes.

"We talked about our plans for the day, but nothing seemed to gel." Cayrolynn spoke to Tip as they walked from the Loft to the house. "What do you think, Tip?"

"Sarah Anna needs help with Christmas decorations for her classroom, the church, and the house. Even if, we travel over Christmas for a couple of weeks, she wants to leave some decorations with lights and red bows on the roadside gates."

Cayrolynn knew some men went unshaven and chewed tobacco on a day off from work. Not this family, everyone dressed for guest and for each other. Sausage, bacon, ham, small breakfast steak patties, fruit, jelly, sorghum syrup from a mill over in Warren County, and scrambled eggs with enough butter to make healthy people fat. Like a gourmet festival, everyone ate to taste each dish and avoid a stomach upset.

Cayrolynn noticed Andy tasted, then found a bowl of bran cereal for himself. Andrew enjoyed being chef, yet he ate a grapefruit with a grapefruit spoon that Sarah Anna kept for him in her utensils drawer. Lexie fixed plates for Matt and Sann, but not for herself. She drank juice.

During a holiday breakfast at the home, Cayrolynn remembered, Maybelle, her housemother, telling about giving her mother-in-law some soybean meal. Later, at a family gathering it became a family joke, so with hurt and disgust, Maybelle avoided family get togethers.

This family affirmed their uncle Andrew with his breakfast of pancakes and there were no jokes nor snide remarks. They showed joy in their togetherness and missed brother Sam.

"We don't know the feelings of Toney nor his children, but we understand that Sam misses his place at this table," Andy said.

"I spoke with Sam last night," Tip said. "We talked about our buying the estate that's for sale on the lake. With our retirement, it doesn't seem wise for Sarah Anna and me."

The extra food went into a bowl to be carried up the hill and left for birds or squirrels. Andy and Tip gathered the dishes and began the clean-up.

Andrew cleared his throat.

"I think I'll partner Sam in the purchase. I didn't tell Sam because I don't know what the in-laws, Moseman and Connie plan. Either way, the guest house would offer a place for my retirement. Also, I need a winter place, too."

"You'll keep the Memphis house, the place with Sam, and a house or condo where heavy winter coats aren't needed?" Sarah Anna asked.

"I think so," Andrew answered.

Andrew doesn't tell this family any new secrets, Cayrolynn thought. They accept him and he accepts them in a belonging relationship more than friendship. And, that includes me, too, she thought. Me, too. Behind her eyelids, she felt the tears and moved to the bath to blow her nose.

"Christmas, and like the little red hen, I need help with my decorating, so who will lend a hand?" Sarah Anna asked.

"Surprise, Mom, when we tramped around the hills
yesterday, we clipped holly and cedar for you." Lexie said
before she went for wet bath cloths to clean small hands and
faces.

"I want to use a larger faux tree in my classroom that I
found on sale after Christmas last year. When you brought
the greenery from the hillside, did you bring a live tree for
the house, Tip?"

"One for the house and one for the church, that is, if
you want to decorate the church tree with Christmon's."

"I like the idea to help decorate your classroom," Rae-
Ann said. "Andy bought tickets for the football game in
Nashville, but we prefer to avoid traffic and weather."

"Why don't we begin with the church," Tip suggested.
Greenery and candles in the windows, the advent table in the
front, and a green pine set in water ready for decoration
nearer Christmas Day. If we decide on 'Hanging of the
Greens' for vesper-time this year, we can be ready. You take
Rae-Ann and Cayrolynn with you to the school, Andy and I will
work at the church, that leaves Lexie, TeJay, and Andrew for
the house."

"Do we all agree?" Sarah Anna asked. "I stacked my
labeled boxes of decorations upstairs in the hallway. We
should meet back here for coffee by one, since the clock

shows ten thirty now."

"Cayrolynn suggested monopoly depending upon your plans
Lexie, for Matt and Sann." TeJay placed his hand on her
shoulder and she felt the blush begin at her breast and climb
to the roots of her hair. No one commented, still they saw.
Cayrolynn didn't understand her unconscious response to his
touch.

Sarah Anna loaded her car, so Rae-Ann and Cayrolynn took
the red Porsche.

"She brings us to keep her company, Cayrolynn," Rae-Ann
said. "She tells the story about decorating with candy canes
one year and getting a tree full of mice. Her first graders
discovered the mice and that caused a stir. She collects all
year to find natural items families can find and use on their
own trees."

Sarah Anna unlocked the building and led the way to her
classroom with Rae-Ann and Cayrolynn following loaded with
various decorations. The school hallway appeared dark with
the wide antique flooring and wainscotting to match. Clean
smells caused Cayrolynn to think about TeJay when he began
school here. Were his stubby little hands rough after work
with Claude and Tip?

"I like big bright lights especially those which flicker
on and off, yet I wouldn't want to cause an electrical short,

so I use small lights with advice from Tip," Sarah Anna said.

"How do you keep the cedar smell, since I see you avoid the live evergreen?" Cayrolynn asked.

"Potpourris, but no fire hazards like wall plug-ins. My students make paper chains from colorful construction paper and snow flakes from lacy white party doilies cut in various shapes. You'll notice some paper or plastic lace coasters to hang with the spray painted cones and sweet gum balls. Pretty gift sacks add color where once I used brown pokes from the grocery."

"They take the tree decorations home?" Cayrolynn asked.

"Yes, and this year Rae-Ann brought me large sand dollars, one for each child. Lexie helped me put their names one each, so I need help with hot glue for the hangers, then put those on the tree."

"Shall we spray the pine cones, gold, and the sweet gum balls, silver, Sarah Anna?" Rae-Ann asked.

"Sometimes, children help me spray paint, but not this year. This year one current little wiggle worm would cause me grief. Please spray the cones and those balls. Use the newsprint to protect the table. My students will help me put those on the tree."

Cayrolynn watched the way Sarah Anna executed her plans and felt surprise to find the room decorated in an hour.

"No one will be hungry for lunch, how-some-ever I put Maude's vegetable soup in the crock pot and we can eat, whenever. Your monopoly game sounds like fun, Cayrolynn."

*   *   *

"Will Lexie leave the children with Sarah Anna, if she goes to visit her college on the mountain?" Cayrolynn asked Rae-Ann on their return drive home.

"She may go, still, I doubt it because the weather becomes dull with an odd drop of rain," Rae-Ann answered. "Her children will go to sleep and she likes the family camaraderie. The campus stays quiet when people enjoy their fireplaces. If this were a day of sunshine, she would find friends outside with their children and other holiday visitors to the campus."

Rae-Ann drove following Sarah Anna. When Sarah Anna turned toward the house she honked, then continued up the hollow road to the spring.

"So, many places of memory here, Cayrolynn. The spring where Claude and Maude lived and the spring at the Old Lonesome Place. I want to go to the store where my folks stopped often after a Sunday afternoon drive and bought me a Grape Soda. When I'm here, I think about people and places, and I miss the youth of my parents when we lived here."

The store seemed never to change with its wide plank
wooden porch. Inside, scruffed linoleum on the floor, and
chairs around a warm wood-burning stove in the back. The
owner didn't recognize either Cayrolynn or Rae-Ann and asked
no questions except to say, "Be careful, now, on these roads,
we may get some ice."

Rae-Ann bought two candy bars and two pieces of double
bubble. She handed Cayrolynn one piece of the gum and put
the brown sack on the back seat.

Cayrolynn knew they went to the cemetery. Tip's truck
stood before the front door of the church. Rae ignored the
truck and drove around the perimeter to the family plot.

"Soon this place will be wrapped in snow," she said.
Cayrolynn walked along with Rae-Ann, then left her. She
walked further past the ageless cedar, and to the front of
the church. Tip saw her and held out his hand for her touch.

"Come see our handy work?"

Andy came from the church ready to climb into the truck.

"Where is Mom?"

"Home. I came with Rae-Ann."

Andy left and walked to find Rae-Ann. Tip locked the
double front door with the attached holly and cedar wreaths
and red bows.

"Shall we be off," he said and like he helped Sarah Anna

he opened his side of the truck and tugged her inside. Cayrolynn looked to see Andy and Rae-Ann, but the downward curve of the road past the church cut off any view.

"Come with me to check the status of the decorations at the house, Cayrolynn. We plan monopoly and the swap-off of reading books to our grand-children. Do you need a bowl of soup?"

"No soup, but I would like to help with the black walnuts, if someone hammers them for me."

"We ask about that, come."

*   Thirteen   *

This Sunday morning, Cayrolynn dressed in a navy dress she crocheted her first winter in Nashville. She felt a need to feel pretty and be special, so she sprayed her ankles trying to use miniscule amounts of perfume. Perfume caused her eyes to water and made mucous in her nose. Her boss, Malcolm, before his death gave her his door prize #5 Chanel.

TeJay parked behind the church. The number of cars verified a full house like the crowd last Wednesday evening for Thanksgiving vespers. Friends and neighbors came because they wanted to speak to Lexie or other children of Sarah Anna and Tip who were home. Just like any church old home week, Cayrolynn thought.

This morning, Lexie wore a royal purple vestment celebrating the beginning of Advent. Cayrolynn understood the Methodist liturgical robe from her years at the children's home. Neither the Baptist minister nor Lavender's Pentecostal pastor wore a robe, but the choir members did.

Women didn't speak from the pulpit in the Baptist church, but Lavender's church called women to be pastors in their churches.

"Not enough hymnals, so we'll sing the Christmas songs we know." Tip led the singing, and the beginning thirty minutes of music seemed short.

"Y'all know Lexie. She brings our lesson this morning." Cayrolynn experienced the climate of the church where the audience appreciated the speaker and waited for her words.

"Today, we begin Advent. Four Sundays with four candles mounted here on the evergreen entwined wagon wheel that Claude found and brought here when we began to celebrate Advent. This hand whittled wheel came to the hollow with our first land grant pioneers.

"Once people used these four weeks for fasting and self-examination. After these four weeks of Advent, we celebrate the twelve days of Christmastide before we come to January 6 and Epiphany. Joy comes to me in being with you this Thanksgiving week-end and your pastor spends more time with his other charge, the Shiloh Church near Bald Ridge.

"We move from our thoughts about Thanksgiving and Thanks Living, to think about The Christ Child.

"Once a preacher named Henry Drummond gave a little talk on Love that D.L. Moody heard. Dr. Moody brought Mr.

Drummond to this country where he traveled giving his sermon, The Greatest Thing in the World. When you leave this morning, please take the tract copy of our lesson and his sermon given to you when you entered for church.

"Mr. Drummond began his message with verses memorized by most of us when we were children. From your Bibles, read or say with me Chapter 13 of First Corinthians. We stamd in honor of God's word.

*   *   *

"These past days brought many remembrances to my family. We came to the hollow because Claude and Maude adopted my Dad. They loved my Dad and over time, they adopted my Mom and us, too. My family adopts a new sister, Cayrolynn. You'll love her like one of us.

"Being here in the hollow and on this hill with Brush Arbor Church, along with my return home, makes me think about the word Love.

"Eros, the Greek word for love includes passion and lust. Eros is the physical bonding of sex. Eros may or may not unite with the lasting agape love of God.

"Storge, not used in the Bible, but the Greek word for love with a family group. The love of parents and siblings for each other, which I think of as love of the heart around the hearth.

"We know philo, the brotherly love. Philia and Adelphos together make the word Philadelphia and characterizes our Christian friendship with each other.

"We think about eternal agape love that today brings joy. And, we think about worldly eros love, when entered into without soul and spirit becomes bitter memories with sin, hate, guilt, and death.

"Before daybreak, this morning, I awoke and felt a need to watch the sun come from the Cumberlands across the barrens and hilltops to our church, then across the hollow to the hills of middle Tennessee. You and your families experience this awakening, too, at Easter when we meet here in our graveyard behind the church for Sunrise services.

"I came downstairs and found Uncle Andrew with a first mug of coffee. I didn't follow my desire to watch sunrise because of our overcast with weather that seems more like the hills move to capture the clouds and gives us serene solitude.

"In our conversation, Uncle Andrew told me about a place over-looking the Mississippi River where he likes to watch sunrise. It's a place where his Dad lost his life to the River on a stormy night.

"My favorite place is here on this ridge line, but on the Texas coast in a community named Freeport, we visit a small travel park that borders the port. When we go there, we stand looking up at the tankers, stretching like mountains from the water to the sky. When dawn comes and the early morning mist dissaptes, awesome describes the sight of those ships in first sunlight.

"God takes the blindness and sleep from our eyes and reveals his Son. The disciples knew fishing boats and the apostle, Paul, traveled the waters in good weather and storm.

"So, on this first Sunday of Advent, we think about the word Love, and we think about our God so great who removes the mist of fog and clouds from our worlds, and we meditate on the birth of the Christ child who places His agape love within us, body, soul, and spirit, and abides with us.

"He places His footprints on the mountains and seas. To end our service, I asked my Dad with TeJay and Cayrolynn to sing a closing Christmas song."

"Silent night, holy night." Cayrolynn joined them to sing the verses, and those present sang along on the chorus.

During the final prayer, TeJay took Cayrolynn's hand and they left by the back door. They drove down the hill before the others left the church. When she returned to the Loft to change into a sweater and jeans, she self talked, "I was glad when they said unto me, let us go into the house of the Lord."

*   *   *

Sarah Anna planned her Sunday lunch so that Lexie, Rae-
Ann, and Cayrolynn helped with coffee, ice tea, and milk.
Lunch came soon after the family returned from church.
Busy talk diminished, then quietness as they ate.

*   *   *

Cayrolynn remembered Lavender's philosophy. "Some women
spend all afternoon cooking and starve their families before
food gets placed on the table because of their need to show
personal power. Their husband's must stay outside and wait
or they get nagged to help in some way. Men escape to smoke
a cigarette that kills with cancer or heart problems."

"Did you do that Lavender?"

"It's later in dreams or remembrances, we see our
shortcomings and failures," Lavender answered.

*   *   *

Before they finished their Sunday lunch, Lance called
Lexie. When she returned to the table, she needed to go to
the airport in Nashville to meet him.

"Lance called from Tetterow to say I must meet him with
the children because their corporate jet lacks passengers.
We can avoid the commercial flight and be home sooner with
less hassle. Who can drive us?"

"Sarah Anna and I need to enjoy our grand-kids, so we'll

drive the van, turn it in, and collect TeJay's truck.
Do I hear any objections? Then, with agreement, TeJay you
might give me the paper work for the van rental."

Even before, Sarah Anna, Tip, Lexie and the children
left, Uncle Andrew asked Andy and TeJay to ride with him to
the interstate for Sunday papers. Cayrolynn and Rae-Ann sat
at the table enjoying spiced tea.

"When the house clears and everyone goes, we clean-up
and put-away, Rae-Ann," Cayrolynn said.

"Sarah Anna keeps all in order, so we face little work.
You wash and pack the dishwasher while I dry and put away,"
Rae-Ann suggested. "We might look at a video and take a nap
here in the den, or if you like, we can go to the Loft and
look at your suggestions for the art pieces you plan for me."

"You choose a video or a CD for us to take to the Loft,
then when the men return, they can enjoy the den and we won't
be disturbed with their conversation sparked by newspaper
reading," Cayrolynn suggested.

"I'll come soon, Cayrolynn. First, I want to take a
walk along the road to the Ol' Lonesome Place and use the
remaining film in my camera. Come with me," Rae-Ann said.

"You go. I need a quiet afternoon."

In an hour, TeJay came with his brief case.

"You read a book, Cayrolynn? Rae left Andy a note, so I

came to find you. I plan to take myself to Tip's work space and finish some nagging tasks."

"This book Sarah Anna brought from the library, and I find it difficult to put down. My time with your family keeps me busy and it's fun, yet I keep wanting escape to the ending of my book," Cayrolynn said.

"Now, I know you don't need me, however if you do, come downstairs. Don't expect the family until after dark."

At dusk, Cayrolynn finished the book and felt surprise to see sundown when she arose to close the blinds. Sarah Anna feels the loss of family when her home reverts to pre-vacation emptiness, she thought. Closure of music, the finale; or closure of a book, leaves loss of feeling if it's over. Cayrolynn left the Loft and went to the quiet empty house. She returned to look outside and realized the lack of rental cars. Tip's truck stayed parked down by the walnut tree near the orchard and Sarah Anna's car under the covered carport off the deck, but no others.

She expected to see Rae-Ann watching a video and enjoying the logs flickering behind the fireplace screen. Never did she come to the house when Sarah Anna wasn't home. Now, Cayrolynn went upstairs to look for people. The door to the room where Uncle Andrew slept stood open. Andy's old room showed order and no luggage. Strange, no one said good-bye before they departed.

Rather than stay here after everyone left, Sarah Anna went with Tip to the airport. Cayrolynn turned on lights. She turned on the oven and began the task of making hand-shaped biscuits without a cookie cutter. Maybelle made hand-shaped busicuts when some unhappiness came to their children's home. "A good pan of biscuits with butter, black berry jam or apple butter, and hot chocolate will help our heartaches," she would say. Cayrolynn pushed the biscuits into the oven when she heard the truck door slam.

"Who's here," Sarah Anna called after she opened the back door.

"Only me, Sarah Anna. I went to the Loft and finished my book, so I failed to say good-bye to Rae-Ann. When I came a few minutes ago, I found an empty house. I made biscuits for our supper."

"Surprise. I never knew you could make a batch of biscuits."

Cayrolynn took place mats from the drawer and began to set the table. Sarah Anna disappeared up the stairs. TeJay and Tip came from the backyard.

"With all our eating, we eat again, Cayrolynn?"

"Time to finish up the leftovers and enjoy dessert."

"Smells like fresh bread to me," Tip said.

The biscuits came from the oven brown, ready to eat, and not burned as Cayrolynn feared. TeJay pushed a CD of music from a hammered dulcimer that gave a quiet background for their conversation.

"You should be rejoicing, Lady Love," Tip told Sarah Anna. "You made our home a happy place this week-end."

"You mean an answer to our prayers. I'm regretful our son, Sam and his family couldn't come."

"Don't despair, Mom. He'll come as a surprise one day," TeJay said.

"I find your home like a resting place, warm and complete. It gathers and then, sends everyone away ready to face their next ventures of life," Cayrolynn said.

"Tip and Claude worked trying to make this house livable before I came. After the death of my grandfather, my grandmother moved from her farm into Memphis to live with my Mother. All her furniture, except for a few pieces, remained at the old homeplace. She listened to Tip talk about remodeling the house, then insisted we use her furniture."

"Unbelievable to leave furniture like yours unattended," Cayrolynn said.

"I think she worried about vandals and fire, so she dust covered everything and a tenant couple lived on the place," Sarah Anna said.

"Our heat here in the house, during that first winter, came from logs and the fireplace. We put in the elaborate heating system later," Tip said.

"My plans included returning to Memphis during the summers to finish my teaching degree. After I came to this drafty house, I wanted to leave the hollow and move back home. I remember those terrible cold days of ours."

"Another oft told tale by my Mother, Cayrolynn. She sees the house today, and talks about that first winter before I came," TeJay said.

"One night in March, I awoke to hear a freight train. I knew trains, which I heard all my life, so I disregarded the sound. Then, it hit me, we lived in the country with no railroad for miles. I pushed Tip and we both rolled and tumbled into the closet with our bed covers. Tornadoes mean disaster."

"Cayrolynn, you open my Mother's memory bank that keeps all the stories we begged to hear again and again as growing children," TeJay said.

"The difference comes with the details. She tells you, Cayrolynn, but she shortens the telling because we can match her word for word," Tip said.

"Please allow me to finish," Sarah Anna said. "Our telephone lines came from the barrens, not from further down

the hills. The telephone rang, Tip went to answer, and
Claude and Maude checked on us. He helped me return to bed
and he went to build the fire. During that time, I dozed off
and in half sleep dreamed. When I awoke, peace came about my
life here. I never needed to leave nor experienced
homesickness again."

"Sam knows this story and you hope it gives him peace
when holidays come and he misses you'all?" Cayrolynn asked.

"Exonerates his heart and ours, too," Tip said. "Now, I
go with you to remove your research from my workshop to your
car, TeJay, and to see Cayrolynn to the Loft."

"I'll put things in order, Cayrolynn," Sarah Anna said.
Thank you for our supper and we'll never forget you can cook,
that's forsure."

They walked out the back door into a mountain gust that
made Cayrolynn reach for the banister beside the steps. She
felt such happiness with the compliments for her meal.
Tip went ahead and reached the workshop door before TeJay and
Cayrolynn.

"Remember to lock behind yourself." TeJay held her for
a moment then kissed her on the forward. "And, I plight thee
my troth," he said before he released her and followed Tip.

* Fourteen *

According to her previous plans, Tuesday morning, Cayrolynn drove to Nashville. She sang along with the radio, even so, it took two hours before she reached the <u>Artist's Lair</u> where the owner took her work on consignment. The original country store merged into a gallery, art consignment shop, art supplies, primitive art and antique furniture, with various other items useful to decorators.

Before she arranged consignment of her work, she read the owner's contract that said, no crafts. She didn't understand. Some items seemed rather mundane to be classified as art or for home decorating.

"I'm not an artist," Cayrolynn said.

"You're an artist," the owner said, "and I like your work. I'll sell to decorators who look for unique wall pieces."

She parked in the alley and took the boxes with framed needlecraft from the trunk of the car.

"Anybody, around?" she called. She placed her work on the long work table. The owner came from the front and began his pre-acceptance examination.

"All these will sell before Christmas. I plan to close up and take January off. Nice car you drive, Cayrolynn."

"Belongs to a friend of mine. You remember my friend, Beatrice, she borrowed my car. Since I work at home, I don't need a car for every day commute."

"Shall I send you the money for these or will you drop by?"

"Best, I'll call. Some money before Christmas would be nice, but I guess you know that."

*   *   *

The positive feed-back about her work gave Cayrolynn the impetus she needed for the clinic. His comments about her car caused her to park three blocks away when she reached the doctor's office. She didn't want envy or jealousy from anyone fighting for life.

Few patients sat around the reception area, and these forlorn undernourished clients caused a climate of depression. She could remember the smell of the cigarettes of her Mother, the loss of weight before they knew about the cancer, and the tattered magazines in the doctor's office that matched the appearance of the magazines she saw here.

"Your lifestyle contributes to your health, Cayrolynn," the nurse said. "You show a five pound gain in the past two months. The miracle of healthy living comes when patients try to get well and people around them, help. Do you have a good living situation?"

"Yes. I want to live and be free of pain."

By the time, she returned to her car, she felt pains of hunger. Two and time for food. Fast food helped.

Her last errand meant browsing through two craft stores. She bought needlepoint patterns, yarn, and one book for counted cross-stitch. When she finished and returned to the car, she felt indecision. She couldn't decide if she should go home or call TeJay. If she drove, sunset would disappear before she came to the hollow. She hesitated. She never called TeJay at his office. Turmoil of emotions jumbled her speech causing a lisp. The cell telephone made swift connections.

"TeJay, I'm at Green Hills."

"I want to come pick you up, Cayrolynn. Tell me where you parked, so I can find the car."

"I'll park nearer Hillsboro Pike and open parking spaces where you'll see me."

"Give me ten minutes."

She watched TeJay's truck turn at the light and come to

the car. She opened her door and stood waiting until he
parked beside her. When he came home at night, he spoke and
asked about her day, but seldom touched. Now, he reached for
her, stood holding her, and placed a kiss in her hairline.
Caution kept her silent.

"Please follow me to the Condo. I'm working with a
client and I'll return to his office. Then, meet you back
at the Condo, soon."

After Cayrolynn sat before the television watching the
evening news, she thought about her reception by TeJay. When
a man loves a woman, she takes first place and her call
prized. Life turns on small emotional accords. She stood
and went from room to room making a careful examination of
the condominium. She self-talked.

"This glow that I feel might not last, but for now I
wear my rose colored glasses and pray favor for myself."

Dusk passed and night came before she heard TeJay
calling for her at the back door.

"We can spend the night here, but I think we'll drive
together to the Loft."

"It meets my approval to stay here, TeJay. I can go
home tomorrow."

"No. Off with the lights and electrical stuff and out
the door."

She didn't comment, but helped put the place into order before she took her purse and went to the car.

"You ate lunch?" TeJay asked.

"Yes. Why don't we go to the cafeteria in the mall for our supper," Cayrolynn suggested.

"It catches me by surprise each time we share our thoughts and they match," TeJay answered.

"Then, you leave your truck here?"

"Do you need little red tomorrow?"

"No," Cayrolynn said. "No traveling tomorrow."

"Tip needs a day in town, according to what he said, during our car ferrying over Thanksgiving, so tomorrow he can come in with me and solve my our vehicle problem. I need to exchange this car, I think, and get one you enjoy more."

TeJay began to hum 'Christmas is a coming' and then turned on the car radio to NPR. Both chose salads and vegetables for supper at the Hickory Hollow mall, then took I-24 for home. They drove through Tip's new electronic gate at ten.

"Anyone still awake, here?" TeJay called to the house. Sarah Anna opened the deck door.

"TeJay, we tried to call you when Cayrolynn didn't return. Your cell took messages."

"Sorry, didn't hear the page and forgot to look."

Tip and Sarah Anna sat watching a cowboy western, but ready for bed. "So, do the good guys win?"

"Foolish questions. Foolish answer. And, did you get a report from the doctor, Cayrolynn?" Sarah Anna asked.

"Gained five pounds, but no change except for some new prescriptions."

Tip clicked off the television and suggested hot chocolate with a bedtime snack.

"Turkey Day helped you add those pounds, Cayrolynn, now before Christmas, you should add another five," Sarah Anna said.

They laughed with the joy of mirth, but Cayrolynn knew they wished a miracle for her.

"Will you go in with me tomorrow, Dad?"

"Sure. Do we leave at six?"

"Yes, or thereabouts."

TeJay walked swinging her hand across the yard to the Loft, then stopped in the downstairs laundry. She climbed the stairs, but heard him lock the outside door and return to the house.

In the morning, she listened to the wind. Bare branches from the oak scratched against the eaves making sounds like a coded message. With the sound of fierce gusts this place returned to the starkness felt two hundred years ago before the time of land grants and first settlers.

Fatigue, she thought, and the spirit of lethargy. The tiredness experienced by women who once lived here. Their use of lye soap made in outside kettles, then lifting water from the spring to the wash pot, and to galvanized tubs elevated on wooden horses with a scrub board. Washdays took all day Monday and ironing all day Tuesday.

She opened her blinds, then returned to bed and lay thinking about the surprise she hoped to share with TeJay when she knew she was healed. Meditation led her to the softness of thought between daydream and sleep.

When she talked with TeJay, she felt his attention, but when he went to work, she couldn't remember exactly what being with him was like and what all this meant.

"I'm not your buddy," he said. "Beatrice became a buddy for Aubrey. Maybe, she didn't sign up and put her name on any list, but she stayed his buddy to the very end. That's called altruism, I think. We're partners."

"Why, TeJay, what makes us partners?"

"Contract friendship. You give a commitment to me and I give myself in commitment to you. Marriage gets discounted in the world of law. It becomes a contract to be ended in divorce if emotions change or things don't work out."

"You talk about covenant with a three fold cord?"

"In marriage, either written or verbal contract, neither
person may agree on all the terms even when the vows get
spoken. Each thinks they can load their mate with some
idealist fairy tale about how things should be."

"We never married, TeJay."

"Our commitment lacks papers for a court of law. But,
God willing, one day it'll take the permanence of legality."

Cayrolynn lay listening to the bombarding wind and
watching the sway of the stalwart oak outside her Loft window
with its last few leaves and she thought about her
conversation with TeJay Now, she remembered his hands on the
wheel and the speed that covered the miles. She wanted no
friend nor personal sounding board to run TeJay's ideas past,
nor a woman friend for prattle.

TeJay didn't slouch in the driver's seat. He sat tall
in command of the vehicle he drove like he sat tall at his
desk at his work and made his life decisions endowed with
sturdiness of character. In her thoughts, she couldn't see
his face, but she remembered the smell of the deodorant he
wore that permeated the car. The smell of tension and the
smell of sweat became his smell that filled his car, not the
softness of the bath powder that kept her dry.

"When I make my commitment to you, TeJay, I feel like I
should fill out some form as though I apply for employment

and you can check my references to determine if I fit the mold of your expectations."

"That's a question of mine, Cayrolynn, that you carry the subconscious inferiority because you work free form as an artist and not a pay check job. I hear the questions about what do I bring to the marriage or what do I put on the table and why this feeling of fear?"

"We keep plowing our theoretical thoughts. I can't add a big pay check to the bank account each month, so am I a luxury, expensive, and unnecessary?"

"Cayrolynn, you follow the equal sign of the equation, one plus one equals two. Two minus one equals one. For myself, I'm already into the equals two bit and there's no turning back. If we continue this discussion, soon you'll cry. No tears. We may need the marriage covenant sooner. Being around you makes me fear to lose you. Free floating anxiety with a terrible case of jealousy, I think."

"In my mind, I keep seeing the ring worn by a woman married to an attorney, who knew Beatrice. She wore his diamond ring, enough for a family fortune, she drove his car, and lived a status life, but her husband, she never saw," Cayrolynn said.

"We'll put a large calendar on the kitchen wall. You'll mark our times together, and circle if they're quality times.

You must list every way, I say, I love you."

    Cayrolynn remembered the yarn and other purchases left in the car from yesterday. Even with motivation, she lacked energy to be up and working. This quilt that covered her bed brought thoughts about someone who worked coverings for a winter that cometh. The muted colors showed faded cottons from washing and drying on the line in the sunshine. It appeared as a log cabin pattern with whatever scaps available. The petite stiches caused her to question if it came with Sarah Anna from Mississippi or with Maude from West Virginia. Maybe, this quilter as she worked spoke prayers over the quilt for needed rest and peaceful sleep. Prayers that asked the Lord's healing for fever, or sicknes, or heartbreak. She smoothed the quilt with her hands before she arose and made the bed.

*   Fifteen   *

"These days before Christmas I need my substitute back-up routine. I'm pushed by one legal case, too." TeJay talked and moved his hands in a circular fashion that showed tension. He never talked with his hands. "Most musicians work their contracts, however I'm available."

"Will you be staying in town on other nights? Cold weather with troublesome road conditions begin in December."

"Only on the nights I work with a band or I find I'm too tired for the commute home."

"Will your space with Shafe be available, so I can stay in your Condo?"

"Sure. My explanation didn't come out right. Erase. Cayrolynn, I need to stay in town and I want you to stay in my Condo instead of here in the Loft."

"Thank you for the invitation and I say yes."

Even though she decided to go to Nashville, she tarried at the farm. Artistic equipment and supplies meant major

moving. Staying in the Loft kept her focused to her diet and
pre-Christmas projects.

*   *   *

"When U-en-zs going to town, Cayrolynn?"

"Sarah Anna, you shock me when you use this Tennessee
word. Do they say U-en-zs in Kentucky? I never heard it in
Alabama?"

"Don't know. I must ask. Colloquial, I think."

"I'll go Saturday morning and return here Sunday
afternoon. I said yes, but too much hassle."

*   *   *

Often in the Condo, she experienced insomnia. On Sunday
morning, she arose early, read the paper, and dressed for
worship. TeJay knocked on the back sliding doors.

"Always up early, and I want to worship with you this
morning. These Advent Sundays point toward Christmas Eve. I
like the candles and readings setting the season apart from
most of the year. All part of my heritage that I enjoyed, so
I want to go with you. Am I invited?"

"Of course. I miss Brush Arbor Church with warmth from
the large butane heater, however I enjoy traditional worship.
I want to go downtown to join the wise men who sought
Christmas."

"Shafe came in last night. No problem with my staying

at his place, but his parents and two aunts come to town tomorrow. Did you look in the paper for a special program like Hanging of the Green?" TeJay asked.

"I did. Special music with carols and bells this morning, then I need to return to the Loft."

"I missed buying you supper last night, so I'll buy you lunch today. You didn't appear and I expected you."

"When you're working, you get a divided self. You need your breaks to relax and most restaurants need their tables at this season. Beatrice took me to see <u>Amal</u> <u>and</u> <u>the</u> <u>Night</u> <u>Visitors.</u>"

"How about tasty toasty waffles ready for the toaster and hot maple syrup?" TeJay moved to make fresh coffee.

"TeJay, do you give focused attention to any person who talks to you?" Cayrolynn shook her head. "It amazes me that no matter what you're doing, when I speak, you give me complete attention. Do you do this for everyone?"

"I think I do. Some people attend to several projects at the same time and fail to hear or see nuances. It may show my loss of hearing. Any person, who counts and talks at the same time, loses their place in counting or fails to hear all that's said. Who's most important? If a person goes about their chores, then the chore becomes more important than the person. When someone treats me that way, I want to put one foot in front of the other and walk on out the door," TeJay answered.

"I like your complete attention when I speak, but I want to smooth the crease across your forehead."

"That wrinkle comes with my poor vision, I think. I need glasses or contacts, otherwise, I frown trying to see and the wrinkle stays. My mono-eyebrow covers my birth defect. No eyebrows."

*   *   *

Often Cayrolynn self-talked aloud putting sound into the Loft. "I must get outside. Exercise and brisk breezes. My tasks dictate and I forget to eat. I forget to pitch baskets. I'm getting bored. I need a change of direction."

She acknowledged the progression of days toward Christmas. She met deadlines in her work that meant manipulating time to reach her goals. Friday afternoon brought the anticipation of the week-end and Monday morning, the clock and the calendar.

"I smell smoke." She stood with the basketball. "I smell smoke." First, she looked at the roof of the Loft and across the hill, nothing. The house showed no sign of smoke. More like intuition than smell, some fire somewhere took her attention. She walked and looked toward the homestead, toward the cemetery and Brush Arbor Church. Smelled. Then, walked back to the laundry, and took the telephone from the wall. Tip's work number on the blue paster stuck out from the telephone book. He answered.

"Outside, I smell smoke. I see nothing, but it's toward the head of the hollow. I think."

"Thanks."

The binoculars stayed on the top shelf of the closet. Nothing came into view except deer. She remembered, Tip kept a few cattle up the hollow. He kept his land posted to keep hunters from an accidental mistake that killed a cow. Seven deer seemed to move toward the Ol' Lonesome place.

She returned to the basketball and tried to control her emotions and the impetus to get involved. Soup and fruit for me and a nap, she thought. Close work makes my eyes tired.

*   *   *

"Cayrolynn, it's time for a cuppa." Sarah Anna came up the steps bringing a fresh apple deep dish pie. "The smoke blows ashes. Tip called me at school and he thinks it's a controlled burn now. We lost the homestead and the old barn near the spring at the head of the hollow."

"So, did Tip say where it began?"

"At the cemetery. Someone cleaned and burned along the circular drive. They failed to listen to advice about wild fires this year. Whoever thought no fire remained, but it sneaked along the ridge line. No one noticed or reported until you called Tip. It's our land and our loss."

"Our pot of green tea waits along with your dessert. Did you want me to go with you to look?"

"Tip will come for a mug of coffee and a bath soon. It's a common emotion to go see. You come with us, if you wish. I dread looking at the remains of the homestead."

"Lexie took me there. Claude's uncle hid behind a door when the northern army came through. Someone in blue killed him and someone in gray repaid by killing the man in blue. TeJay said Claude and Maude told many stories about the house. That day with Lexie, I felt some other person kept us company. Were there ghosts do you think?"

"Of course. Yes, of course. Maude's sixth sense seemed to know about people from the cemetery who stopped by. She followed a hillside path up to the cemetery and church. I must go for my camera. When Tip comes, he'll expect me to be ready to go see the hollow. Tip doesn't handle trauma well, and loss of the homeplace may cause despair."

"Did you lose walnut, cedar or other original trees?"

"Claude contracted for the virgin timber cutting when he moved here, so it's not a financial loss."

"Information about the fire and Tip's concerns solves

some of my curiosity, and you know your pie is my favorite.
Thank you, Sarah Anna."

*   *   *

Cayrolynn looked from the Loft windows and watched the
seeping darkness flood the hollow. Along the ridge line,
dots of fire burned a log or the roots of some still standing
tree. TeJay came and parked below her window, then came
upstairs.

"I'm glad you're here, TeJay."

"Me, too. I think the fire creeps along one of the fire
breaks and that protects the pastures. Did you talk with my
Dad or Mother?"

"Briefly."

"Tip will suffer. I called Sam. Sam takes a flight
tonight and be here by morning."

"Why, TeJay? I don't understand."

"All part of our family, Cayrolynn. Tip's Mother, our
grandmother, kept her savings sewed inside the lining of a
carpet-bag valise. Tip took his meager things in the valise
when he moved with Claude and Maude. Maude hated the dirty
thing and took in down an alley and threw it in a dumpster.
Tip experienced hysteria. He lost consciousness, so Maude
called Claude home. Claude asked paramedics to awaken Tip.
When he heard Tip's story, they retrieved the valise. Smelly

garbage filled their house. Claude took the clean dried
bills to the bank. He and Tip opened a savings account
together. When Tip joined the Army, he sent his savings home
for the account. During Tip's time away, Claude and Maude
took the money and bought the farm. Some land, they bought
from the county tax roll of unpaid taxes and other acres came
from owners who wanted out. Tip came home and couldn't find
Claude and Maude. The banker told Tip about Cannon County
Tennesse and the empty bank account."

"Tip told you this?"

"Maude told my Mother. We don't say much about love in
our family, but we show it. Watching Tip and Claude work
together meant watching pure love enough to see it. When Sam
comes observe the rapport between Dad and Son."

"You and Andy felt jealousy?"

"Not really. Lexie could pour on sweetness thick."

*   *   *

"TeJay," Sarah Anna called, "Come for supper, and you
too Cayrolynn. Tip wants to show you the homeplace."

"Thanks, Mom. Come, Cayrolynn."

"Maybe tomorrow, not tonight, TeJay."

*   *   *

Cayrolynn felt a need to tell Beatrice these happenings.
"I feel like an orphan again calling you, Beatrice. Our

hollow went up in smoke today. The terror of wildfires and it continues to burn the side of the hill from the cemetery to the pasture."

"Cayrolynn, I planned to call you. TeJay sent us a form about some insurance you bought while working. We returned the forms. Your medical situation came out with many technical terms. TeJay wanted to know the definition of Sjogren Syndrome and I told him fibromyalgia plus other factors make up the syndrome. I think he looked on the internet and wanted a more personal definition relating to you."

"Do you think TeJay can write to the insurance commissioner and get more money for me?"

"I think so. More than you currently receive, maybe."

"When my boss, Malcolm, suggested the term insurance, I couldn't believe any need. Now, this money means more freedom for me."

"You'll leave the hollow, Cayrolynn? I can't believe you'll say good-bye to TeJay."

"The check in my spirit never goes away. I want to go to Florida and see the cemetery with graves for my Mother and Lavender. I need closure for my early life and those years before the children's home."

"TeJay might take you to the Gulf and be a support."

"No, Beatrice. I need to find my young self without anyone along to chaperone."

"Cayrolynn, you spend days working with your hands and time thinking about your life. The abused rejected wife or the chemically imbalanced teen rebels, but you're beloved. TeJay will do all he can to help you find yourself. Believe me."

"If you would come for me, then I'll sleep over until the trauma of the hillside fire dissipates. Tip and Sarah Anna go to Houston next week for Christmas. I'll leave my gifts for them here and see them when they return."

"Okay, Cayrolynn, I need to come now. I should be there by seven, so please be ready. Tomorrow, I take vacation time and go spend Christmas with Aubrey and his parents."

"Thanks, Beatrice, I shall watch for you."

After Cayrolynn packed, she left an open note for TeJay on the counter. "I plan to stay with Beatrice pre-Christmas, while you work and your parents go to Houston. Beatrice plans to go to see Aubrey. Cayrolynn."

* * *

Before dawn Beatrice packed her car, then returned for words of good-bye. "Cayrolynn, I ask you this week to take a memory walk wherever you lived around here. Don't get into confused thinking about the ring you wear and the naive wife

of the attorney you met at Thanksgiving who thinks TeJay
needs you to acquire partnership. This week, you listen to
me, you'll receive Christmas roses, and telephone calls."

* * *

Christmas Day at noon TeJay came to get Cayrolynn for
their trip to the farm and to open gifts.

"Everyone says we make time for our greatest treasure,
but this holiday schedule kept me busy and stressed to the
limit. I apologize and ask your forgiveness because my "have
to's" overwhelmed me."

"TeJay, no reproaches and no guilty excuses. I need my
friends and feel so insecure, but I knew I should come to
Beatrice's apartment and I have enjoyed complete peace.
Thank you for calling and keeping me up-to-date about all the
going-ons."

"Last night, I mentioned our going to the farm for our
gift time. We eat at the Waffle House on the way, then go to
the farm. I hope we can stay until Tip and Sarah Anna
return. Okay, with you?"

"Yes, sir."

"I see your eyes that smile and I see no grudges."

"TeJay, people in divorce can't speak peaceably because
they hurt. That's like Joseph and his brothers. Don't bring
false accusations. Did Tip and Sarah Anna leave us heat?"

"If all the thermostats get turned to zero, the pipes freeze. Sarah Anna left us Christmas dinner packed in trays in her refrigerator."

"That news makes me happy, TeJay."

"She gave you the tape of an old movie she knows you like, so we'll watch the movie and enjoy the gas logs in the fireplace. Sound like fun?"

"You, betcha."

"Tip found you a loom, now you can learn to weave."

"Don't tell me all the surprises." Cayrolynn found she laughed and cried from an overload of emotion. TeJay stopped on the side of the interstate and wiped her tears, then gave her a Christmas kiss, when he said 'Christmas Gif'.

*   Sixteen   *

Advent, Christmas Day, Boxing Day, the twelve days of Christmas, and soon comes Epiphany. Cayrolynn opened a book of <u>WHISPERS</u> by Amy Carmichael before setting her work agenda for the day. These verses concerned praise. Praise in all things.

On Boxing Day, the day following Christmas, Andy and Rae came to the farm. Plans for Andy and Rae to spend time alone in the big house seemed right. TeJay needed time with his lap-top, so he remained in Tip's shop. Cayrolynn began learning to use her loom.

When Rae and Andy drove into the yard, she and TeJay went to greet them. Andy seemed to pout when he realized they planned to stay at the farm these few days.

I find it difficult to forgive, Andy, she thought. Why would he hit us so hard with his rude question about a date for our wedding? A soft answer turneth away wrath, however I wanted to say, none of your business. Why would TeJay say

Ground Hog Day like we made a decision? Now, I mess up my
morning with negative thoughts.

Cayrolynn pulled the cord for her blinds and saw a misty
cloud hovering that made the house and backyard translucent.
This fierce storm with icycles and blown snow against the
fences inspired a desire to fill the Loft with good smells of
allspice in the oven and apple cider simmering in the bean
pot. She stirred the makings for banana spice muffins, and
filled baking cups with batter before she placed these into
tins and into the pre-heated oven.

After she finished her make-up, she pulled on wool pants
over thermals, socks knitted for sledding, and chose a warm
Christmas sweater. She tried the television, found a snowy
screen, then turned it off and began listening to a guitar CD
played by TeJay.

Her cell phone buzzed. "Cayrolynn?"

"Yes. I'm busy like the little red hen this morning."

"Rae says Andy didn't sleep well. The medicine he took
caused a skin rash, and now, he seems to hallucinate. She
fears trouble for Andy."

"What can I do to help, TeJay? Should I come over?"

"Thanks, but tread with care because I didn't shovel a
pathway."

To go to the big house proved a hassle. Turn off the

oven, turn off the lights, place the muffins into a picnic carrier, and pull on the winter parka. TeJay opened the back door, took the muffins, and helped her inside.

"I started coffee, Cayrolynn."

"I'll find something for breakfast, and I'll use your mother's egg cups."

TeJay put eggs to boil, while Cayrolynn chiseled slices and giblets from the pre-cooked country ham found in the back of the frig. She wrapped the ham in wax paper ready for warming in the microwave.

Rae came into the kitchen and poured a cup of coffee. She took a napkin to blow her nose because tears flushed her face like a dripping from snow on the roof. TeJay stood, put his arms around Rae, and kissed her cheek.

"I'll sit with Andy while you talk to Cayrolynn and drink your coffee."

"Will you take Andy to the hospital, Rae?" Cayrolynn asked.

"I called Lexie and talked with Uncle Andrew, who plans to fly to Nashville. Andy's parents left last night, so they plan arrival today. One medical friend of ours lives in Woodbury, and he plans to bring a stand with a bottle IV that he thinks will help. When Andy feels better, I want him to come home with me. He needs sunshine and rest on the beach."

"After your coffee, muffins, and ham, maybe you should take a shower and dress for today. Do you want an egg?"

"Yes, please. I need breakfast because tension seems to take my strength."

"I'm not needed here, Rae," Cayrolynn said. "I want to complete several unfinished tasks. Call me if I can be of help." Footsteps to the Loft required patience. She wished for a guide rope like the banister for a foot log across a flooded creek.

Some days she couldn't work, but this morning the repetitive stitches added to her emotional quietness. She heard a car start and peeked through a slat to see the driver. The cloud shifted east with enough lift for her to see Rae. Maybe, I should go to the house, she thought, then remembered contagious germs. Maybe, I could follow Rae to the cemetery, but Rae needed time for planning if Andy took a leave of absence.

The triptych panels made with stitches and fabric paint lay across the coffee table. Cayrolynn continued working without fatigue or noon-time hunger. She heard the car return. The door downstairs made a squeak when opened, then she heard Rae call.

"Cayrolynn, Cayrolynn, may I come upstairs."

She crossed to the door, opened it wide, and said,

"Sure, Rae, Sure you may come visit."

Rae came bringing the coldness of winter and a red nose.

"I drove to the cemetery. When I bought this car, my
Dad suggested four wheel drive. I never know when I'll be
called to a place where sand presents problems. Ice and snow
gave me no fear except I might slide off the mountain going
there. I drove into our family space and opened my door
before I realized a wind blew across the mountain."

"Felt like Alaska?"

"Oh, so cold. The peace and untouched white panorama
made me think of heaven and angels. I imagined I could hear
my babies singing and dancing a beautiful ballet in heaven.
Claude and Maude loved my family and Andy's, so I know they
enjoy my three babies.

"Often with a virus, a patient gets well in a day or a
week. Last night, Andy woke me with his talking. I turned
on the light, then realized his high fever. He kept asking
for the measurement readings. Sometimes when a patient
declines toward death, they get into a strange conversation
that resembles talking out of their head or hallucinating.
My premonition concerns his convalescence. If my diagnosis
proves true, Andy needs quarantine and no work for months."

"You paint with black paint, Rae. Wait for your doctor
friend who brings the IV, and for Uncle Andrew. You glimpsed

your babies with Claude and Maude, now fears and fatigue
limit clear thinking. Drink some milk and doze off in Sam's
room. I'll call you when our family comes. You need rest if
you take Andy to Mobile."

Rae took Cayrolynn's suggestion. She went into Sam's
old room and closed the door. Cayrolynn stood looking at the
hollow toward the east. The hills appeared smudgy black
holding gray clouds. Stark trees held icicles that bent
branches and caused an occasional cracking sound. Cold rain
seemed to freeze when it spattered the snow covered parking
behind the house.

Sarah Anna's cold weather soup for supper, she thought.
From the freezer downstairs, she took two packages
that she defrosted and warmed in the micro-wave. One package
went into the crock-pot and the other into a soup tureen
ready for the oven after she finished the corn sticks.

Rae awoke at six surprised that she slept so long. She
began to get ready to return to the house.

"I won't come there, but you come here, Rae," Cayrolynn
suggested. "You can take corn sticks for supper and send
TeJay for the soup."

When TeJay came, Uncle Andrew followed him up the
stairs. "Thank you for thinking about supper, Cayrolynn. My
Mother and Dad should arrive soon. They traveled bad roads,

but didn't stop after they heard about Andy. Dad called around noon."

"And, how do you enjoy this weather, Cayrolynn?" Andrew asked.

"Great weather for a book or work on one of my projects except Rae came and slept. I stayed quiet by taking a nap. I'm disturbed about Andy's health."

"Andy's pneumonia seems like a hospital bacteria with some symptoms I don't recognize. Days before Christmas, Andy seemed too tense. I told Sarah Anna, but not Rae that I think Andy suffers from some form of arthritis. I'm not sure what this means for the future."

"My Mother told me that you think Andy needs a different practice. Did you tell Andy?"

"No. Andy chose research, however he excels as a brilliant doctor. From first grade, Sarah Anna saw Rae taking care of Andy. I tell you this with discretion, TeJay. During their years at Knoxville, in both achievement and I.Q., Rae outpaced Andy. We decided it best for Rae to go to med-school in Birmingham not Memphis."

"You found it easy to implement your decisions concerning Andy and Rae?"

"Rae's parents need her and she feels her responsibility. Older people, who suffer from dementia, need help and both parents need Rae."

"I never heard that," TeJay answered. "I knew Rae's parents worked to help her with med-school tuition. She lived with them during her residency at the Mobile Infirmary."

"Cayrolynn, forgive us for family talk," Andrew said.

"Should I go into the bedroom and close the door?"

"No," TeJay said. "Some of this I never heard, Cayrolynn. I want you to listen with me."

"I refrain from discussion with Andy about his leaving the lab. I feel he and Rae should live together unless they decide to divorce," Andrew said.

"True, we see Andy as brilliant and sensitive. We never knew what he thought when Rae miscarried, nor when she lived with her parents in Birmingham and Mobile. Maybe he took advice from you Uncle Andrew when he made decisions about Rae and the consequences. Emotional factors enter into fighting against poor health. Does Andy see another woman, or do you know?" TeJay asked.

"I don't think so. He felt distress that I didn't bring Rae to Memphis."

"Andy may respond to the medicines and rest. We hope. What further prescription will you suggest?"

"Go with Rae to the warmer weather where she lives, also

three months leave of absence."

"And, before he returns to Memphis, you'll dismiss him
from the practice."

"I'm buying the estate with Sam and Toney.   Before
summer comes, I plan to move there.   Branson experiences
winter with ice and snow.   I hope to spend the harsh weather
months near Andy or Lexie."

"Andrew, does this mean you plan to retire?   You don't
seem that old," Cayrolynn said.

"I'm not ready to decide yet.   This illness of Andy
brings to crisis a turning point.   I need to talk with Sarah
Anna and Tip, and I shall."

"You two talk serious on an empty stomach, so I suggest
you eat Sarah Anna's soup.   I think Sarah Anna said she
copied this recipe from her Grandmother who lived in
Mississippi."

"We need to back up Rae at the house.   May we take the
Crock Pot over?" TeJay asked.

"Of course.   When Sarah Anna and Tip come, you'll need
more soup and cornbread."

In a few minutes after he went to the house, TeJay
returned.   "I need to eat my soup with you, Cayrolynn, and
make telephone calls."

Cayrolynn opened the oven and filled TeJay's bowl.

She took corn sticks from the wrapped aluminum foil. TeJay began searching the phone book for numbers.

"Fred, I'm Andy's brother. Rae said you planned to send out some medicine. I hope you'll come, too."

"I can understand the highway patrol bringing you. Our parents need help because they should be home by now. I'll thank you, if you can mention them to your driver."

*　　*　　*

"Hi, Toney. May I speak to my brother. No parents and I feel anxious. Did they call you? (Pause) If they arrived in Nashville, they'll appear soon. The roads seem like an obstacle course. Fred'll come soon."

TeJay replaced the telephone and looked at Cayrolynn.

"Well, what do you think of our family problems, Cayrolynn?"

"Surprise. It bothered me that my Mother sent me to the Children's Home without any discussion with my Dad. When I spoke about my feelings with my houseparent, Maybelle, she told me to leave sleeping dogs sleeping."

"My Dad said Uncle Andrew didn't like identical twins nor married couples in med-school together. Today, he tells us a different view. When they come home, I'll talk to Dad. If I'm critical of my Mother, she'll despair. If she participated with Uncle Andrew, she carries guilt. I know because I know my Mother."

"You expect them soon, and I think I hear a car or truck."

"Fred. I must go see."

TeJay left an empty soup bowl. Before he went downstairs, he pulled Cayrolynn's hair. She felt happiness for the touch and gladness that she took time for her shampoo this morning. She self-talked, "Small affirmations allay my fears, my envy and jealousy. Am I so ego starved that I can't share TeJay with his family and Rae who suffers more than I know?"

*   Seventeen   *

Near mid-night, TeJay looked for lights in the Loft
before he called or went across the icy driveway.

"Cayrolynn, why do you sit here? Can't you sleep?"

"No sleep, TeJay. When I experience tension while
working on some creative project, I can't sleep."

"I understand that emotion. Sure. When I get caught up
with a case, even in my sleep, I keep working on arguments."

"I'm trying to finish these scenes for Rae's office and
I lack a vision of her wall space. Not seeing where she
hangs my work makes me feel inadequate. From her comments,
my three fold triptych fits and Tip helps me with the frame."

"Forget the doubts. Your work meets approval, I'm
sure."

"And, how's Andy?"

"Sleeping. He awoke and showed surprise that Fred,
Andrew, Rae, and I kept him company. Didn't eat. Drank some
water and went back to sleep. Fred decided to spend the

night, and that means he stays watchful until morning.   I
need to talk, Cayrolynn."

"Shall we make coffee?"

"Sure, unless you think the caffeine unwise."

"No matter, soon everyone goes and I return to quiet
views of the hollow where black buzzards circle and a keen-
eyed hawk makes a dive at any movement."

"I want you along when I talk to Tip. You must
understand, I waited for you all my life and you take first
place with me. At age twenty or twenty-one, I fell for Rae.
Proximity I think, with no other girls around, and I failed
to date other girls, I met. I took classes at MTSU and
worked my music on the week-ends. That summer, I stayed here
in the Loft. Rae bounded up the stairs and into my room. I
caught her hand and pulled her down to my bed where I
studied. I kissed her. Tip put his head in the door and
said, 'Son.' I'm not sure Rae heard him. I know she didn't
see him."

"Were you able to talk to Tip?"

"I thought he wanted me, so I went to find him. When I
asked if he needed me, he told me I should read the book of
Proverbs. Then, I knew he called me down. I felt rebellion,
embarrassment, and parental discipline. I'm a man, I
thought."

"You didn't come home for awhile."

"Less and less. Sam and I might have talked during his
decision time, if I'd stayed here. I'm glad Sam didn't
commit suicide. In my own selfish thinking, I couldn't see
the problems of my family."

"Do you think Sam linked himself to Rae?"

"Maybe. Sam followed footsteps after Tip. He tried to
keep his grade point average to the letter like Tip's and Tip
achieved straight A's with his brilliance. Sam took off to
Branson, but now, he likes his work and community lifestyle.
Toney and the kids make his life complete."

"Subjects like Rae and Andy, you never discuss with
Tip or Sarah Anna?"

"Right. To what purpose, what would be gained?"

"So, how did Andy get married?"

"Fell into it. Even today, he never recognizes Rae's
value."

"And, that makes you angry."

"Until you showed up, Cayrolynn, my lifestyle and my
life, too, stayed empty at minus zero. These past four
months offer enough time for us to know if marriage is right
for us with or without your medical reports."

"Do you think your Uncle Andrew plays God? He decided
the medical schools for Rae and Andy. Andy faces Hobson's

choice with no choice about his job. Now, your uncle buys
Sam a house and will he decide options for Sam and Sam's
children?"

"I want to talk to Tip. I can't talk to Mother because
she was ready to marry Dad the moment she met him."

"Who paid for your Mother's college?"

"All my family secrets and you get loaded with my
problems."

"Don't forget my story, TeJay, and all my problems. I
never wanted a boy friend because I lived with the examples
of my parents. You're blessed with parents who love each
other. No matter, why Sarah Anna married Tip. She worships
the ground he walks on and you know it."

"Sarah Anna loves Tip, but with jealousy and in a
possessive way. Lexie broke her arm in the cemetery. Did
she tell you?"

"No."

"The church needed someone to play the piano. Sarah
Anna found a teacher from Wayside School who agreed to come
play while they sought for a person in the community."

"I thought Lexie played the piano?"

"After she took lessons, at age ten or so, she began to
play. Lexie told Mother she thought this teacher pretty,
however she began to notice her smile. Lexie became jealous

of the smile Miss Piano gave Tip. In her small heart, she
wanted protection for my Mother. She couldn't decide if she
would quiz Dad on the way home in the truck or if she would
ask questions at Sunday lunch. She decided to use the
question in the truck approach."

"Lexie doesn't miss much does she?"

"Correct. This Sunday she sat in the arbor in the
middle of the cemetery thinking about how she would phrase
her questions. Tip called to her, but didn't hear her reply.
He began to back out of his parking space. Most of her life,
Lexie played tag or race and jump over the cement boundaries
between graves. In her imagination, she planned to run and
trip for a dramatic premeditated fall. She thought she could
race along and then this fake fall would get Dad's attention.
Lexie never cried like a cry baby, but she planned to cry."

"Schemes often work, but I fear Lexie became humpty
dumpty."

"She missed a step and hit a cement urn positioned on
the corner of one plot. This heavy urn, slipped, overturned
and fell when Lexie hit against it."

"Gives me goose-bumps."

"Maude said angels care for little girls. The urn hit
the edge of the boundary and stayed there. Lexie lay
stunned.

"Tip didn't see, but Miss Piano did and she came running in her high heels across the gravel parking area. Her screams seemed to wake the sleeping graves near Lexie. My Mother, stood, inside, near the windows, talking to a friend, and she heard. When she looked outside, she saw Dad opening his truck door in a hurry. Solicitous Miss Piano tried to touch Lexie, but Lexie screamed in panic.

"They drove home in Mom's car with Tip holding Lexie.

"Later, when she sat in Tip's lap while they watched television, she asked Tip why he married our Mother. Do you love my Mother, Dad? Tip found himself emotional when he tried to answer Lexie's fears. 'Your Mother is a busy lady with you, and me and three sons, but I sure do love her and you do, too. Don't you?' Lexie said she nodded, but she began to pray for God to move Miss Piano away.

"Sarah Anna heard Lexie's questions and it gave her a clue about the accident. Lexie wouldn't allow any one to touch her or hold her but Tip. She needed reassurance. My Mother told me, it was a good question, because she needed that reassurance, too."

"So, Lexie received no injuries during this experience except for the trauma?"

"When she kept complaining with an arm ache, Tip took her for an x-ray. She needed a cast on the left arm, also

she fractured her nose.   Miss Piano left and Charlotte came
to play, and she plays by ear."

"Lexie told me Charlotte couldn't play because of an ear
infection.   When the infection cleared, she could play
again."

"Charlotte brought her son Franklin, who sat in the
wheel chair and still does.   He and his Dad sat at the end of
the front pew behind Charlotte while she played."

Rae-Anne called from downstairs.

"Please come up Rae, I'll make you hot cocoa."

"Fred told me to leave him be, and find a bed over here.
May I borrow Sam's bed, Cayrolynn?"

"Of course, TeJay tells me family stories and he rejoins
the men at the house."

"I kept talking to Cayrolynn and didn't telephone Lexie.
Even at midnight, I think I'll call her."

TeJay talked on the phone, while Cayrolynn checked for
blankets and Rae's comfort.

"I'm asleep, Cayrolynn.   Thank you for checking, but
when I face problems, I tend to sleep instead of rolling and
tumbling."

Cayrolynn found TeJay gone when she returned to the den.
The music continued, so she turned off the player and the
lights.   Before she went to sleep, she thought about this

family. Each child felt part of the life of Tip and Sarah
Anna, but they married and lived their own lives. Commitment
seemed so different for these men, and beyond comprehension.
She remembered the mad barking of wild dogs that chased a
female dog in heat. Life basic and fundamental, vulgar and
coarse, yet life gentle and kind with a love both physical
and emotional.

Lavender held her once during a bad time and cleansed
away her tears. Tonight, she longed for Lavender.

When Cayrolynn awoke, she felt wide awake and not
needing the soft dozing of some mornings. She went to the
bath and brushed her teeth and hair. This morning, she
pulled her hair back into a pony tail, and pulled-on jeans
with a red sweater. She opened the blinds to the east,
looked out at the winter morning, and felt disappointment in
seeing no sunshine. The panorama of snow encompassed the
wide angle of a camera vision. The quietness of a perfect
snow covered hollow seemed rare for her ears unaccustomed to
lack of noise. When she looked for Rae-Ann, she found Sam's
bed made with the rainbow quilt Maude pieced from flour sacks
and quilted the winter before her death. She heard the door
downstairs open and close, then TeJay's call from the bottom
of the stairs.

"Cayrolynn, I need to go to town. Can you go with me?"

She went to look down the stairwell at TeJay. "I want us to
go into town for breakfast. Fred said Andy slept a good
night. My parents will come by noon, and I want you with me
to finish some errands."

"Sure. I should wear a coat?"

"Warm jacket, with cap and gloves."

She went into her closet and reached for her leather
jacket and her purse. When she returned to the stairwell,
she found TeJay dressed in his leather jacket and ready to
leave. Minutes later they left the farm.

"I need thinking room and the best way seems for us to
return to the Condo. We need breakfast, a big breakfast with
pancakes for me. How about you?"

"Not hungry, but you inspire me."

Cayrolynn watched TeJay take the icy back roads across
the hills. Stone fencing marked some fields, barbed-wire
cattle fencing outlined others, and some seemed idle and bare
with no fencing.

"Quiet and cold. I find this so beautiful, TeJay. I
question the lifestyle of early settlers in the 1800's and
those of the war, maybe fifty years later."

"Winter in the heart with too much stirring these past
few days. I wish we could stop and walk in the spiky ice
along the roadside, both making scrunchy sounds, but since

neither of us wear boots, we won't. Early settlers lived
food, clothing, and shelter. Maybe, a day like today offered
a time for reprieve with beauty and inside work. Harsh, all
the time, harsh, Cayrolynn."

"Did you leave reading materials at the Condo?"

"No. I want to enjoy our friendship, maybe play checkers
and tell jokes. Heard any good jokes, lately?"

"One of the problems of relationships, according to what
I hear, concerns boredom. I hope you won't be bored with me."

"Shall I answer that by stopping like by these snowy
woods."

"I know that poem. Tell me about your law practice."

"One partner decided to retire and move with his
daughter and her family to California. Another partner moved
to a firm in New York that handles international law. Often,
they asked me to become a partner. For many reasons, I
refused. Since I met you my life changes, so now; I want
permanence."

Cayrolynn found it easy to listen to TeJay, who spoke in
a masculine tone with authority, but she knew nothing about
this work that he talked about.

When they stopped for breakfast TeJay ate, but Cayrolynn
decided orange juice and cereal. Without words,
the fibromyalgia and fatigue symptoms penetrated their meal.

"If we planned a day with skiing in the Blue Ridge or near Park Cities above Salt Lake, you would need eggs and ham."

"TeJay, my musing concerns your ancestors who settled here and fought off blue coats and you think about the luxury of winter vacations. What a contrast."

"Good thoughts. Even while I put together a legal brief, shows I work like my grand-pappa's. Some of my ancestors wanted the life of a country yokel, others wanted to move west. Onward, they moved to Arkansas and Texas. Which reminds me, do you own essentials at the farm and Condo? I forgot to ask if you have clothes and make-up both places."

"Clothes, makeup, yes. You dress in a hurry, TeJay, every morning and follow a pattern. I'm out of practice, since I haven't worked in a year."

"Do we need to return to the Loft for anything you left?"

"Thank you for asking, TeJay. When I cleaned the Loft, I separated town from country. Most don't differ, but city stays in town."

"I need to ask you more specifically about your money, Cayrolynn. You need to pay self-employment tax, maybe some income tax, and you need money to cover your artistic expenses. Nitty gritty of living, money."

"Most people can ask their parents for loans. From the beginning, I knew I must be frugal."

"What's the saying? God meets our needs, but not always our wants?"

"The desires of our hearts and I'm thankful for mercy and grace."

"Our firm handles few divorce cases, but most research says sex and money cause most conflict. I haven't offered you an allowance for the Loft. My Dad likes to give Mother pocket money, he says for non-essentials. Your lifestyle in the Condo needs a different budget than living in the Loft."

"So, if you meet my cash expenses in the Condo, tell me the ground rules."

"You tell me, Cayrolynn. To think people live on love, when reality is money, seems immature and impossible. Help me, Cayrolynn, and next year we'll file income taxes together as a couple."

*   *   *

They parked under the back canopy and both went inside. Often, Cayrolynn felt an indescribable emotion. Lavender said she understood, but no one could feel this crazy, Cayrolynn thought. TeJay turned and noticed her eyes, now large straining to see. "Copper penny for your thoughts,

Girl Friend." She shook her head, then climbed the stairs.

The telephone rang and she heard TeJay answer. After he
finished talking, he came to find Cayrolynn.

"The call came from Fred. He said, Rae decided to get
the emergency medical crew to take Andy to Murfreesboro and
from there a medical helicopter will take Andy to the
hospital in Mobile. Rae says she needs Andy where she can
take care of him."

"What did Uncle Andrew say, and your parents? What did
Andy say?"

"Fred gave Andy a shot to make him sleep. No one was
consulted nor were they around when the medical crew came to
pickup Andy and Rae."

"TeJay, the surprise stops me. She stole her husband."

"I know, it's unbelievable. Fred says he thinks Andy
needs quarantine until they determine what's wrong. He
thinks Rae took charge to protect the parents. If Uncle
Doctor knows, he didn't say. Rae sat with Andy, so she must
have seen or known she needed him with her."

"Do we return to the Loft? What do you think?"

"We stay here. Too much talk and too many emotions
floating around. I think I'll go work at the office for
awhile, and can you be at peace here, Cayrolynn?"

"Sure. I'm glad we're here. I need to read a book and

think of others. It's a good day for exercise inside with all the machines and the pool. When will you come home?"

"Don't expect me. If Shafe's around, we need conversation. Bye, Sweet."

Cayrolynn leaned her head backward on the chair, then thought it better to stretch and be comfortable.

"Bong, Bong," What the clock? She stood to walk down the stairs and into the foyer where the grandfather clock with its grand eloquence struck the hour. She self-talked. "The clock stopped when the grandfather died. I'm alive and well. Time for me to exercise and swim or soak in the hot tub. TeJay took himself from the farm and the trauma of family decisions. When he returns, he can find me enjoying the amenities of this complex. I have no intention of hibernating at the farm."

*   Eighteen   *

The bamboo basket attached behind the mail slot in the
front door of the Condo held a yellow memo about a UPS
package held in the office. TeJay walked out the back door
and around to the office. When he returned, he brought
several magazines and a package from Lexie.

"Don't be surprised; she sends unusual gifts."

"Here, these scissors from the drawer. Open."

"Lots of packing even though I see nothing breakable.
This for you, Cayrolynn, and this for me. Look, a handsome
sweater, and for you, what?"

"A book. Look, not for one year like a calendar, nor a
journal with lines for writing, although I can do that, but
structured for the Twelve Days of Christmas. It suggests
Photo Album, Day Book, or Scrapbook. Large, 18x18, and
covered in Tartan Plaid with an embossed gold name label
"Twelve Days of Christmas." Engraved, underneath the title
in ornate calligraphy, "Cayrolynn." All these added extra

pages means a keepsake for years to come."

"I warned, Lexie sends unique gifts."

"Show me your sweater, TeJay."

"Imported and brought home by Lance or purchased from some international shop. Looks handmade with intricate patterns and yarns. Do you think the Middle East, either Turkey or Greece? Kilim, what does that mean?"

"Find the dictionary because Lexie makes us ashamed with our word knowledge and not finding more creative gifts for her family. What did you send, TeJay?"

"I sent money. Very crass. Toys cost money, also she needs to choose for herself and Lance."

"Your Mother keeps memory books, so I must use my new gift book to keep birthdays, Christmas, and days of celebration."

"The song "Twelve Days of Christmas" became a favorite with us like "Over the River" at Thanksgiving. We sang the melody by rounds and other times, we divided the lines and tried to out do each other with our parts."

"Lexie saw my diary compositions of rhymes and verses, so she knows my delight in receiving this book. I shall stay busy these twelve days, forsure."

*　*　*

First Day of Christmas: My True Love Gave to Me A

Partridge in A Pear Tree (12/25) Wednesday. Christmas Day and celebration of the birth of the Christ Child represented by a partridge: the only mother bird who will die for her young.

Second Day of Christmas: My True Love Gave to Me Two Turtle Doves and A Partridge in A Pear Tree (12/26) Thursday. Two Turtle Doves represents the Old and New Testaments with the foretelling and coming of Jesus.
The day after Christmas Boxing Day: boxes collected for the poor. Small monies called mites. Rae-Ann and Andy came to the farm.

Third Day of Christmas: My True Love Gave to Me Three French Hens, Two Turtle Doves, and A Partridge in A Pear Tree (12/27) Friday. Three French Hens represent faith, hope, and love found in I Corinthians 13.
Andy's health involves everyone in the family. Snow, ice, and clouds fill the hollow with winter whiteness.

Fourth Day of Christmas: My True Love Gave to Me Four Colly Birds, Three French Hens, Two Turtle Doves, and A Partridge in A Pear Tree (12/28) Saturday. Colly birds were taken into the mines to warn of gases or lack of oxygen. They represented Matthew, Mark, Luke, and John.

Fifth Day of Christmas: My True Love Gave To Me Five Gold Rings, Four Colly Birds, Three French Hens, Two Turtle

Doves, and A Partridge in A Pear Tree (12/29) Sunday. Five gold rings represents the first five books of the Bible, also called the Torah or Pentateuch.

Sixth Day of Christmas: My True Love Gave to Me Six Geese A-Laying, Five Gold Rings, Four Colly Birds, Three French Hens, Two Turtle Doves, and a Partridge in a Pear Tree (12/30) Monday. Six Geese A-Laying represents the six days of creation in Genesis.

(Cayrolynn noticed a red flyer stuck in their front door advertising a cosmetic and color coordinated fashion seminar to be in the Condo Clubhouse. Nice, she thought, if I am here.)

Seventh Day of Christmas: My True Love Gave to Me Seven Swans A-Swimming, Six Geese A-Laying, Five Gold Rings, Four Colly Birds, Three French Hens, Two Turtle Doves, and A Partridge in A Pear Tree (12/31) Tuesday. Seven Swans A-Swimming represents the gifts of the Holy Spirit. Romans 12:6-8 lists: prophecy, helps, teaching, exhortation. giving, leadership, and mercy.
New Year's Eve: TeJay took Cayrolynn to dinner with Shafe and some other friends.

"Dress pretty and we'll go eat when I come from the office, and then, I promised to fill in extra with a band until twelve."

"You would like for me to stay with you at a table until you finish the playing and ready to come home?"

"No, you're like the good little trooper who sticks with me even when you're tired or bored. Please, no rejection, but I watch you and you won't tell me when fatigue strikes. I'll bring you home, then I don't worry about you."

Eighth Day of Christmas: My True Love Gave to Me Eight Maids A-Milking, Seven Swans A-Swimming, Six Geese A-Laying, Five Gold Rings, Four Colly Birds, Two French Hens, and A Partridge in A Pear Tree. (1/1) Wednesday. Eight maids a-milking represent the blessed's of the Beatitudes found in Matthew 5, the Sermon on the Mount. The servant maids-a-milking were considered the lowest in the culture. New Year's Day: TeJay watched football and talked on the telephone. Cayrolynn worked out at the Clubhouse, enjoyed the precision of needlepoint containing bright colors, then read from a Christmas book sent by Sam and Toney.

Ninth Day of Christmas: My True Love Gave to Me Nine Drummers Drumming, Eight Maids A-Milking, Seven Swans A-Swimming, Six Geese A-Laying, Five Gold Rings, Four Colly Birds, Three French Hens, Two Turtle Doves, and A Partridge in A Pear Tree (1/2) Thursday. Nine Drummers Drumming represents the nine flavors found in the fruit of the Spirit in Galatians 5:22-23.

Sarah Anna called with wishes for the New Year. "We miss you Cayrolynn, so don't stay gone for long."

Tenth Day of Christmas: My True Love Gave to Me Ten Piper's Piping, Nine Drummers Drumming, Eight Maids A-Milking, Seven Swans A-Swimming, Six Geese A-Laying, Five Gold Rings, Four Colly Birds, Three French Hens, Two Turtle Doves, and A Partridge in a Pear Tree (1/3) Friday. Ten Piper's Piping represents the ten commandments. Snow and ice gave TeJay an excuse to bring yellow work papers with his laptop over from Shafe's to work in the Condo and scribble all morning. Cayrolynn awoke early and took a trip to the exercise machines, then she went swimming in the oversized hot-tub. She washed her hair in the shower at the Clubhouse. The water and exercise rejuvenated her energy and gave her a healthy self-confident feeling.

TeJay went off to the office and to a music appointment. Cayrolynn became engrossed in her needlepoint creation for a green velvet pillow, so with the background music and the focus of her work, she found it difficult to stop the flow of her attention until after midnight.

Eleventh Day of Christmas: My True Love Gave to Me Eleven Ladies Dancing, Ten Pipers Piping, Nine Drummers Drumming, Eight Maids A-Milking, Seven Swans A-Swimming, Six Geese A-Laying, Five Gold Rings, Four Colly Birds, Three

French Hens, Two Turtle Doves, and A Partridge in A Pear Tree
(1/4) Saturday. Eleven Lords-a-Leaping represents the eleven
disciples who remained after the death of Christ on the
Cross.

Winter storm weather, however TeJay called from the
office to warn he needed to work all day. Music filled the
condominium and Cayrolynn worked at calligraphy.

Twelfth Day of Christmas: My True Love Gave to Me Twelve
Lords A-Leaping, Eleven Ladies Dancing, Ten Piper's Piping,
Nine Drummers Drumming, Eight Maids A-Milking, Seven Swans A-
Swimming, Six Geese A-Laying, Five Gold Rings, Four Colly
Birds, Three French Hens, Two Turtle Doves, and A Partridge
in A Pear Tree (1/5) Sunday. Twelve Lords-a-Leaping
represent the twelve points in the Apostles Creed.
Chapel Church, this Sunday morning, smelled of cedar and
eucalyptus, a sermon by a visiting speaker thrilled to be in
Nashville, and praise like an over-turned rainbow receiving
and returning a cappella notes written all in sharpes.

*   *   *

Cayrolynn looked at the wooden Christmas Advent calendar
Sarah Anna gave her with the four weeks of moveable numerals.
She cherished this gift with notations about candles.

Her own pen and ink drawings edged the Twelve Days Book.
Here and there, thoughts written in calligraphy, made the

book personal. "I'm finished, TeJay, want to see?"

"Sure. Your notes for these days are written in third person; not personal with I, or me, or we, or us? I like your work and it's our reminder from year to year. Couldn't you add some cherished words in the margins to show us special to each other?"

"I will. The book doesn't include Epiphany, TeJay, so I think I'll add a section. Christmas Day yields to Epiphany and these have been wonderful days for me."

"Our family never felt the after Christmas blues. I think we celebrate all year. My Mother followed her remembrances from her Grandmother and our Great-Grandmother."

"Epiphany comes like the new year and brings anticipation for my healing."

"Two agree in prayer and I do agree with you, Cayrolynn."

Epiphany. (1/6) Monday and the day the wise men came to Bethlehem. Cayrolynn missed the eastward view from the Loft looking to snow cold hills, yet she felt glad she stayed in Nashville at the Condo. First, Tip took a cold and then, Sarah Anna experienced fever and stayed in bed for a few days.

January winter added snow, with snow laying around waiting for some more, according to hill predictions that new snow joins the old.

"TeJay, I have this longing to work on my new loom Tip found for me. No expectation for you to commute, but Sarah Anna stays home with her school closing due to weather and the roads. Most of the tasks I brought along, I finished, already. My thought is you might take me there and leave me for these January weeks?"

"Since my Mom stays home, sure, but I'll miss you. Friday is a good day for me, and we can go then. I don't think you should drive alone with this weather and some roads closed."

*   *   *

"This is Rae, Cayrolynn. Is this an acceptable time to talk? I'm at the office this afternoon, and I wanted to ask how are you enjoying winter weather these days?"

"Rae, thank you for calling. We plan to go to the Loft tomorrow morning. I missed saying good-bye when you left the farm. I'm a person who needs closure. I like a day that ends with a wide screen sunset."

"Cayrolynn, please talk with TeJay about my report on Andy. Fred and I discovered Andy works on a HIV research project and by accident he became infected. He planned to take his life, but Fred and I said no. Fred gave Andy a sleeping potion and we moved him by helicopter. Andy awoke

in my apartment with me and with Fred. I didn't talk to
Uncle Andrew nor to the parents. Andy belongs by marriage
covenant to me, and I plan to enjoy our relationship until
all the medicines stop working. Maybe, the Lord will stop by
or send his angels and leave a blessing, for Andy and me."

"These years, I've struggled with my health and I know
love is the best medicine, Rae. Your parents live in
assisted living at Point Clear?"

"I'll not neglect my parents. They encourage me in my
love for Andy."

"For some weeks, I dream of a flower pot. The flower
lifts with a top layer of dirt. Then, like a bed of fire
ants, the pot is filled with larva that look like white and
pink shrimp. They squash easily. The dream occurs and I
find it difficult to forget."

"Do you dream in color? What color flower pot and
flower?"

"Blue pot with water catcher on the bottom and a purple
hyacinth with a wonderful aroma that fills the room."

"I dream in color and smell, too. Cayrolynn that sounds
like germs in your bloodstream dying. What do you think?"

"I think so, too. The Psalmist says, I shall not die,
but live and magnify the name of the Lord. My friend
Beatrice is a Buddy to Horace who has HIV. I hope you find

good medicines for Andy.   Did you tell the parents and
TeJay?"

"Fred planned to stop by, also Andy called his Dad, but
I didn't speak with them.   Enjoy your winter days in the
Loft.   Gather holly and willow branches for your Laurel
Bloomery pottery jug and pitcher."

"God is good all the time, Glenda Rae-Anne.   Blessings."

During this conversation, Cayrolynn sat in TeJay's
recliner.   Now, she slid to the floor and lay trying to
relax.   Her fetal position placed her body in a coil.   She
didn't try to move.   After a bit, she felt her eyes close and
when she awoke, she felt cold and couldn't move.   Often, when
she awoke at Lavender's, she experienced sleep paralysis.
Once she told Maybelle because two girls suffered from
traumatic emotions.   One girl would faint or fall to the
floor with the least upset, and another girl turned a red
almost purple which stayed for several days.

"I hope I out-grow the sleep paralysis," she told
Maybelle.

"Unless you experience emotional trauma, your life will
offer no cause for the paralysis."

Now Cayrolynn lay awake, unable to move.   She began with
an eye lid.   Nothing.   One toe.   Nothing.   She tried relaxed
breathing and it helped.   Also, she dozed off again.

"Cayrolynn, why are you on the floor?" TeJay asked when he entered the Condo after dark.

"I guess I watched television and went to sleep, TeJay."

"Here, I'll help you up." Cayrolynn gave him her hand and felt happy to see the paralysis disappear.

"You heard about Andy?"

"Rac called and asked that I tell you. How did you hear?"

"Fred came from Mobile and stopped to talk to my parents. Rae and Fred showed wisdom and for now, we wait to see if we're needed."

*   Nineteen   *

"Cayrolynn, on a clear day, you can see the barren ridge at the head of the hollow." Sarah Anna stood looking east from the Loft windows. "One year our buses couldn't travel our county roads, so we missed every school day in January. I don't like for children to wait for the bus in cold weather."

"Last night, I slept under the new white down-filled comforter you gave me for Christmas. Thank you and it keeps me warm."

"The forestry people told Tip they think someone set the cemetery fire, and the same person set the homestead. Willy Bert and a cohort evade being found. We need to be careful with our security. I know you are, Cayrolynn, but a word of caution."

"I hear you, Sarah Anna, loud and clear. I'm glad Tip unpacked the loom, and set it up for me. I need some instruction and practice."

"What do you plan first?"

"I think a wall hanging made with cotton thread. I feel motivated and ready to look at books in the library or illustrations from the WEB."

"I find you busy, so I know you experience energy. Often, I seem motivated but no energy to execute my plans. When I was younger, I'd pull everything from a closet and replace in order. Now, I try to complete one shelf, then another. To pull everything out might discourage so that I could never finish with the clutter."

"If you go to the house past the workshop, please tell Tip I experiment with the loom. TeJay helps Tip today, I think. Maybe, I can finish something to show my efforts."

* * *

Roads cleared and bus drivers completed their routes. Cayrolynn missed Sarah Anna. Cold winter sun, then shade while a cloud warned of snow again. Cayrolynn knew someone stayed at Ol' Lonesome. Someone frisked Sarah Anna's freezer downstairs, but no way to prove any breaking and entering.

Cayrolynn ate a corn muffin in a cup of milk for lunch. In the county paper, she read about the bank robbery. The reporter said the banker ate a fried egg sandwich, before he returned to work.

The school bus traveled the ridge line going to and from

the barrens. In the afternoon, she used the binoculars to
watch its hesitation with each gear shift. After she watched
the buzzards circling near the hill top, she moved her view
toward the hill climb road, and recognized the blob of yellow
that looked like yellow play dough. The over-sized bus
hesitated and climbed using all its power. Now, the bus
stalled with no movement toward the east. At the edge of her
view, some towering tree lacked anchor and began to descend
across the path of the bus; slowly at first, then hard and
fast with a crash. The bus seemed caught in the upper limbs
where no leaves obstructed the view. The road seemed to
leave the hill and move to the hollow below bringing the bus
down, too.

Cayrolynn watched the slow motion transfixed. She
reached for her cell telephone and called Sarah Anna.

"The ridge bus can't make it up the hill. I think
they'll need fire truck ladders for the children to climb
out. It seems blocked to the east but the way seems clear
from Wayside."

While she watched, Cayrolynn saw someone swing on a rope
with someone holding tight and then drop into the tree with
the bus. He swung the rope back for another person to ride
up to the bus. Nothing seemed secure and braced. The drop
from the back of the bus went downhill and couldn't be

navigated. The bus driver secured his feet on the tree and then the two men began to bring out the children and place them on the tree. Each child braced against branches. The older children held the younger and the wind blew the hair of those who lacked caps. Cars came down the hill, but no pathway opened for people to reach the bus. The asphalt crumbled and took a car down the incline.

Sound carried across the hollow and Cayrolynn heard terror.

Tip's truck went up the gravel road to Ol' Lonesome and parked. She saw him swing on a lower rope, then catch the rope the two men used. She could see Tip take a child and hold the rope while the child held tight. Tip's repetitive trips brought children down to the shelf rock near the spring at Ol' Lonesome.

Cayrolynn knew she couldn't take the car and go there, so she called Sarah Anna again.

"Sarah Anna, Tip needs help at Ol' Lonesome where he leaves children he brings from the bus."

In a few minutes, Sarah Anna drove up the gravel road and other cars and trucks followed.

"What are my thoughts?" she asked herself. "Time for a nap, so I better put myself in my work chair and be diligent. Absolutely nothing so bad as Sarah Anna and Tip returning and finding me in sleep paralysis."

*   *   *

TeJay came at dusk. "Cayrolynn, why all the lights on the hillside road?"

"I'm glad you're here. I watched a mud-slide push the bus down the hill. Your parents went there. Would you check on them?"

"They drove into the back yard before me. Did seeing this accident cause you stress?"

"Yes. I saw people going to help, so I watched, then began my work on the loom."

"Tip and Sarah Anna carry change and trauma well, and may not talk much."

"I need soup and an early night, please, TeJay. You check your parents and unless I hear another word, you'll see no lights here."

*   *   *

Sarah called from the house to ask if she could come over.

"Sure, Sarah Anna. I've been expecting you. TeJay says you're taking a week from school."

"I'm making soup for some children and their families. Most of the children on the bus will miss a week, too. I'll be over."

Cayrolynn sat before the loom with hands folded and no
work. Sarah Anna came without her usual cheery self nor a
loaf of fresh banana bread.

"My internal clock awakens at the same time each morning
even though we stayed up late. TeJay kept us company at the
hospital until twelve, then he went to the Condo. Tip and I
came home around one."

"How did you leave the children?"

"One child, they transported to Vanderbilt and the
others will stay a few days. Parents or grandparents stay,
too."

"What does this mean, Sarah Anna?"

"The slide seemed to have no cause and would have
occurred without traffic. The children received cuts,
bruises, some broken bones, however most suffered from
trauma. 'What might have been' became the conversation
instead of what happened."

"Who were the men swinging on the ropes to rescue the
children?"

"Willy Bert and his friend lived at Ol' Lonesome and
kept the ropes for quick escape to the upper road. Their
wives could pick them up and bring them food or clothes."

"You and Tip didn't know?"

"We didn't know. The sheriff didn't try to apprehend

them yesterday, but he'll pick them up today. Tip says the parole board will make concessions for their courage."

"They operated with drugs and car stripping, I think Lexie said."

"Now, they get another chance and I hope they go straight. TeJay will talk to them and Tip, too. How are you Cayrolynn?"

"I want to live here. I need to talk to the doctor and be checked again. Anemia causes weeps. Once stress caused sleep paralysis, so if I'm at the Condo, Beatrice can help me get medical attention and changes in my medicines."

"We miss you when you go."

"I miss you. Can we have a cup of coffee or tea? Somehow, I missed asking when you came."

"I need to join Tip, he sleeps late. We plan a lazy day with delivery of my soup at dusk. Call if you need me, otherwise I think I'll spend time calling to check on my students."

*   *   *

"This is Lexie, Cayrolynn. Tell me about yourself and all the happenings at the farm. My Mom says she and Dad think they may be fighting a virus."

"Lexie, as you know, yesterday turned cold and groggy. The bus slipped with a mud-slide on the ridge road and I

think the state road people are there today trying to patch
to make the road passable to local traffic. Otherwise, the
detour around takes so much time."

"My Mom says Willy Bert turned himself in to be picked
up today. Did you see him?"

"No, Lexie, except at a distance I watched two men and
the bus driver taking the children to safety. Tip helped,
too. When the weather turns bad, I use every pre-caution to
avoid chill. Your Mother came a few minutes ago, but didn't
stay. I hope it's fatigue and she can avoid a cold and Tip,
too."

"She told me you want to return to the Condo."

"Lexie, you're into small time stuff this morning. Yes,
I need to see my doctor. Now, tell me about yourself;
otherwise, we sound like street gossip in the courthouse
square."

"My parents don't sluff off on life. It's serious
everyday with them. The hillside fire, Andy's going home
with Rae, and now the mud-slide with the bus accident gives
them nightmares and it may take time to settle into a quiet
structured pattern again. They're blessed to fill jobs they
like and stay busy."

"You encourage your parents Lexie and I hope you can
come home again soon."

"No long good-bye, Just good-bye, Cayrolynn."

Sounds came from the house and Cayrolynn saw the propane truck filling the tank near Sarah Anna's green house. The storm cellar held plants to be brought out at the end of frost. The green house gave Sarah Anna and Tip a hobby plus green salads all winter.

Lexie's homesick, Cayrolynn thought, and I am, too. She still has a home to come home to, but there's no place for me on the gulf coast. I am thankful, Sarah Anna and Tip welcome me here.

*   *   *

Often, Cayrolynn packed everything to go to the Condo. Today, she took very little. On the way, she tried to decide if she should go to the Condo or stay with Beatrice.

"In our last conversation, she lectured me," Cayrolynn spoke aloud. "My psyche needs approval and quietness, not the upheaval of rejection, so I must stop off at the Condo. Decisions come in many ways and approval by others contributes to final outcomes. So, TeJay, you'll find me in your space, tonight."

*   Twenty   *

TeJay put his key in the back door and shoved. Fresh
bread and good kitchen smells greeted them.

"Who's here? We're home."

Sarah Anna came from the hallway with Tip following.

"We came into a warm house left with your dryer running
so we expected you soon. I brought food, and Tip and I are
cooking for you two. Tip followed your instructions to find
your outside key, so we let ourselves inside and I hope you
don't mind."

"Great. You know our favorites, cornbread for Cayrolynn
and yeast biscuits for me. And, I smell meatloaf."

"Your Mother felt the agony of memories. This day's the
anniversary of the time Sam left us, so with the snow, the
cabin fever became too much."

"We feel blessed you came and doubly blessed that you
cooked us supper. I see you found the new tableware
Cayrolynn bought and it does look pretty."

"Tip starves, so if you two will wash your hands or whatever, we'll eat."

Sarah Anna felt at home with the bowls and cookware Cayrolynn collected. TeJay asked his Dad to return thanks, then silence prevailed while they began their meal.

"You said this day's the anniversary when Sam left home."

"I can see how a person can be pushed into a complete breakdown," Sarah Anna said. "I was fortunate to have my family during that time. Lexie and Andy were still in high school."

"I understand the trauma, Sarah Anna," Cayrolynn said. "We're glad you two came to see us, today. TeJay and I are having our first big fuss."

"What, Son."

"Before I tell you, let me ask a question, Dad. Over Christmas, Uncle Andrew talked to us about Andy and Rae. Did you know he separated them?"

"Your Uncle went through a stage," Tip answered. "He thought siblings and couples and twins shouldn't attend the same medical school which isn't true. At the time, we didn't understand, even though he told us. Only after Rae moved to Alabama with her parents, did we understand that Andrew managed her medical school acceptance. We're not part of his shenanigans," Tip explained.

"My Brother caused us problems all along," Sarah Anna added. "Now, he's pushing Andy out of his practice or research lab and Rae will pick up the pieces, I think. I hope."

"It's not a happy time for Andy and Rae." Tip said. "We fear for Sam and Toney because Andrew becomes part of their plans with his purchase of the estate where they'll live."

"Was Rae a consideration for Sam's leaving home?"

"TeJay, we don't know. Rae was the sister and you know that. Our answer is that circumstances seem to turn out right for Sam. Toney's a good wife and Sam's work is making him a wealthy man. Andrew's wise to invest in Sam and his family because Toney and her parents include him. He'll have people in his old age which he needs." Sarah Anna answered.

"So, tell me why you and Cayrolynn are debating." Tip said.

"TeJay wants us to move into a large elaborate condominium that I don't like," Cayrolynn answered.

"There's a real estate complex a client needs to unload that I like, and I believe it'll make a good investment," TeJay said.

"You went to look and we came. Could we go see?" Sarah

Anna asked.

"Sure. I'll call the security people and we'll go now.
We should take your car, Tip. It's easier for the four of
us."

Cayrolynn sat beside TeJay, who drove, and Tip sat in
the back with Sarah Anna. Even with the wait at traffic
lights, it took only a few minutes to reach the ten floor
apartment house constructed from an old warehouse.

They took the elevator to the eighth floor and entered
the apartment foyer. All the drapes stayed closed, but they
turned on the lights and saw an apartment furnished by an
interior decorator rated A plus.

"Do real people live here?" Sarah Anna asked.

"Does look like pictures from a Sears catalog, I think."
Tip walked around the large grand salon and asked to open the
drapes with the electrical opener on the wall.

"It's so beautiful, Cayrolynn. You must tell us why you
don't like it." Sarah Anna commented. "I think it looks so
comfortable, so rich and inviting."

"It's my woman's intuition, I think. Then, it's a
showplace lifestyle that I've never lived. I don't know how
to give parties to help TeJay get and keep clients. It
scares me. These two small bedrooms, one for guest and one
for a maid, but no space for my work hobby. No westward sun

in this place, only the oblique rays coming from the east. I
need to be where we can park our cars outside our door with
space for me to go walk and with a neighborhood grocery where
mothers push babies in their carts."

Neither Tip, nor Sarah Anna, nor TeJay answered. They
looked and admired, then drove back to the Condo.

"I see your reasoning, Cayrolynn," Tip advised. "And, I
see why you like the city lights downtown, TeJay."

"Cayrolynn doesn't want to garden, so we need the Condo
with lawn service. We must work out what we want and she may
be right that we need to stay here and not sell."

"Sometimes, we do know things by intuition," Sarah Anna
stated. "Cayrolynn, the place is called the Broadside, why?
I don't understand the name."

"Broadside like a broadside ballad, I think. Like a
song poem printed on one side and sold as a poster or
painting. The apartment building faces one way and lacks
views even though there are windows. Mostly, I would miss
the walk on the sunny side, always on the sunny side."

"How do you feel about the wall paper?" Sarah Anna
asked.

"Maroon or wine, but not the red of scarlet, embellished
with felt or velvet design like a Moroccan tent or harem.
The dense musky smell seems like incense, like a perfumed wax

candle burned to the end of the wick."

"Do you read Edgar Allan Poe?" Tip asked.

"Poe writes in despair, I think. Quote the raven nevermore that should be evermore, and yes, the apartment's minus touches of Emily Dickinson. In high school, my teacher said Poe's cottage in New York is positioned in a park. Homes develop with people and your country home holds rural canvas and denim for hard wear by children, and the Loft is dressed in red and green gingham. This Condo shows purple and yellow brocade with white lacey second curtains."

"You need a house to help you get well, and somehow, this new apartment's not a Broadside for you, but a Brothel. Do you see it as a Brothel?"

"Sarah Anna, you dig deeper and I couldn't think why I didn't like the place. Even if I saw a need to redecorate, TeJay would say yes and do that for me. What you're saying is correct and I don't want to move there."

"So, now my parents enter into our ruckus."

"Your Mother and I must decide about our retirement and the farm. We talked about selling out, but now, we aren't so sure. With Claude and Maude, it became a family place, 'the old homeplace,' and that's no longer true."

"Where did you think you would move?" Cayrolynn asked.

"To a house that smells new in a retirement village,

where we can play golf, and fish, and play dominoes with other retirees all night."

"I don't believe you," TeJay said. "But, until Cayrolynn and I work out this decision, I don't want to get mixed up in your moving off and leaving us. But I ask, do you think you would get your money out of the homeplace?"

"Probably not. That's one reason to sit still. Claude and Maude bought the original one hundred acres. With the tree farm acreage we bought, all together, we own about five hundred taxable acres. Much of the land's hillside, as you know," Tip said.

"Farms need families. When we harvest our nursery stock, the land needs replanting. Our burn needs either hand planting or by plane, and I guess with pine," Sarah Anna said.

"Sarah Anna and I talk about our plans. Andy likes the farm, but his life changes. Lexie plans her life in Texas. Sam stays busy and never comes to visit. Now, TeJay finds his commute, even with good roads, impossible."

"Don't get into confusion, Cayrolynn. My parents talk and re-talk what they think. It's preliminary to eventually coming up with a plan. Advice from a national farm or ranch realtor or realtors in Nashville or Atlanta might be appropriate."

"Tomorrow, before you leave," Cayrolynn said, "please go with me to my consignment gallery. It's closed for the month of January, but the owner's often around, if he's not in Florida, and I would like to show you both, his set-up."

*   *   *

Tip heard the rain before he heard the telephone. Sarah Anna turned over and asked if they should sleep late or get ready to leave. Cayrolynn didn't answer the phone, so Tip said hello.

"Dad, come with me to breakfast and you can bring something back for the family."

"Sure, TeJay. I need to shower and wipe off a few whiskers. Give me fifteen minutes and pick me up out front."

"I feel like turning over and taking one last nap. No one pushes us and we shouldn't push ourselves." Sarah Anna pulled the blanket around her head and disappeared.

"TeJay invites me for breakfast and I'll bring you an egg sandwich on wheat bread."

Cayrolynn came downstairs, but heard nothing, so she returned upstairs to work until she heard some stirring. Near nine, she went to the kitchen and made coffee. Even though she heard nothing, Tip came in the back door with bagels and donuts.

"I brought along an egg and ham sandwich for each of us,

Cayrolynn. I ate with TeJay, but I got hungry. Sarah Anna
needs coffee when she awakens. She says it's related to her
metabolism."

"Shall we eat, or will you check on Sarah Anna first?"

"You eat, while I check on Sarah Anna."

"It feels so good to see you here, Tip, since TeJay
needs less stress from the commute. It's raining and cold
this morning with slush. This weather brings out wishes for
hot sassafras tea or chocolate, a wood fire, and music. Your
being here for a couple of days would be nice."

*   *   *

After Tip and Sarah Anna returned Cayrolynn to the Condo
from their trip to the consignment gallery on Hwy 96 and said
good-bye, the separation trauma doubled Cayrolynn over with
tears and she sobbed to herself. "I want to go to the Loft."
She lay on the floor with small couch pillows and the will to
relax. TeJay found her there, sleeping, with a hiccup in her
sleep and dry tears that smeared make-up. He covered her
with an alfghan from the back of the couch and went across to
Shafe's condominium to call his parents.

"Mom, did Cayrolynn seem upset when you left?"

"No. She said she wished she could come with us, but
she didn't seem disturbed. We experienced grief when we left
her like leaving one of you with Maude when we went off to

work." Sarah Anna gave the telephone to Tip.

"You're only an hour away, Son. Since Cayrolynn came to us, she feels like our child and we know she needs to be there with you, but we miss her. Do you-uns still fuss?"

"I know," TeJay explained, "she doesn't like my suggested change for the Condo, but probably it's more than that. She must be feeling some emotional stress related to her health."

"If you haven't seen the shop where she sells her work, you should go for a tour of the place. The owner keeps one section for primitive antiques and artistic endeavors. It looks like an organized garage sale. His private warehouse barn, for decorators only, carries pieces with big price tags."

"You enjoyed your trip with her?"

"Yes, we did and I think she did, too."

"Expect us this week-end, Dad. If she experiences homesickness for the Loft, then we'll be there week-ends, forsure."

TeJay put supper in the microwave and set the table, before he went for Cayrolynn.

"Cayrolynn. Cayrolynn, listen up. Why are you on the floor?"

"TeJay, I must have relaxed here before I took a nap."

"Supper's ready. Come with me across to Shafe's."

"I'll come. Give me a minute."

Cayrolynn creamed her face and the new make-up brightened her rested appearance. Early dusk presented a winter sky with the frigid coldness of the season. Cayrolynn wore a sweater but the chase across the driveway left her shivering.

"So, unwise to come without a jacket," TeJay said. "You enjoyed your field trip with the parents?"

"Yes. I hated to see them go, even though we'll be there again soon. This moving to the new Condo, really bothers me. It's not the villa, here's the brownstone villa complex, and that's the high rise hotel. It's fully furnished, however I looked at furniture and art today with Sarah Anna and Tip. I don't want a home that looks like a hotel room."

"Go back to the beginning. I come home to find you on the floor? Why?"

"When they left, the world closed in on me. I lay on the floor with hopes to relax."

"Be truthful, Cayrolynn. I need to know. Were you thinking about self-extinction?"

"No. Didn't think of that. No. Tip kissed me on the forehead and Sarah Anna kissed me on my cheek. I remembered

Sarah Anna telling about Be Back and I knew they told me Be
Back or until the next time. Like a child, I guess my
emotions steered out of control much like homesickness."

"Did anything happen to hurt your feelings?"

"No. Except, I needed some thread and your parents went
with me into the craft store on our return trip. The price
on the shelf said two dollars and the scan at the registrar
said three dollars. I questioned the price and the girl gave
me a curt answer. Tip told her the extra charge meant cash
registrar fraud. She was upset and we were upset. When she
didn't call her manager, we left the thread on the counter
with no purchase."

"This happening shouldn't have upset you."

"But, it put a dark spell at the end of our outing."

"The folks left, and no thread purchase, so what then?"

"We turned out the lights before we left which meant we
returned to a dark Condo. Somehow, we didn't turn on much
light when we returned. Maybelle turned on all the lights in
winter because lack of light makes us mope and be grumpy."

"You hit the doldrums with tears and failed to turn on
the lights or make some hot soup or cocoa. Or, do you see
another problem? Why does this Brothel word stick?"

"Well, we aren't married."

"We'll get married."

"No. We will not."

"We will on Easter morning at the sunrise service at Brush Arbor Church. No matter, if you live one day or one hundred years, you'll marry me and whither I go, you'll go."

"Must we live at the Brothel?"

"Cayrolynn. Shut up. Ours must be a covenant marriage, not a co-habitation."

Later, she would think about their relationship and know people carry secrets that cannot be put into words. Telling isn't what happened because only the two people in relationship know the spoken and unspoken communication that happens between themselves. What's the glance or the touch or the telephone call that says more than the words spoken?

*   Twenty-One   *

At midnight, Cayrolynn answered her cell phone that she
hid beneath her pillow each night.

"Cayrolynn, I need empathy. Aubrey's sister called me.
I expected him to die soon, but not this afternoon. Their
funeral home will come for his body in the morning after the
doctor fills out the death certificate. On my way home from
Atlanta, I thought about grief."

"Beatrice, I stay awake reading tonight, so our hearts
must communicate with intuition. Many poets and authors talk
about sorrow like John Gunther in <u>Death Be Not Proud</u> or
C.S.Lewis in <u>A Grief Observed.</u> I found a picture book about
Mother Teresa that said she never wanted a person to die
alone. Aubrey made the right choice to go to Atlanta with
his parents and experience his heaven going with his family."

"I understand about Aubrey's death, Cayrolynn. I like
the word home-going because it's an eternal trip."

"Will there be a funeral?"

"Yes and no. Aubrey wanted cremation. His family will decide. They plan a graveside service in a cemetery once rural, but now urban. It's a family plot where his parents placed their markers and one for Aubrey, too."

"TeJay wants to talk to my doctor at the clinic. Will you work tomorrow and will you be there?"

"Yes. Blessings and thank you for your words of friendship, bye, too."

*   *   *

Cayrolynn continued to read for two pages to the end of the chapter, then enclosed a marker and placed the book under her bed for easy finding. She turned off her light and found a comfortable stretch to go to sleep. She tossed, then slide to her knees beside the bed to say prayers for all these people her life touched.

*   *   *

Friday came with nothing said about their week-end trip to the Loft. Cayrolynn packed.

Sarah Anna called.

"TeJay said nothing, so I don't know our plans, Sarah Anna."

"You're a thrifty soul, Cayrolynn, so I decided to treat you from the January sales with new towels and bed linen for the Loft. I washed the lot and put the Loft in order, so we're waiting for you."

"Did you hear from Rae?"

"We did and they plan to come at Easter. Andy isn't returning to Memphis. Rae says they plan to live near her parents at Gulf Shores. Andy'll work at a lab in Mobile with abbreviated hours to match hers at the pediatric clinic. Otherwise, all's the same with them."

"I have a letter from Lexie that you can read. She included some clippings about Fat Tuesday, Mardi Gras in Galvaston and a book that tells about Lent, those forty days, Good Friday and Easter. Sarah Anna, tell me how your family celebrated Easter."

Sarah Anna felt some need to continue the telephone conversation. When she talked to Lexie, Rae, or Toney, each swapped happenings, but with Cayrolynn the conversation never seemed complete.

"One year for Christmas, Maude and Claude gave us an electric maker for boiled eggs. We found pleasure at Easter with dyed red eggs, hide them and find them, lost and found, but we all liked the candy marshmallow eggs best. Claude worked with a man whose family celebrated with red eggs and a pre-Easter night meal. Toney tells me Sam bought a boiled egg maker and they enjoy red eggs at Easter."

"Is this a ritual from a church?"

"Russia or Greece, I think.   Call us if y'all come to supper, Cayrolynn."

*   *   *

TeJay came from the office early and made no mention of the farm.

"I called your doctor and asked if we can come to see him at five. My interest isn't to interfere in your medical records, Cayrolynn, nor do I mean to be secretive or selfish, but I want to ask what the doctor knows about you that I don't know. Love shouldn't be blind and I want the best for you and for me. Do you understand?"

"I think I understand, but I wish instead of talking to Beatrice you would ask me. Trust, don't you know? I see no problems with your plans. None. If they need a blood test, this sweater allows easy access to my arms. So, I'm ready to go."

"I made the appointment, but no talking to Beatrice. What will we be looking for? Iron poor blood?"

"Anemia, maybe. I'm healthy and I shall not die but live to praise his holy name. The changes after my boss died caused so much stress. I know healing's in my body either with medicines or miracles."

"I didn't ask for a clinic visit. I asked for us to go over your records."

Beatrice didn't appear, so Cayrolynn felt she must be gone for the day. Often when she came, she would sit for an hour before the nurse took her back for blood work and consultation. Now, the nurse-receptionist took them into an office to the doctor on duty. Professional visits come with a planned courtesy. They sat before the doctor opened her file.

"This test shows a stable condition. Tell me about your stress situations in the last six months."

"Before I came for tests, my boss died with the virus and I left my job. My housing situation changed and I moved in with Beatrice who works here. I met TeJay and moved to his parents farm where I can work on my art, and get exercise and fresh air."

"Tell me about your sleep, any apnea?"

"I sleep well, but I experience sleep paralysis after some traumatic happening."

"Explain."

"Some prisoners came by the farm and took a truck. We had a hill fire at the homestead. TeJay's brother was diagnosed with HIV. The hill mud slide took the bus with children down the hill. Sometimes, I move between the farm and a Condo in town."

TeJay began to talk, but Cayrolynn couldn't seem to

listen or even to get her breath.

"Cayrolynn, will you marry TeJay?"

With her breathing problem, she felt the tears. She could only shake her head. She arose from her chair and went to the small lab across the hall. She turned on the water and hid the sounds.

When she opened the door, TeJay waited for her and they didn't return to the doctor's office. TeJay asked her to wait until he brought the car.

"Did the doctor change any of my prescriptions, TeJay?"

"No, he wants you to keep an appointment you have for a physical."

"Yes, I know. Your Mother wants you to call her, if we can be there for supper."

"I'll call her while you get ready. Okay with you that we drive there tonight?"

Cayrolynn didn't listen to TeJay's telephone conversation with his parents. Going to the the clinic left recollections of doubts. Aubrey died.

"Ready to go, Little Red Ridinghood?"

"Yes. Big Bad Wolf."

* * *

From the valley road, they could see the farm house aglow with light. Cayrolynn thought this must be the view

TeJay saw each night at the end of his hour commute home.

"Looks as thought your parents are expecting company with all the lights."

"This week my Mother faced each day with the question if the buses could run on the icy hill roads. She never liked to miss days due to weather, but now she holds fear for another accident."

TeJay drove near the back deck steps and they went inside for greetings before he parked the truck under the Loft.

"Eat first, then we want to show you Christmas photos from our trip," Sarah Anna said.

"Several shots we'll frame for our upstairs hallway, but we bought a new album and now it's full," Tip said.

"Dad, you should've been a photographer."

"Don't tell him that because we would've starved."

Tip brought a leather covered album with the plastic sleeves filled with Christmas photographs.

"Your Mother wrote explanations on the backs, and she typed some names and dates for each that you'll see."

They sat on the couch discussing each picture. Children grow, mature, and make school accomplishments. Cayrolynnn saw the blessing of Sam's family for these grandparents.

"Pride and joy, our grandchildren, and I think they'll

come for Easter," Sarah Anna said.

"Andrew bought the house and gave it completely, deed and all, to Sam and Toney. They asked us to come help them move, but it doesn't fit with our work schedules nor our January weather."

Cayrolynn noticed TeJay remained quiet. She knew he talked several nights with Sam. Whatever arrangements Sam made with Andrew, TeJay gave advice based on the experiences of Andy and Rae.

"I hope Sam can spend a week showing the farm and where he grew-up to Toney and their children," Cayrolynn said, "that is, if they get to come. I think he must miss this place."

"The Mississippi farm of my childhood belonged to my Mother's family and often when I drive into the yard here, I remember my Grandmother coming to meet us while drying her hands on the flowered bid apron she wore."

"Sarah Anna's memories account, in a large part, for our rebuilding and the additions to this house for our home here. So interesting, to be a farm family, and now have an ordained Chaplain daughter telling us about her plans for celebrations of Resurrection Sunday, I think she said," Tip said.

"But, you grew up in Detroit City and I think about a relative of Lavender's who lived there," Cayrolynn said.

"They drove a big car, I remember, and wrote to Lavender, but never came to stay, often or long, because of their jobs."

"I never returned to visit in Detroit after we married. Sometimes, I think about that. Everybody seems to be from some other place," Tip said.

"Our cemetery goes back to 1815 and some of those first family names continue. People with roots. You enjoyed family history, TeJay. You and Claude. Claude liked to sit you on his wood chopping block. Do you remember his long reminiscences?"

"I remember I liked to help chop the fat pine kindling splinters making them ready to begin the fire in the stove or fireplace. Maude hated that ax.

"Claude lived in Detroit for fifty years, and he would get people talking and matching-up kinfolks with everyone in the county. I never found him boring, but Andy and Sam would go rambling off or inside to bother Maude. Much of what I learned, I remember." TeJay answered, then asked, "Will we have sunshine this week-end, Mom?"

"No, rain."

"I may need to return to the office, but Cayrolynn can expect me by the time she gets up. That is, if she sleeps late. When she's here she awakens at dawn, but in town, I think she sleeps until noon."

*   *   *

Cayrolynn didn't hear the car when TeJay left the next morning. Rain peppered her window when she awoke. The ring on her finger caught her attention, and she remembered that before long, she would wear the symbol of legal significance.

She turned on music and dressed in a red sweater left by TeJay in the Loft years ago. Before she spread her bed, she artfully made her face to look clean and professional. I don't go around looking like an unmade bed all day, she quoted to herself.

No noise came from the house, and she didn't open her blinds to the east. When she looked to the west, the stark tree farm acreage stood wet and leafless like India ink pen drawings. She self talked. "Right brain, or left brain? Either way, my fingers find work and I'm so happy. Will I die? Someday, yes. Am I afraid? Yes, because of pain. No for the final victory. Jehovah-Shalom."

*   *   *

Sarah Anna called and then came for de-caf tea. This morning she brought graham carrot muffins. Cayrolynn appeared happy, however Sarah Anna noticed rivulets where tears marred neat make-up.

"You went to the doctor and how was the appointment?"

"I'm doing fine and I need to continue to avoid stress

situations. I recounted all the upheavals here since I
came."

"Can you think of current thought patterns that give you
stress, Cayrolynn? Do you push yourself too much with your
art projects?"

"Today, I feel sad for Aubrey who died and Rae with
Andy. I feel unsure with TeJay because he liked Rae and now
she'll be free to marry him. And, the wife at TeJay's office
said, her husband told TeJay no partnership without a stable
marriage and probably kids and a house in the suburbs."

By this time, the water began to seep from Cayrolynn's
eyes.

"Cayrolynn, you know I can't listen and watch you cry
without telling you what I think. TeJay loves you, and we
love you. Glenda Rae-Ann never suited TeJay. TeJay told us
about the pressure at the office and he would accept none of
it. He loves you, also Tip and I know so."

"He never says or shows it."

"Yes, he does in many ways and you need eyes to see his
outpouring. Start with the friendship ring you wear. That
ring isn't to impress his bosses. Andy and Rae wore rings
that said, true love waits. TeJay picked up on that phrase
and plans the right time and place to marry you.

"I know TeJay talks with meaning, but often an

explanation might give me more assurance."

"Before TeJay met you, Tip saw the gate to Claude's place open and went to see. TeJay used Maude's advice to get strenuous exercise rather than a drink from a white lightening jar. I think those partners in the firm feared TeJay might leave and take those clients he brought with him. When the partners put pressure, he came home and talked with us."

"I try not to fear. I guess I find fear, then make a pity party that invites no one but me and it causes tears and headaches."

"The longer you live in the hollow, the more solace it shares. Maude seems to indwell the homeplace. Claude put a swing on the front porch with heavy springs attached to the rafters. The swing kept an up and down movement along with the back and forth. I miss the swing and the gourd dipper for the spring that Claude put on a nail under the house."

"Lexie told me a girl with her baby seems to live at Ol' Lonesome."

"Tip never heard hill stories until he moved here and he thinks they're superstition. I hope the Ol' Lonesome story isn't whispered since the school bus accident. I wish Lexie didn't share that story with you. Lexie thinks you belong to the hollow, so you need to know the stories.

"Some stories came from Ireland to the Appalachians and Maude remembered them from her childhood. The way Maude spoke you would think they happened yesterday or this morning. North Alabama Indians and Cherokees from north Georgia gave us words that we continue to use like Fido, their word for dog. Maude used the word buggerman to threaten and scare my children. No more hearsay tales this morning, Cayrolynn. Enough for now. When the rain stops, use the wetness as an excuse to wrap warm and tramp in the water run-off wearing your new red galoshes TeJay found for you that match your sweater. Life must be lived and enjoyed in small happenings."

Sarah Anna went to the house and Cayrolynn thought about the advice. She remembered Lavender. "Better watch your step girl, your mother-in-law runs this show. A word to the wise is sufficient." Lavender spoke proverbs like Benjamin Franklin. She liked lilac bath powder and toilet water that came in a set at the five and dime at Christmas or the dark blue bottles of Evening in Paris.

*   Chapter Twenty Two   *

"Cayrolynn, I came thinking we could have lunch."

"Did you look for me in the rec room, TeJay? Such a cold day outside, but excellent for easy exercise on the machines. Remember the red folder in my mailbox about a workshop? I signed up, in case, I lived here and not at the Loft. We listened to a lecture about faces and the presenter came with a variety of masks. She talked with us about facades along with make-up."

"Can we go now? Even if you aren't hungry, we can find a salad somewhere."

"I'm hungry. Just a few minutes for me to be ready and did you have a good morning?"

"So, So. Don't dress up, either pants or skirt."

"With jacket, I know."

When she returned, TeJay continued to sit at the table, reading. She watched and knew his focused mind didn't tell him, she sat beside him. When he turned the page and wrote on a yellow pad, she moved.

"Oh, you're ready. I think I'm thirsty, so a bottle of water to carry along."

She felt emotional imbalance and blushed. TeJay kept her waiting, and now, his unconscious control made her tense.

"Did you wait long for me?" Cayrolynn asked.

"An hour."

"And, it made you angry?"

"No. The office seemed noisy and I needed space and concentration. Why do you ask? Are you angry?"

"I feel like I'm five years and having a temper tantrum."

"You want to lay in the floor and scream or turn inward with depression?"

"I mean I'm jealous of anything or anyone who keeps you from me."

"Would you prefer a sandwich here, Cayrolynn?"

"Yes."

"Your morning left you with stress. Sit. First, a cup of bullion from the microwave, then toast in the toaster, then ham with lettuce and tomato," TeJay directed.

Cayrolynn went upstairs. She felt she should make the lunch, but not with this upheaval. She knew the screaming of her insides wouldn't settle until she could cry. Dry eyes with no tears and she couldn't relax.

"Come Cayrolynn, you'll feel better with a cup of soup." Tears came then, building like hot springs bursting. She crawled into bed and covered her head. TeJay left her.

*   *   *

Cayrolynn awoke with dreams and sweat. She turned back her quilt and realized the thermostat needed to be lowered. Tear stains matted her make-up put on with such precision at the workshop, so she spent a few minutes creaming off the old and replacement with the new. When she came downstairs, she thought TeJay went to Shafe's or to his office. He continued to sit working on papers that littered the table and the floor surrounding his chair.

"I'm sorry I collapsed and I wish you didn't see me or endure my upheaval."

"Why, Cayrolynn, why this emotional collapse?"

"My morning involved too many stimuli that leave me huffy. When I drink too much caffeine, I feel like this and need to sleep it off."

"Did you make friends at the workshop?"

"I met some people, women who don't work, but think they may go to work. Congenial group and everyone's kind. Did you finish your legal brief or whatever you worked on?"

"I finished and I need to run my notes down to the

office.   I could put them on the computer, but I think I'll ask someone at the office to do that for me.   I waited until you awoke, so you can go with me.   That is, if you wish?"

"Yes."

Drive time traffic filled the roads.   Cayrolynn didn't follow TeJay into the office but stayed in the truck.   TeJay stayed minutes, then returned and drove them to the cafeteria.

"You must eat, Cayrolynn."

"I will.   I never miss meals.   Lunch was the exception."

Cayrolynn knew she took too much from the line, but she wanted to keep TeJay from any complaints about food.   Prunes and cottage cheese, mushrooms in a spinach salad, paprika sprinkled broiled fish, several squash goulash, and garlic toast.   When they unloaded their trays, she noticed TeJay matched her choices.   Often he would choose according to what she took from the line.

This cafeteria filled to over-flowing for lunch, but now, for supper, intermittent seating left them with freedom to talk.

"Was our trip to the farm this past week-end helpful?"

"Yes, but I don't want to be at the Loft without you, and, if you need to work on Saturday, then we'll go when you finish."

"We should go to church with Tip and Sarah Anna. They accept our excuses, but their friends want to know us, or they want to know you. Church is a community place for them; a place where they share problems and others understand. Answered prayer is real for them."

"You said Maude walked to church, so tell me how she climbed the hillside. She must have gained sustenance there."

"She did. She made herself a rope pull to help her climb the hill without falling. After Claude died, she suffered like most widow women. Men seem to marry again, but most women remain alone. Some experience a depth of loneliness with their sorrow."

"Do you work with estate settlements?"

"Not really. When we advise clients about estate planning, we share like a committee, to be sure we don't forget some helpful aspect. After senility or death occurs, our suggested advice proves itself as either right or wrong."

"One of the women in the group, Jo or Josephine, plans to sell her condominium and move to Texas to be near her children."

"And?"

"Part of estate planning, I think. I asked her which condo because I thought you might think about her place,

if you really want to make some changes. It's a condominium
on ground level without stairs. Your having three bedrooms
helps because Tip and Sarah Anna can stay in one."

"Your acquaintance at the workshop, will she sell her
furniture with the condo?"

"I didn't ask. She collects Llandro and invited us to
come see her collection that her husband brought her from
Spain."

"Did you talk with Beatrice recently?"

"Today. She helps a teacher who took on a pizza
delivery route because she has two boys and she wants them to
work. She wanted me to know they enjoy the car of mine she
bought."

"Beatrice seems to enjoy taking on helping projects."

"She likes to help, but I don't think she meddles in the
affairs of others. With an extra quotient of nurturance,
she's vulnerable to being taken into a helping role where
she's needed."

"And, she continues to work at the clinic and that's a
small salary job."

"Either for men or women, jobs bring money and power,
even personhood. You know this, TeJay. When a person's
poor, they're subject to the forces like no food, poor
housing with no utilities, and lack of clothes to give

themselves a feeling of self-worth."

"I took a sociology course and the professor kept explaining everything according to the concentric circles of a city. Our farm life didn't prepare me for the changes that occur when people move from the center of town to suburbia."

"I keep wanting to tell you about the women in my workshop group, yet I know that's the lowest step in conversation when we talk about other people. I guess it's judgemental conversation, too."

"Do you think talking about ourselves fits higher or lower than talking about others?"

"I don't know, but I do know that I keep thinking about my present work project, too."

"And?"

"I'll show you even though I'm in the beginning stage with a canvas backing and small merging of the alphabet. Color makes the designs. I don't label it a tapestry, but a mural."

"I keep thinking about my work, too, Cayrolynn. My client makes money with his corpus of country songs. He promotes, contracts, and becomes a publist for a couple of road shows with singers not well known."

"My work needs planning, but the execution gives me thinking time. With your work, thinking and plotting, stays in your mind, I think. Sometimes, you seem like a million miles away and I know you are trying to figure something out," Cayrolynn said.

"People live their own lives and getting mixed up with problems like charge cards and over-charging, divorce and bankruptcy, and taxes leaves very little left over for quality of life. Live on love can mean a lifestyle of harmony or disaster."

"I live on love," Cayrolynn teased.

"Don't I know it."

Like double exclamation marks, their laughter came.

"We can talk about world affairs or we can talk about ideas of merit. What's next on the list?"

"Sometimes, I listen to talk radio or television panels, but I prefer the cadence of music. The faster the music, the faster I work. The faster the music, the faster I eat."

"I don't hear background music, tonight. We use several canned tapes in our office with choice either turned on or off, either vocals or instrumentals, and either classical or country."

"You leaf through the newspaper in the mornings."

"Scan only. Keeps me ready to talk with a client. Do you look at the paper for ideas?"

"Often for clippings that I save because the ideas make

sense to me. Someday, I want to put together a scrap book."

"What did you see recently?"

"Today, I saw a proverb by the man Lexie quoted at Thanksgiving. 'I shall not pass through this world but once. Any good therefore, that I can do, or any kindness that I can show to any human being, let me do it now. Let me not defer or neglect it, for I shall not pass this way again.' by Henry Drummond. It appeared in a magazine about calorie counting that one of the women passed around at the workshop."

"Do you memorize easily?"

"I do, TeJay, by writing down each phrase until I can write lines without looking and eventually all."

The table waitress came to ask if they wanted complimentary coffee. Both said, no. Much of their meal, they didn't eat, but Cayrolynn asked for a take-out-box for left overs. When she took a box home, it gave her an easy lunch. Tonight, her thoughts didn't include food. This time, TeJay remembered to help her up to the bench truck seat. On the way home, he stopped for gas. Someone who knew him came over to talk. Both went inside to pay, and Cayrolynn sat in the cold truck, but TeJay understood and returned before her feet seemed to tingle with cold.

"Too cold to fill up, too cold for conversation, and did you get cold sitting here?"

"I didn't. I find it interesting to watch people. The man next to us put in two dollars worth. One man filled his tank and an extra gas can like for a lawnmower. Some vehicles came with one lone driver and others carried occupants."

"Did you know that intelligence is marked by observation? I seem to miss what's happening around me."

"You consider yourself a dummy?"

"Back to first ·agenda. Do we discuss ourselves, other people, or?"

"I know. World affairs, ideas or theory."

"Maybe, when we get home, we should watch a video about cowboys, or clowns. Which?"

TeJay drove under the carport and Cayrolynn felt glad to stop all the chit-chat. Some television and a movie along with needle craft and busy fingers brought less demands.

"Cayrolynn tell me something."

"Sure. TeJay, what?"

"When you lived in the house full of women, where did you leave your sewing equipment?"

"The same ·clear plastic box I use now, this one, and it stayed in the hall closet."

"Did you allow anyone to use the thread, needles, and scissors?"

"Of course. We kept an ironing board, iron, and pressing cloth there for all to use. No problem because we mended and then put everything into the closet again."

"If a person with germs used your needles and left dormant infection and you by accident stuck yourself? This is hypothetical and open ended?" TeJay didn't tarry with his question but went to Shafe's.

Cayrolynn locked and checked the doors when he left. She couldn't answer TeJay and his thoughts. Maybelle said don't solve your problems at night, so she made the room tidy and climbed the stairs. I never wanted to be selfish, even when teachers didn't want us to share pencils because of germs. I kept my homework hidden, but I helped anyone who asked me how to find the answer. Oh yeah, okay, so tomorrow brings another day.

*   Chapter Twenty-Three   *

"TeJay shows me an acceptance I don't deserve,"
Cayrolynn thought. She knew she tried to overcompensate when
she felt inadequate. Self understanding with feelings of
inferiority caused her to want to make-up for some personal
lack. "What can I do to prove myself."

This contrary thought pattern nagged at her thinking
like a premeditation for a crime. She self-talked.

"I don't need to impress him with clothes, or make-up,
and certainly, not with education or money. He says nice
comments about my art endeavors, but I feel so inadequate.
He does appreciate me, but how can he see me except in an
inferior way? I'm a nobody with these medical symptoms."

On Friday night the last of January, she called her
friend, Marthee, who helped her move to Nashville from the
children's home.

"Marthee, this is Cayrolynn and I need help."

"Sure, if I can."

In the background, she could hear the television and children.

"Don't let me keep you on the phone, if your family needs you. My problem concerns my lifestyle. I have a friend who wants to marry me, but I feel so inferior. Do you remember my singing at our house on Sixteenth Street, when we entertained aspiring musicians on week-ends?"

"Of course, you liked to sing like your Mother."

"My friend plays substitute as a back-up for groups around town and I would like to surprise him on Valentine's with the poem I quote and a couple of songs. Do you think you and Pitt could go for late supper that night and take me to the place where my friend TeJay will play?"

"I can ask. Week nights are difficult for us because I continue to work mornings as a teacher's help and Pitt works two jobs. Nights, he works the radio disk jockey deal and days, he continues to sell cars. But, I'll ask, Cayrolynn."

"I'll need you and Pitt to help me set up the act. Remember Hosea? Hoe leads this group and I need Pitt to ask him, if I can surprise TeJay?"

"You know how to network, Cayrolynn. I get so busy, I don't keep up with you and it's so nice for you to call. I'll try your party planning. Ingenious. And, I hope we can make it work for you."

Now, Cayrolynn felt sneaky with doing something behind TeJay's back. Would she tear up her nest? The wise woman builds her nest, and a foolish one tears it down. Would he understand and say thank you for this surprise gift she would give?

For a week, Cayrolynn waited for Marthee to call in answer to her request. Often, when her thoughts returned to the projected plan, she felt a pressing impulse to cancel. She didn't, but in her heart she prayed alot.

"Cayrolynn, we can't get away on Valentine's night. Pitt called Hoe and received a yes answer. You call Hoe and this is his number. He told Pitt, as usual, he'll do the vocals, then bring you on at the last to close out the night. Most people will be gone, so if your voice cracks, it won't matter."

When she said good-bye with all the niceties spoken, Cayrolynn lay on the couch thinking about the conversation. The emotional upheaval during the past weeks never entered her thinking. Now, she touched her face where tear stains often eroded make-up and lost mascara drew raccoon circles around her eyes. Could she perform without her heart bursting? Did alcohol help her Mom through the tension of being on stage?

Cayrolynn pulled on a switch of hair grown longer since

her last trip for a hair cut. Sometime in her childhood, she unconsciously chewed during tension. When she noticed, she took herself to the bath and carefully wiped away the wetness. Lavender said, Cayrolynn, don't chew on your hair. Maybelle said, Cayrolynn don't chew on your hair. Now, she said, "Cayrolynn, don't chew on your hair. You know better."

The force of her desire to sing gave her courage, so she called Hoe.

"Sure, Cayrolynn. I won't tell your friend, TeJay, but we'll all be watching the straight faced one to see his reaction. Someone said they thought he dated Aubrey's friend. Is that you?"

"Aubrey's buddy, Beatrice, lived near Aubrey's apartment and I stayed with her after Marthee left and the house broke up. Do you remember Beatrice? She works for a doctor?"

"I think so. Don't let me down, now, Cayrolynn. Been a few years since I heard you at the house, but you do a good job when people aren't watching you. Just remember that and you'll do fine."

Valentine's Day came. TeJay brought her roses and took her to dinner, then went off on his bass fiddle assignment. At eleven, Cayrolynn finished putting on the party dress she wore the night TeJay met her. My Mom's dress, she reminded herself. Peter Pumpkin doesn't take his wife partying. My

Dad hated any man who admired my Mom. Jealousy and hatred.
I hope TeJay likes my Valentine surprise.

She called a cab and arrived a few minutes before
twelve. In the front lobby, she handed a note to the
attendant for Hoe. The hostess came with directions to a
side table and took her there. She felt sure TeJay didn't
see her. TeJay did see her and felt shock, then disbelief.
He kept his eyes averted and continued the essential beat.

"Where is she?" He tried to watch the hostess to a
table in the dark, then lost her. Near twelve, Hoe stopped
and gave an exclamation about Valentine's Day. "Now, a
friend of mine chooses to surprise her friend tonight with an
act she learned from her Mother. You are on, Cayrolynn."

She changed words from "You are my sunshine," to you are
my sweetheart. Singing took on a lower Alto sound and the
tones came precise and clear. Automatic with no thought, she
sang and then repeated Robert Browning's words, "How do I
love thee, then back to "You are my sweetheart" with Hoe and
the audience helping. No one noticed TeJay. He couldn't
play. His heart kept turning over and he wanted to run.

Hoe remembered her repertoire and asked for Knoxville
Girl, the one song Cayrolynn hated and planned to write other
words for the melody. This mournful ballad from England in
the 1700's wasn't appropriate for the Valentine's Day

message. She abbreviated the verses and sang the feller into marrying his sweetheart.

Finally, the end came with people calling for more. Hoe took her over to the side door where TeJay waited.

"She is a dear, TeJay." Hoe didn't wait for a comment and TeJay put his arm around her shoulders.

"Where's your coat?"

"In the foyer, with the hostess."

"Wait. I'll get your coat."

With people milling around no one noticed, so he picked up her quilted cashmere from a chair and returned to help Cayrolynn put it on. Even with the coat and the car heating fast, chills caused Cayrolynn's teeth to chatter and her body shake. Before he reversed, TeJay pulled her close and said, "Thank you. Best Valentine's ever."

At home, TeJay parked behind Shafe's condo and walked her around the building, across the driveway, and left her at her front door.

"Thanks. You did surprise me, forsure. Do you think the tension from your performance will keep you awake?"

"My tension from the day and week of waiting. I did it and I hope you like my singing for you. Thank you for the roses and special dinner tonight."

TeJay placed a kiss on each cheek before he used his key

to let her in the door, then went to Shafe's condo.
Cayrolynn feared the left over tension, but sleep came with
no problems. When she awoke, she lay thinking about Hoe and
her surprise for TeJay. When we give a gift, it's our
choice. TeJay said thank you, however she couldn't discern
if he felt the delight she felt in giving the performance for
him.

*   *   *

Sam heard the telephone before he opened the garage for
business. He knew TeJay went to the office early to talk
with him because he needed a sounding board.

"I told you, TeJay, to walk softly with the girl. For
months you prize her, and now your emotions fail you and you
want to zero out. It's the same old story for you, TeJay.
How did it happen?"

"Everything, our dinner, great, then she came with a
surprise song for me and it turned me off. Almost, I
couldn't wait to bring her home. Love turned to hate."

"Teen-age, puppy love crush. If this hate grows, you
must ease her out. After the honeymoon comes reality. My
greatest fear for you comes true. You expedite divorce cases
and you see the aftermath of love gone sour, and I hoped it
would never happen."

"Don't lecture me, Sam."

"You need help. The folks love her, and you're in distress."

"I want a wife and I have been waiting for a long time."

"I liked Toney, however our marriage came before love. Now, when she walks into the garage and I'm not expecting her, my heart turns over. During the short time before my decision to marry Toney, I went over what Tip and Sarah Anna told us happened to them at Dauphin Island. Sure, the draw of sex caused the contract. They decided to make a contract to build their lives together. When the gloss is over, can you make a contract to yourself and to her to take care of her?"

"I did that already, Sam. I already promised myself and Cayrolynn to keep her until she dies."

"And, that's what marriage and family is all about."

"All the love and care my heart felt, left me."

"Go back to the beginning and think through how you felt from the beginning. Take away the gloss and see if in hard reality you can keep your promises to yourself and to her. Toney and I didn't sleep together until after Manny was born. Hate is difficult and being Sarah Anna's son, I think the hate emotion will pass and you'll know a level headiness that will return a better love to you and see you through her fatigue problems."

"Good sermon, Brother. Sometimes, I miss Claude, especially when I seem to hear him when you're talking."

"Did you ever think that Claude might be Tip's Dad, and our grandfather?"

"I wish you never said that or thought that, Sam."

"I think Sarah Anna married Tip to leave home, but she loves our Dad. Andy loves Rae except he never got around to married love. They experienced a brother sister love and I hope with Andy on the beach with her, they'll find the covenant love they should have. As for you, TeJay, did Cayrolynn see your change in desire for her?"

"I think not."

"Then, call the parents and send her to the Loft until you can work these emotions out."

"She says she doesn't want to be there without me."

"TeJay get Tip to help you. Don't hurt the girl. Love is a gift and you know this."

After TeJay finished talking to Sam, he called Shafe's office and obtained his out-of-town number. After sunset, and his office closed, Shafe returned his call.

"I'm still here in Louisville with no final assignments, job-wise. Vera knows I'll not live with her parents. This hold-up with our marriage seems to be winding down. Her aunt plans to move with Vera's folks."

Most times, when TeJay worked late, he called Cayrolynn and now after he talked to Shafe, he called her.

"Listen, Cayrolynn, I work late and I want you to call your condo workshop friend to see if we can see her condo. We need to obtain her asking price, if she wants to sell."

"Do you want me to call you back, TeJay?"

"No. Only if she wants us to come tonight. It would be better one day next week. Just talked with Shafe, who wants to return to his condo and we'll need for you to stay at the Loft. Does that meet with your approval or do you concur?"

When she placed the telephone back on its' rest, Cayrolynn knew by insight, her discernment was true. Like her Mother, Sue Selaco, sent her to the children's home, TeJay needed to sweep her out the door. At other times, she might have called Beatrice. In her heart, she knew she tried to stabilize her relationship with TeJay and failed. The surprise song didn't work and worse, it turned him off. She went into her bedroom and took her Bible from her night stand. True promises come from the Psalms. I walk with you, and I'll not fail you.

Cayrolynn didn't cry. She sat with her head in her hands feeling lack of words and enmeshed in spider web fears.

The telephone rang and it was Sarah Anna.

"Did you and TeJay enjoy Valentine's?"

"Yes. Did he call you to ask about me being in the Loft while he works out some living arrangements with Shafe?"

"Not yet, Cayrolynn."

"I think he will. I thought he already called you. He asked me to call about another condo owned by a woman in my workshop on Tuesday morning who said she wants to sell."

"You'll be living here again soon? We want you here and you know that. If TeJay calls us, we'll assure him that we want you. He knows how we feel."

Cayrolynn couldn't find a telephone number for Jo. Then number found and no answer. She put on a sweater and walked to push the bell of the condo. No answer.

When she returned home, she realized she failed to close her drapes and her reflection glared back at her. The failure web that hedged her in thought consumed her thinking and showed on her face. Before she closed the drapes, she deliberately smiled. It took a few minutes to get over the despondency, and put her mind on her work which was her mural in process. Before her fingers began to divide green embroidery threads for the brown burlap backing, she turned on music.

*   Twenty-four   *

By nine on this winter evening, Cayrolynn felt the
fatigue of her emotions with eye strain and knew she should
be in bed. Other times, she might have dozed on the couch.
Instead, she double locked the Condo, turned out lights, and
went upstairs. In the morning when she came down, she self
talked.

"I need to go to the Loft. It's the action I can take.
Eat my cereal, pack little red, and go."

Cold sunshine and an open road. Cayrolynn sang along
with the country station and marveled at the file of jokes
the announcer must keep to make advertising intervals
sparkle.

Tip built an electronic gate that opened like a garage
door with a push on a digital control panel. Cayrolynn
pushed the correct numbers and drove into the farmyard paved
for parking.

No wind and no sun here in the hollow, just surrounding

winter coldness like the rejection she felt in the Condo.
Coldness wrapped her like summer air-conditioning in a super
cold shopping mall and she anticipated the warmth in the Loft
after she pushed the thermostat forward.

"I am home. I am home." She sang and greeted each room
and felt a glow like each room spoke back, "Welcome."

No urge to take her things from the car, but a need to
eat. Hunger. She took from the fridge a frozen lunch that
she placed in the micro-wave. Toast made from frozen bread
with a sprinkling of garlic and smidgen of smeared margarine
then placed under the oven broiler. Now, make it pretty, she
thought. Use a yellow place-mat, my pottery dishes, and
stainless with a heavy pressed glass tumbler filled with
fresh spring water. Need some watercress, she thought.
An apple for supper last night, cereal for breakfast, but a
good lunch for this hungry soul.

Television came not from cable, but a dish planted
further up the hill. At mid-day nothing of interest. She
went for her needle-craft and began work. Joy came with work
by her hands and the almost finished mural.

"Cayrolynn. Are you here?"

"I'm here, Sarah Anna. It takes me by surprise that
when I work my focus relieves me of any sense of time.
You're home and I'm glad. Did TeJay call?"

"No call, but you both know you're home here. My
supper's ready except for corn sticks, so I think I'll bring
my papers and grade them here, if you agree?"

"Yes, please, Sarah Anna."

Cayrolynn changed the music to a softer blue grass while
Sarah Anna went for her canvas bag holding pens and papers
and motivational stickers. Both worked along, with no need
for conversation. Eventually, Cayrolynn remarked, "Silence
reigns and we get wet, except that I find it easy to be with
you Sarah Anna without the need to bare my soul."

"Me, too, Cayrolynn. I notice Lexie sent you a book for
Lent like the one she sent to me. Did you begin yours?"

"Yes. I read a book first by skimming the chapters.
These readings sound like 'do this and live,' but I decided
each noun is an adjective of affirmation for me."

Cayrolynn reached for her book partially concealed under
a work basket. Sarah Anna went to the fridge for water and
returned with a glass of cold apple juice.

"Would you prefer hot cider, Sarah Anna?"

"No. Better this way. Tell me an example your noun-
adjectives."

"Pain or masks, voices or charity.

"You see these words as affirmation because you define
each before you read the explanation by the writer."

"Maybelle told me to listen to a radio preacher, then define his sermon for myself. One preacher chased a rabbit which is what Maybelle called getting off the subject. He talked about dyed hair. At one time, he worked in a coal mine, and he said that God gave him his coal black hair."

"How does that fit your words?"

"Masks. Does he tell me about himself and expect me to accept his definition for my hair color."

"Did your housemother talk about this sermon?"

"Sure. She said the Bible's filled with lives of women we should read with wisdom. I remember she said hair is a woman's crowning glory."

"Did she approve of color and beauty routines?"

"Course. Saturday night wasn't just a bath for us. My brown hair needed a touch of red to make it shine. One girl with white hair needed more blond to look polished. She kept nail polish for us, not red polish that chipped, but clear to make our hands look neat."

"When you talk about your Mother, Lavender, and Maybelle, I understand, you were fortunate in the women who helped you grow up."

"Sarah Anna? Cayrolynn? Anyone here?" Tip called from the laundry room downstairs.

Both answered and both went down the stairs.

"How about some supper? How are you little daughter?"

"Fine. You can see."

"Come with us, Cayrolynn and we'll eat," Sarah Anna
encouraged.

"Think not, Thanks. No exercise, today, so I'll throw a
few baskets, until I get too cold."

They left her with the basketball, and in a few minutes,
Cayrolynn went into the laundry room, took a heavy jacket
from a peg, and a ball cap before returning to the yard and
the exercise of throwing baskets. Tip came to the deck and
stood watching her in the dusk, then went inside to talk with
Sarah Anna.

"Something's wrong, you know. TeJay doesn't call us and
Cayrolynn appears. My friends at work tell me that when an
engagement strings out without marriage, over time, they see
each others clay feet and romance leaves. It becomes like
two relatives living together or two friends. Romance comes
with a new face and new interests. So, the engagement breaks
apart and often someone gets hurt."

"Children get hurt, Tip. No children here except I see
Cayrolynn as a child and I hate to see her get hurt. For a
little while, I worked on papers and talked to her. I'll go
back when we finish our supper."

"Maybe, it's a good time for me to work in my workshop

and see if she has other needle-craft for me to block and frame or for me to help her with. So, I'll join you there after I watch the news."

"I don't expect TeJay. He'll breeze in on Saturday and be caught up in some pressing litigation. All these years for him and no marriage, so I guess I thought this time would be different." Sarah Anna finished in deep thought.

"Don't despair, Sarah Anna. The good Lord works in ways we can never see. Right? Right. I'll be there in a bit. What do I say, I'll just mose-ey on over there."

Saturday afternoon TeJay came home. He brought a movie for the parents to watch with them, so he didn't get caught with Cayrolynn alone. By early Sunday, he left.

Sunday morning, Cayrolynn dressed and went to the interstate for breakfast and the papers. In her heart, she felt the need for worship, but without explanations to Tip and Sarah Anna. She drove to the mountain and joined the student congregation in the chapel at Sewanee. Singing and a sermon about the meaning of Ash Wednesday and Lent seemed matched to her needs.

Never did she wander out driving, but today she looked at the map and decided to turn down the mountain road to Alabama. She met no cars nor trucks on the descending blacktop incline and after some driving near the Alabama-

Tennessee line, she came to a railroad which she paralleled
into town. Before she took the four-lane with markers to the
interstate and the National Park Service sign for a Cave, she
stopped at a Dairy Queen. The hot dog with chili and a coke
took care of hunger.

An older matron suggested she enjoy a milkshake. The
kind advice caused her place an order.

"You don't live around here and these mountain winds
will lift you over to the Tennessee River."

The woman moved to talk to some friends and Cayrolynn
took an information folder about Russell Cave. Since the
milkshake proved too cold to drink, she took it along secured
in TeJay's coffee holder. At the cave, she stood outside in
the park and watched fish swimming in the creek that flowed
to the cave.

At the visitors center, people watched a filmstrip and
the guide suggested they follow her for a tour. Cayrolynn
tagged along following two teenagers who seemed to show off
for her. One family group with grandparents, parents, and
two small girls went first. Two women, who seemed to be
school teachers stayed last, then wove into the group and
became first.

Most of the questions concerned the Indians who lived in
the area and would have come to the cave. Cayrolynn found

herself asking questions along with the others.   When she
returned to her car, she felt remorse that the lecture ended.

"I know your car," this woman not on the tour, came to
speak.   The man, who seemed her friend, watched and Cayrolynn
felt uncomfortable.   Never did she see such a pencil of a man
so completely tall, straight, and thin.

"Yes, It is a beautiful car and it belongs to a friend
of mine."   Cayrolynn edged away and walked to the building.
In a few minutes, the woman came into the building where
Cayrolynn washed her hands and she continued her words.

"I hope you'll invite us to your wedding on Easter
Sunday.   Your car belongs to TeJay Hillabee and he's a friend
of our son, Shafe Morris."

"Yes.   I'm Cayrolynn and of course, you're invited.
TeJay told me.   I'm glad I met you.   TeJay tells me you stay
in Shafe's condo often."

Cayrolynn felt the closeness of the conversation and
needed space.   She exited the building and went to the car
and left before the couple returned to the parking lot.   Any
explanation would bring questions, so she fled and turned
west, by mistake.   She found herself in a small village with
a road turning north up the mountain.

The paved road became one lane and brought anxiety.   She
questioned if she should turn around and go back to Russell

Cave. "No place to turn around," she self-talked. "Tip
advised no back road exploration and by default I failed to
heed his advice." Finally, she came to a main road and
turned east down a precarious two lane before a town, and a
road north to the interstate. With thanksgiving, she met no
vehicle and experienced no automobile problems on the lonely
road. The trip took all afternoon, therefore she drove into
the Loft parking after Sarah Anna and Tip went to vespers.

Neither Tip nor Sarah Anna came home early on Monday
night. Cayrolynn felt sure Sarah Anna stayed for a faculty
meeting and Tip took his time doing errands before coming
home. She didn't try to call them, but spent her time
getting ready for her trip to town come Tuesday morning.

After Sarah Anna and Tip left for work, she backed
little red from the garage. She went to the Condo, parked
under the canopy, and imagined playing hop-scotch, into a
square of tile and out, then to home space and back again.

Inside, everything looked the same. Walking room to
room brought meditation, praise, and prayers that all things
worked out. When problems came, Maybelle would walk through
their cottage singing and blessing everything. Out goes the
bad and in comes victory, she would call forth blessings for
people and places, clothes and shoes, and anything considered
a problem.

Alone in the Condo, Cayrolynn used words of blessing. She went out the front door and locked, then went to the workshop in the community room.

"We talked about color, clothes, make-up, hair, food, manners, exercise, now our topic today concerns temperament. Our personality and values yields outward behavior." Vanessa, the leader, began and gave out a profile check list to help center the discussion on topics to be covered.

"Out of the binding tangled threads of life, we look for wonder. Even in the midst of failure, we look for enduring grace, and how do we seek and find?"

Cayrolynn realized during the past two days, she spent thought trying to make her life make sense.

"I feel as though my life is so unfinished," Sharon spoke. For some unknown reason, maybe tension, the group laughed. The laughter brought a togetherness of camaraderie.

"Think about taking a reproach and unforgiving, how do these words expose your thinking?" Vanessa asked.

No comments by anyone.

"Our lives change and without change it would be impossible to live," Vanessa talked.

"I wanted to take my life, go to sleep forever, but I heard someone say, life's like a bus, wait fifteen minutes and it will change," Eula said.

"It's true, you know, memories like unburned log stubs stay in the ashes, but minutes tick by and life changes enough to go on living." Gayle moved, slightly, when she talked and the movement showed her sleekness and energy.

"Ashes belong on the refuse pile, and my moving back to Texas shows me, sometimes, we need the courage to throw away more than ashes or memories," Jo said.

"You want to ad-lib here, Cayrolynn?" Vanessa asked.

"Your lecture on make-up returns and I need answers to keep bad thoughts from showing on my face or putting unwanted tones in my voice."

These weeks together brought contributing thoughts from these women and Cayrolynn understood why she needed to be part of the group. The affirmation came like a ray of hope or faith. Thought patterns crystallize into burdens, burdens of words, then inescapable walls, and the dark past of fences. When the group ended, Cayrolynn moved to talk to Jo.

"I have a friend who looks for a Condo to buy, Jo."

"Yes. The director said someone asked. Can I show you my place or show your friend? Come home with me now to look."

When they went in her front door, luggage stayed on the front rug, and Jo explained her arrival before the group meeting.

"I didn't think I could get here in time for our workshop, but the journey and time presented no problems. I never want to be a beauty queen, however the presenter's worth her money."

"Agreed. I want to see the Llandro you collect."

"I packed several pieces for my daughter in Dallas. When I move, I plan to mail my collection, piece by piece."

Cayrolynn didn't comment on the collection with oo's and ah's. She admired the works of art and said so. Then, she took time to look at the condominium floor plan.

"This Condo belonged to the builder before he moved to another site to build another complex. You'll notice the extra closets and baths. The back workroom has a guest bath and space offers so many decorating possibilities. Before I met my husband, I worked in a furniture store."

Cayrolynn didn't tarry but said all the appropriate comments and thank you's. When she returned to the canopy parking for the car, no truck or car parked in the second space, so she didn't go inside. She planned a trip to leave her work at the consignment shop.

To be sure she stayed relaxed, she stopped for fruit juice and a deli sandwich that she finished eating when she parked in front of the shop. Customers took the owner's attention, however he gave Cayrolynn a receipt for her work.

One other errand, seeing Beatrice at the clinic, then she returned to the Loft. She sang all the way home. With all the rejection and unknowns in her life she feared a bad report that didn't happen.

Sarah Anna drove through the gate and Cayrolynn pulled up behind. "Been to the clinic and got a good report, so I'm praising all the way home."

"Great, Cayrolynn, come along and have a spot of tea with me."

"Happy to." Cayrolynn parked and felt the joy of being asked. Sarah Anna took brownies from a container in her cabinet and brought cups with hot water from the microwave.

"So, you went to town and do you feel really tired?"

"Oh, no. I missed drive time traffic in Nashville. What do you hear from everyone?"

"Rae-Anne will call you, I'm sure. She says this time of togetherness is God-sent for both of them. She takes days off and they visit with her parents and enjoy the beach."

"And, Lexie?"

"She considers birthing another child and some traveling with Lance whenever he goes off with his work."

"And, Sam and Toney?"

"You and TeJay need to go see them and we do, too. They move into the big house and enjoy every minute. Little

sister gets her own room, but the boys double up.   The boys
decided they want to leave guest rooms for family when we
come.   Manny, their oldest told me this, and I assured him
we'll be there, forsure."

Cayrolynn enjoyed her hour with Sarah Anna, then went to
the Loft.   Later, when she went to see Tip in his workshop,
she planned to tell him about her stop to leave her finished
work.   She didn't expect TeJay's call when the telephone
rang.

"My Mom said you have a good report, today."

"Yes.   I went to my workshop meeting at the Condo
community room and Jo's ready to show you her apartment.   She
asked me to come see, even though she came from Texas this
morning."

"Did you like it?"

"Not sure.   See what you think, TeJay."

The short conversation supported other impressions.
Since the night of her gift in song, he became a different
person.   Love turned to hate.   Now, she knew she must
begin plans to leave the Loft and this family.

*   Twenty-five   *

Weather reports said bad weather on this dark Thursday
morning.   March first and it comes in like a lion.   Another
program interruption and counties named with probable hail
and tornadoes.   Most days Cayrolynn watched few television
programs, but today she switched channels to find recent
plottings about weather.   Many dire weather predictions for
Middle Tennessee, she thought.   When she went outside, the
atmosphere stayed too warm, windy, and overcast.   The gray
white laced clouds boiled across the hollow.   Small new twigs
with tips of green leaves scattered across her path and
caused her to hurry inside.

Near the laundry room door hung a heavy yellow vinyl
slicker and on the ledge several flashlights.

"These you should find in the dark, if they're needed."
Sarah Anna warned her about weather when they explored the
root cellar together.   "Just because we never use this root
cellar as a storm cellar doesn't mean it serves no purpose.

After the storm hits, we can look outside and see the
destruction. My memory makes me cautious."

When the electricity went off, she knew the weather
closed in. She took the raincoat from the peg. It hung long
and covered most of her clothes and shoes. Outside, buffeted
in fierce wind, she went toward the root cellar. An uneasy
quiet seemed to grip the homeplace.

Tip hinged a heavy iron bell on the door supports of the
cellar. Cayrolynn tripped and hit her head. Pain. When she
squeaked the door open, she saw spiders. Fear. Since
childhood, spiders gave her traumatic fear. Impossible to
use this cellar as weather protection, so she moved to the
east of the house thinking she would find another place for
safety. Beside the brick steps to the front porch might
offer protection.

She needed the flashlight because the overcast became
like midnight. In her haste to scurry up the incline to the
cement underpinning for the porch and steps, she missed her
footing. The fall threw her on the soft mulch used to
surround strawberry vines and against the brick border.
Intense pain encompassed her ankle along with the throbbing
of her head.

The sound of fury came nearer and she burrowed into the
ground trying to stay close to the earth and holding onto a

pyracantha bush positioned in the corner by the steps. She pulled the coat tight and heard the sound of huge airplane engines. Boeing 747, she thought. The sound moved on up the hollow and away. All became quiet before the rain and hail came popping her and slamming into the mulch. Later, she thought she must have fainted. She felt alive and dry. No need to move, so she didn't.

Sarah Anna tried to telephone Cayrolynn. No answer. She helped get children on buses and even took one child home. Reports about downed trees gave questions about whether buses could travel their routes. When the school upheaval slowed, she went to check on her house and Cayrolynn.

The tornado took a skipping path. The same path it took that spring before TeJay came. Trees on the road caused her to park her car and walk up the incline through the orchard to reach the Loft. Her useless umbrella crumbled.

The door to the root cellar stood ajar, so she picked her way across the back parking. With all her vocal power she screamed for Cayrolynn. When she pushed against the cellar door, she saw snakes. No sign of Cayrolynn and now the sheets of cold rain pounded against her wet clothes and matted hair. Tip came from the hill and joined in her search for Cayrolynn.

"Where is she Tip? How can we find her?"

Trying to maneuver around the house proved more than an obstacle course. On the way, they saw the yellow raincoat. Both reached her together.

"Are you hurt? Are you okay? What happened, Cayrolynn?" Tip and Sarah Anna asked questions together.

"I'm so glad you're here. I hurt my head on the bell at the root cellar, and I fell trying to reach the corner here by the steps."

They pulled to lift Cayrolynn who couldn't stand. Her ankle buckled and she screamed. With help she leaned against them and moved across the front porch and into the front hallway.

"Sarah Anna look at the bump on her head. She may have a concussion and her ankle seems either broken or sprained."

"Help me, Tip, she needs the recliner or the couch."

"Shock or delayed shock takes its toll, so try to be detached," Tip said. "I'll cover her, Sarah Anna, you go for a warm shower and dry clothes."

Cayrolynn closed her eyes and went to sleep. They debated if they should take her to the hospital. The telephone rang. Sarah Anna listened to the one-way conversation she heard while Tip talked to TeJay.

"Cayrolynn didn't go to the root cellar because we saw

spiders and snakes there. She hurt her head and her ankle. We are deciding whether to go to the hospital emergency."

Tip ended his conversation and said, "Your son's on the way home and he suggests we call Andy's friend Fred."

"Fred, Cayrolynn has a bump on her head and a swollen ankle. What do you suggest?"

"Sarah Anna, he says don't move her. Keep her warm and he'll come soon."

Words sounded fuzzy to Cayrolynn, not distinct. She knew Sarah Anna turned her on the couch and she could hear TeJay talking.

"If anything happens to her, I think I'll die."

Other voices, planning for a bed, mattresses on the floor, changing her into pajamas, going to the bathroom and drinking warm milk, actions that blended with instructions and explanations. Then, the quiet darkness prior to sleep.

During the night, she felt the strong touch of TeJay's fingers on her wrist checking her pulse. No rejection, only the quiet assurance of care.

When she awoke, she saw Sarah Anna near reading the paper.

"Did I over sleep this morning, Sarah Anna? Is it Saturday?"

"No. You didn't oversleep and it's Friday. I'm here because of the storm yesterday and our concern for you. How do you feel now?"

"I don't know. If I can go to the bathroom, please."

"You have a sprained ankle, so lean on me and don't fall."

When they returned, Sarah Anna settled her in one of the recliners and went to make toast.

"The doctor says calcium will take away the blue bruise on your head. We need to soak your sprained ankle in hot Epson salt water. Do you feel better, now?"

"I feel weak."

TeJay and Tip came in the back door, each with questions about her well being and Cayrolynn felt shyness. When she looked at TeJay, she blushed. Sarah Anna asked them to return the mattresses to their correct beds and she wouldn't allow any questions.

"Cayrolynn isn't ready for an inquisition. After we eat breakfast, then we can talk."

"Would you like milk toast, Cayrolynn?" Sarah Anna showed concern. Cayrolynn nodded no, but continued to nibble and dip one corner of her toast into her coffee..

"I want us to move Cayrolynn to the Loft," TeJay said. "If your friends come by, then we'll be in the middle of their conversation. She'll find better rest in the Loft, than in one of the upstairs bedrooms. When we finish our breakfast, if you'll help me, Dad."

"Sure. We want her here, but you're right. Our telephone rings and the activity level will increase. Cayrolynn will find recuperation easier in the Loft."

They sat her in a chair and took her to her bedroom in the Loft. Before they reached the top of the stairs, when her arms encircled both Tip and TeJay, she moved her lips to TeJay's ear and kissed his cold ear lobe.

TeJay gasped and Tip asked what. Neither stopped and with Sarah Anna's help, she settled into bed and went off to sleep again.

During the afternoon, she dozed between sleep and being awake. She knew Tip stood at the door and saw her uplifted hand with a non-verbal greeting. Tip gave messages with a salute, or wink, or small wave and Cayrolynn saw his gestures as affirmation more valuable than any multitude of words.

Sometime later, Cayrolynn heard the chain saw. Sarah Anna came to determine the consequences of the noise.

"Are you awake, Cayrolynn?"

"I'm awake, and so lazy."

"You have endured an ordeal. TeJay went to the office to bring some working papers here, so he can stay for a few days. Tip's beginning to subtract our large oak from the paved backyard. Were you there when it hit the parking area?"

"No. I didn't know it toppled. I went looking for a safe place and the root cellar door wouldn't budge. Also, the darkness made me afraid of the spiders, I saw. I hit my head on the iron bell so hard, it clanged. My thought was to reach the front of the house, but I stumbled and found it too difficult to stand."

"The yellow raincoat told us your whereabouts."

"I need to go to the bath, Sarah Anna. My ankle hurts, but not this bump on my head. Am I all blue? I think I must have fainted when I fell."

The chain saw made impossible noise. When she returned from the bath, she asked Sarah Anna for a pain tablet.

"I have a prescription for pain in my purse. Please may I take one capsule?"

Sarah Anna brought the water and gave her the medicine. Cayrolynn knew the usual effects meant sleep. If she could return to sleep, then the noise would be no bother.

*   *   *

Somewhere on the way home, with an open interstate, TeJay pushed on the pedal of little red, then saw the patrol car waiting in the curve of the median. No question,

TeJay knew he asked for a ticket. He moved to the slow lane and cut the speed. In seconds, the blue lights came behind him, so he pulled to the side emergency lane.

"Sorry, officer. Wasn't thinking. Problems right now seem too much."

"You passed our radar down the road at 110. Truckers drive with a governor and you need one for this car."

TeJay didn't argue, just accepted the ticket. When he came to the exit at Beech Grove, he drove to the top of the hill and into the wayside cemetery. The aggravation of the ticket, plus the fears of yesterday caused turmoil. Now, he bowed his head on the steering wheel. Prayer became real and today, he needed strength. "Please God, please return the gift of your love to me for this woman, Cayrolynn. Like a bird that flies away, my affection leaves and disgust takes its place. I need your love for her to fill my heart. I need mature agape love that comes only from you."

In a while, TeJay drove home. Sarah Anna came downstairs when she heard his car. Tip followed.

"She asked for pain medicine, and even with my reservations, I acquiesced."

"We can ask the doctor when he calls or comes by, but I think you did best to humor her. Is she asleep now?"

"Yes. Tip began the disposal of the tree. His saw

needed gas, so he'll wait until she awakens to begin again."

"Be sure to tell us, if you need us, TeJay."

His parents went to the house and TeJay climbed the
stairs to the Loft. In Nashville, the sun was shining, but
here in the hollow, the gray-fog clouds drifted and caused a
dark day.

Cayrolynn lay thinking. TeJay returned and worked
without music or television. She could hear him turn pages
and sigh. If she turned her foot, then her ankle twinged,
otherwise she lay in peace.

"Peace is a gift," she thought. "Love is a gift from
God to TeJay and to me like grace and faith." In a few
minutes, she hobbled to the bath and then returned to bed.
TeJay came with a glass of water and a calcium tablet.

"I need to check on you, Cayrolynn. Is the Loft too
warm and do you want to come to the couch, now that you're
awake?"

"I prefer to stay here without moving. I'm not hungry,
but I thank you for the water. Sometimes, I thirst and it
feels like hunger, so I'll drink the water and take the
calcium for my blue spots. Did you have a good trip to the
office?"

"I traveled with care, however I got a ticket for
speeding which means I slowed a little. Tickets jar my

finances, both the levied fine, plus increases in car insurance."

"Sorry. Your mind ponders my problems and I'm sorry I cause you concern."

"Tell me when you feel strong enough to move to the couch."

Cayrolynn wanted to move to the couch and might have told TeJay except she closed her eyes and soon went to sleep. Sarah Anna came to stay while Cayrolynn slept, and TeJay went to find Tip. When Cayrolynn awoke, she hobbled to the couch and sat across from Sarah Anna.

"Now that you're awake, I'll warm soup for you."

"Not yet."

"When we first moved here, I lived through that tornado. Weather reports and predictions often accompany our spring days, yet no twister returned to our hollow. All these years, and we experienced no others. Now, you've lived through one."

"Tell me, Sarah Anna, did you hear the airplane?"

"Yes, like a big train. And, the wind. Then, the quiet peace. Older people recall some weather event out of all proportion to other happenings in their lives. Storms come along and it's difficult to remember in the middle of stress that after the storm, peace will come."

"Children remember. They remember more than most people realize, I think. My earliest memory occurred when I was about age three. We drove somewhere in a car with white leather upholstery and my parents talked. This, too, shall pass my Dad said. Want to bet me on it? This, too, shall pass. Such an indelible scene and that's all I remember."

"Past, present, and future. Do you have dreams or foretelling visions about what will happen?"

"One time, I dreamed and my Mother kissed me. She smelled so warm like I remembered."

*   Twenty-Six   *

Tip worked along in his workshop being careful to clean
and put his tools into order after each project like a
workman that needeth not to be ashamed. He completed his
sawing of a frame, took glue and put the corners together,
and tapped on a staple to make the corners secure. This task
finished the project, so he took the frame to a side shelf
and left it for drying.

TeJay sat watching his Dad without squirming or talking.
Hand me that hammer, those nails, or that saw became familiar
instructions when Tip worked and his sons helped.

Now, Tip came and sat on the stool across the work table
from TeJay. He noticed the small tension curve of TeJay's
upper lip and a muscle twitch under his eye. Claude told Tip
about these signs and how TeJay begged for attention when Tip
stayed too focused on some task. Those years, Claude
listened to the boys and offered encouragement.

"We took a beating these past few days, TeJay. I don't

think I'll replace any of the fencing. I presume Sarah Anna
stays with Cayrolynn while she sleeps?"

"All is quiet there and I came here thinking we might
talk...some."

"I'm listening. Talk away."

"Since Christmas tinges of negative emotion keep
returning. I find myself taking reproach against Cayrolynn
for no reason. The aspects of our relationship, which seemed
best now seem the worst."

"Like?"

"All the things she doesn't have."

"You want to marry a wealthy woman?"

"Never. Although it wouldn't hurt. Erase. Sarah Anna
hurts when we make selfish remarks, even in jest."

"You've reached a place where you can't communicate?"

"Yes and No. Valentine's dinner went off well, then she
appeared via taxi to surprise me with a song on the stage at
the place where I played back-up."

"Doesn't sound like Cayrolynn. You mean she took the
microphone and sang to you?"

"Yes. And no problem. After she finished her song to
me, the leader, Ho, who knew Cayrolynn from before, asked her
to sing a ballad."

"Did she sing on stage before you met her?"

"When she was five or six, she sang with her Mother in some roadhouses in Pensacola. When she came to Nashville, she didn't intend to try singing. Where she lived, people who tried to find a life in country music, gathered impromptu style, and strummed the night away. Ho remembered she sang this song. Anyway, now, Ho wants her to come again and he'll pay her."

"What turns you off, TeJay? Does she need your permission to sing? I can see a few problems, but why do you resist?"

"This song she sang, Knoxville Girl, started in England as the Berkshire Tragedy in about 1740 or so, and traveled with the settlers. Along the way, it took on different names, like the Wexford Girl, The Wittam Millar, Waco Girl, and different verses with the same mournful tune. I looked it up one time because Maude would tell Claude and me to stop that black cloud singing. Most country or blue grass performers, avoid the song because it's so pathetic. It could have influenced the book the American Tragedy by Drieser. Did you read that in freshman comp at Tech?"

"Can't remember. You know the song and the melody, so why did it turn you off to Cayrolynn?"

"I saw her in a different way. I became the cruel miller, like one of the titles, or the bad boss."

"You say Cayrolynn meant to write other words to the melody. So, tell me the story of the ballad."

"This man either owns the business or works there. The girl comes to work and he walks her home through a cemetery. He gets her pregnant, then in the refrain, when the snow is on the ground, he kills her and throws her in the river."

"Thirty-five or forty verses, huh?"

"Depending on the audience, yes. With a little white lightning and a good fiddle, it got rid of emotional unhappiness with some crying, I think."

"So, Cayrolynn cut it short?"

"I couldn't play and I started to leave. Somehow, it hit me so hard that she might use some transference technique and see me as the culprit. She blames no one for her fatigue syndrome and in my generosity can she see me as her murderer? Sure, I've dated women and dropped them. Some gave me the rush and dropped me."

"You did take her home. You didn't walk out?"

"Not physically, no. But, I walked out emotionally and it's very difficult for me to bond again."

"Sarah Anna and I suspected something wrong. Cayrolynn experiences healing with the stability and care you give her. If you cast her away, I can't respond to what might happen."

"I believe real love is a gift. The good Lord, I

remember Claude's saying, went about doing good after his
Father gave him power and His Holy Spirit."

"Claude took me in and he liked to say when you give to
the poor, you lend to the Lord and the Lord is debtor to no
man."

"I need the Lord in order to keep my promise and love to
Cayrolynn. I know. Women get cancer and the husband moves
out. The husband has a heart attack and off goes the wife.
Sure, other excuses hide the true reason and even if the
couple stays together, divorce already occurs and one partner
will wait for the death of the other. See my gloom, Dad."

"I never looked at Miss Piano, as Lexie calls her, but
to Lexie she was a threat. When parents fight, children get
hurt. Men who need to voice vulgar jokes, or women who
gossip about their bedroom bring disaster on their families,
I think."

"What's the saying, Dad? Point one finger at another
and point three fingers back at self?"

"Selfish fingers. I don't think you come to me for
advice, son. You needed to talk it out and I think you have
done that. Strange how things happen to shake us up when we
get stuck. Did you need a tornado to help you turn your
thinking in a different direction?"

"Dad. My Mother's the mystic in this family, however,

yes, I did need the tornado and the speeding ticket, too. If little red skidded, then tonight I wouldn't be here. I think I know, I've been asked to do something and I've been given a second chance."

"Want to see what's happening upstairs? If Cayrolynn still sleeps with the impact of her tablet, we need to go to the house."

Sarah Anna and Cayrolynn heard the men coming up the south stairs from Tip's work shop.

"Men around this place get starved out," Tip said to Sarah Anna, "when do we get fed?"

"You and TeJay can bring us the pudding along with the chicken salad in the green bowl. I'll make cream of chicken soup for Cayrolynn."

TeJay went to sit beside Cayrolynn on the couch. She looked like a small throw away waif.

"How's the ankle and head?" Tip asked.

"I'm not hungry."

"My cooking is guaranteed to heal what ever ails you, little sister, even if I give you ol' timey advice." Tip said.

Cayrolynn laughed and Sarah Anna frowned.

"Cayrolynn believes you Dad, how-some-ever my Mom knows better. Too bad we can't call for the pizza delivered.

Guess we need to go raid the box and see if we can find anything other than chicken salad."

"Bologna sandwiches might be better." Tip said, then he stood and began his walk down the stairs going to the homeplace.

"Both of you better count your blessings, we could've been blown heck to breakfast, whatever that saying is."

*   *   *

Monday came with March winds. Cayrolynn lay on the couch and tried to avoid thinking about her fatigue factor that reminded her of boats tied to the dock on East Bay. Bobbling along and going nowhere. Once Lavender said either unforeseen happenings or personal actions cause life to switch course, otherwise the pot simmers until it's dry. She knew her relationship with TeJay moved to a different level and the change seemed more adult and secure.

TeJay lost the barrier in his love for Cayrolynn, yet she seemed to be away from him. Those lovely laughing eyes and her quick smile vanished. Their time together seemed less because TeJay worked late at the office or with his music. Cayrolynn spent less time with creative art projects.

When he came from work one evening, TeJay came to the Loft before he went to the house to speak to his parents and change clothes.

"Do I have your permission, Cayrolynn, to enter into negotiation for the sale of my Condo and to buy Jo's space?"

"I like Jo's place. I looked at her floor plan and it seems more convenient and spacious than the Condos where either you or Shafe live."

"You think it gives out good vibes?"

"Good vibrations, yes. It's clean and airy because since she repainted, no one lives there."

"She says you like it. Do you Cayrolynn?"

"Much better than the Condo that you sell."

"Shafe and Vida plan to move as soon as we get our papers signed and ourselves squared away."

"What about Vida's job?"

"We didn't discuss it. I don't know. Do you agree with my suggestion for a wedding on Easter at the daybreak service?"

"Yes. Will Lexie be here for the ceremony?"

"Everyone in my family will be here. I want a couple who cater weddings to give us breakfast."

"You mean here or at the church?"

"Most years, they give us an after sunrise breakfast in the shed used for the church homecoming."

"Isn't it too cold?"

"Roll down clear plastic keeps the wind away, otherwise,

if the weather is too uncomfortable, we cancel the breakfast.
But, that never happens, we go inside for the service and
the food gets served from the foyer. Claude began the
breakfast idea, then Tip found this cook through a man at
work. I'm thinking this year, we'll ask for the big white
wedding tent which they often use for receptions or meals in
the summer."

"Do I need to help in anyway?"

TeJay stood to talk, but now he moved to Cayrolynn and
held her with care. "Yes, it's your wedding and what I plan
needs your smoothing. You must invite your friends and our
community. You must plan where we go following the ceremony.
You must plan what we wear. Do you think this too much, if
so, then we can change our plans and have a house wedding
with only my family."

"May I take a few days to think about what you've said?"

"Yes, of course. I do need an answer for the new condo
and I'll need you to sign some papers for me."

"I like Jo's condo. All my things are here now, but I
can come help with the moving, if you need me."

The gentle holding added peace, but Cayrolynn found
herself chewing on a strand of hair and TeJay rubbed the back
of his neck.

"Your blue head bump turns normal and soon your ankle

sprain will heal. For you. these days of Lent are celebrated
with quietness. I want to marry you, Cayrolynn."

"Maybe, we'll celebrate twenty-five years together.
However, we begin with our first celebration and it belongs
to us. One book of photographs to share and enjoy together."

"Friends tell me about living in Arizona or near the
desert. They find views of the terrain like paintings
stretching across the horizon. Often they'll try to explain.
Then, I tell them I live in a mountain hollow and my vistas
differ from theirs, yet both hold beauty."

"I know when you're at work, you stop and look across
the city and see views I don't see."

TeJay held her close, then moved when he reached for the
remote to turn on the television. She placed water to heat
in the microwave and began making sassafras tea. From the
frig she took tangerines. The gingerbread baked earlier
remained in a covered baking pan on the stove.

"Do you need a meal, TeJay or is my gingerbread with tea
enough?"

"The bread, tea, and fruit fulfills my appetite,
especially the spicy smells that add calories, then pounds
too hard to lose."

"Funny. Smells, yes, taste and touch and eyes to see
the rich brown color and calories if you swallow."

"So, you want me to finish the real estate deals, Cayrolynn?"

"Sure. How about furniture?"

"Been thinking about that. At your art consignment shop, Tip mentioned some decorators make deals with the owner."

"Yes, and you want him to suggest a decorator or help us furnish the place according to our wishes?"

"Somehow, I can't see us asking a decorator to put the place together for us. You know me well enough to choose what I like. You might discuss furniture with my Mother. She gave Lexie some things that belonged to Maude. Also, Tip took a load to Sam."

"Did Jo say she'll leave her window treatments? I noticed plain drapes that keep out visual intrusion."

"We didn't discuss windows, but I'll ask. Do you want to look again before we complete the deal?"

"No. I plan for a doctors appointment soon."

Nagging her thoughts was eyesight. Since the bang on her head and the fall, often she saw either double or fuzzy. If she returned to lay flat on the couch or bed, her eyesight would clear.

*   Twenty-seven   *

"My vertigo and double vision diminishes day by day," Cayrolynn told Beatrice. "Sarah Anna took me to a sewing store to buy some material for my Easter outfit."

"Cayrolynn, do you really want to create your dress?"

"My desire, yes, but my physical endurance leaves me with questions."

"On my day off this week, I'll come to see you and you see how much you get done, before I come. I can bring everything back to a woman I know, who'll put it together for you. I know you can, but I'm not sure it's wise."

When Beatrice came on Thursday, Cayrolynn welcomed her suggestions. Beatrice read the page Cayrolynn wrote to the seamstress and marveled at her precise instructions.

"I fear for Sarah Anna to come from school and see me not working on the dress. I misjudged my energy and my motivational creativity. You understood and I'm so thankful for your suggestions, Beatrice."

"This couple does sewing in their home. They could work in New York as designers, but in Nashville, they do upholstery, sewing, and other projects like costumes for plays or school programs. You'll see their good work and be pleased."

"I put everything in a box and if they need other items, then they should buy those and allow me to pay when we come for the outfit. I wish you could be here when Sarah Anna comes from school. She may or may not ask for an explanation."

"You tell her it's my suggestion. Right now, your world stays small. If you worked and made decisions everyday, this situation wouldn't disturb you. Sometimes, Cayrolynn, we imagine what another will say, and we don't read them right. Best yet, don't say a word unless she asks."

"Now for some lunch that I made earlier. One salad plate for you and one for me because I'm a good cook. An egg salad sandwich with applesauce and green grapes on lettuce plus orange slices."

"I'm glad I see no dessert, but a packet of your sugar cookies for me to take home, please."

                              *   *   *

The boots for hill climbing that TeJay bought gave Cayrolynn secure footing when she walked between the rows of nursery stock. Most days this walk for exercise seemed like an expensive viewing of an arboretum. Many attached brown cocoons stayed secure following the poison Tip used last summer. Cayrolynn remembered the feel of the cocoon with the living butterfly or moth enclosed in the brown paper web.

TeJay's lack of approval for her song reminded her of these lifeless cocoons dangling from discarded Christmas trees like unwanted decorations. The afternoon exercise struck her with fatigue instead of motivation.

After Beatrice left and following the afternoon exercise, TeJay called to say he needed to stay in town. Sarah Anna called to say she took meds for a headache and Cayrolynn noticed Tip's truck missing. She lacked motivation for embroidery, so she cleansed her face, locked all doors, and went to bed at first dusk. She awoke at midnight, chilled and shivering, so she took an extra quilt from the closet shelf.

Often, Cayrolynn found clear insight for a problem when she took a shower. The beating rain on her head jolted a thinking process. Now, at midnight, under warm covers, she saw her wedding like playing paper dolls. Her cake decorated Sarah Anna's table and ready to be served. The family gathered at Brush Arbor church.

Lexie stood at the front among an altar decorated with

Easter lilies. TeJay stood with Tip and she stood with
Beatrice who wore an exact copy of her outfit in pink.
The grand-children stood in array with them. Lexie guided
the vows and the boys spoke with TeJay and the girls repeated
with her. All this could take place at home with Sarah Anna
and Tip but she wanted the church. When? Not Easter
morning. When? Saturday sunshine gave the church light.
In her mind's eye, she saw the wedding panorama without the
fog of early morning and without a sunrise service of the
community of friends.

With her vision complete, Cayrolynn thought, "Tomorrow,
I write it down. I set my plans in concrete so words of
others don't deter me from my plans." In a few minutes, her
eyes closed again and the clock said nine when she awoke.

*   *   *

Lexie called. "Cayrolynn, I hear a bird singing in the
background."

"My hearing lacks acuity. I don't know birds, but I
hear a mockingbird often."

"Tell me about your bruises."

"With a little make-up, they disappear. The vertigo is
less and may be due to an inner ear problem that will
disappear. My eyes seem to be normal again, and I take
calcium that helps the dark bruises. It's a good report,

Lexie."

"You work on your wedding and I'm excited that our family will gather for Easter, see each other, and celebrate with you. Do you make special plans?"

"Yes, and I need your help. I need suggestions so that I don't hurt anyone's feelings. People keep long memories when they fail to be invited to a wedding."

"TeJay says you want me to pronounce the service."

"Would you, please? TeJay and I need to compare our plans, but hear my thoughts. Some mornings, I'm slow, so I think an afternoon three o'clock time at the church with only our family and a beautiful dessert tea here following our ceremony. I would like for the children to stand with us and repeat everything either TeJay or I repeat."

"Do you think Rae will feel hurt?"

"Lexie, Rae told me, she wants us to drop by their place because Andy suggests they not come."

"I agree, even though I didn't hear. And, the sunrise service, did you discuss this with TeJay?"

"You're the first person and I need your thoughts. Often, when TeJay calls, I'm remiss in telling him about early morning muscle rebellion. Dawn isn't right for me."

"Cayrolynn, I think you make good plans and I'm glad. I need to think through what you say. God Bless."

She sat looking at the telephone and thinking about
Lexie before she decided for a short walk along the fence
line. TeJay came when she climbed to the top of the incline
and looked back at the house. She waved and he returned her
greeting. She watched as he opened the laundry room door and
went inside. She felt the redness of blush cover her face
and neck. Shyness caused her tongue to freeze. She stood
waiting without thoughts whether to return to the Loft or
climb further up the hill. Birds flew into the fence row,
chirped, then flew away. Buzzards circled with the slow
sailing calling attention to some unseen object below. So,
she stood, not moving for twenty minutes according to glances
at the gold watch she wore.

TeJay came from the Loft climbing and whistling.

When they touched, he asked, "May I eat a country lunch
at your house?"

"Did you speak with Lexie about my conversation with
her?"

"I spoke with Lexie, but at that time I traveled I-24
coming here. My plans included our discussing the wedding,
the homecoming of the family, and our trip following the
ceremony. Over-nite it seemed to me, I should come home and
spend the day with you."

Cayrolynn smiled. He took her hand and they walked

along the uneven path made by the tractor at the end of the
nursery stock rows. Togetherness for a noon meal that TeJay
engineered might be gourmet instead of country. He went into
the downstairs closet and brought a small can of Vienna
sausage. Cayrolynn took a fresh salad bag with lettuce and
spinach from the fridge and filled two bowls. TeJay added
his meat with wine vinegar and olive oil to his mixture.
After the blessing for this food, Cayrolynn took pre-mixed
ranch for her salad.

"Tell me what you told Beatrice."

"I told her about Mavis Davis, who sold me the material
for my wedding dress. She talked to Sarah Anna the whole
time we were in the store."

"You felt angry, jealous, and very slighted because
Sarah Anna forgot to introduce you and told you about her on
the way home. Jealousy and bitterness will cause a mate to
pick up a shot gun and release someone from this earth.
Trust must be guarded. If I go for a fortnight, you must
know truth and trust."

"Remember your words when I sing for Hoe or go to stay a
few days with my Florida friends."

"Well said. Andy called last night to say they might
not come. His next meeting with our Uncle Doctor needs time.
I promised Uncle Doctor's absence. Andy and Rae'll stay in

the Condo and come with me on Saturday. We'll bring Easter
lilies for the church with us. Lexie and family can stay in
this space with Sam and Tony plus children at the house."

"Do you agree to the wedding at three with a tea-like
reception following the ceremony?"

"Lexie told me about your ideas for the ceremony and the
reception. I agree. Then, you take me to see where you grew
up in Alabama and Florida."

"Uncle Andrew doesn't come."

"I must try diplomacy there and for my Mother. Andy
needs peace with his uncle, but it's Rae I worry about."

"I put on my boots for my walk. Do you feel like a
truck ride and walk around the head of the hollow?"

"Yes. I want to see the spring at the homeplace, and
wild violets growing on the burned over hillside."

                    *   *   *

Dusk came early at the head of the hollow. Cayrolynn
began to move a few leaves from a outcropping of gray rock.
They sat with TeJay chewing on the stem of brown straw from a
clump of wild sagebrush grass.

"You have an admirer in the wild azaleas to your left."

For some minutes, Cayrolynn felt as though eyes watched
her. Now, she stayed motionless to see what TeJay saw.
These were small deer about the size of greyhounds and

munching on the first green leaves of the plant that hid them. Eventually, they moved on down the hillside.

"Cayrolynn, your friend Beatrice called to ask me to bring you to town to get you checked for anemia. She thinks a few days spent with her and maybe some of your other friends might be helpful before our wedding."

"I agree and I can return to town with you or go in the morning. My planning for the doctor's appointment became part of my procrastination and she decided to help me, I think."

"Are there other symptoms I need to know. You stay so quiet with your barriers to being a hypochondriac. What you eat influences your metabolism, but I never ask about emotions. Tell me, what disturbs you because what disturbs you disturbs me, too."

"When I don't have opportunity to talk with you, like now, that disturbs me. The wedding plans seem too big for me. The smaller service with family and time for me to be awake seems to cause less stress."

"You need my help to set limits. When our friends hear our plans, without an invitation, they might appear."

"I know my mind wanders to sensitive areas where I shouldn't go. I try to curb my jealousy and not take a reproach."

"Your jealousy comes from insecurity. Is it a person or circumstances?"

"Someone like Mavis Davis or the women in your office."

"My first comment concerns now and in the future. Never before did I find someone. You have no reason for fear. Remember the words, keep your mind with all diligence because from it come the issues of life. These hills and hollows hold many secrets. Claude's uncle and aunt built a cabin on the top of this hill and used a pulley to bring water from this spring up to their cabin. They had no children, so they took in a young girl. The aunt became jealous, so when the child went to the spring, Claude's aunt followed her with their rifle. The uncle cleaned the spring that day, and he told the young one she could help. Claude's aunt killed them both, but the case never came to trial because she said the uncle shot her then killed himself. The girl was pregnant."

"Tell me what you want me to understand from this hill story TeJay. I can see the unsettled wildness and lack of population that seems so different from now."

"I want you to know, there'll be no reason for jealousy. Before settlers came, Indians roamed these hills. If we dig around the spring, we'll find carved arrow heads. Life with past, present, and future merge and here where we sit. What has been, will be. I don't want us here with cabin fever at anytime. My Dad ate some jello with Claude and Maude and got a stomach ache that night. Thereafter, my Mother would watch and tell Claude to take Maude to the ocean for a week. She told Claude to take care of us when they kept us and we took sandwiches for our lunch."

"After we marry, and it still seems so unreal, will you take time from work, like today, to spend time to talk with me?"

"I promise, Cayrolynn. I promise."

"This rock seems cold and wet and this pocket at the head of the hollow turns dark. The truck will take us home and then, why don't I ride to town with you and I'll stay with Beatrice for a few days."

                    *   *   *

Outside the wind whipped pollen from trees and flowering bushes. Should I wear a mask or take an antihistamine, Cayrolynn asked herself, when she sat waiting for Beatrice to return and take her for the doctor's appointment.

Beatrice kept catalogs stacked in a basket, some with order forms removed from the middle. I don't need to order anything for my wedding, Cayrolynn thought. She continued to turn pages to fill the time and not turn on the television.

No focus, so her thoughts returned to the animosity she felt for Sarah Anna and Tip. The working space at the Loft belongs to me, she self-talked. When I am there, they impose and make me a child. TeJay belongs to them and I don't want to meet his old girl friends.

She glanced at the catalog with no thought for what she saw. Her tears hit the page. Through the wetness of tears she saw a case filled with costumes for Bozo the Clown. One good pity party and now she sat looking at the makings of a circus clown. Is that me, she questioned herself. Do I play the part of a fool and will I awaken like my Mother screaming at my Dad. He left with words to kill us all, and my Mother called her friend in Alabama to come for me. Before she came my Mother told me, "Cayrolynn, you must go, so please take my advice. Be happy and find joy each day. Life offers more and it's not the dishonest lie of addiction with your Dad's bottle nor the spirit of infirmity with my cancer."

Beatrice came breezing through the door. "Slow day and lots of time slots for you to see the doctor. Sandwiches for my lunch, then we'll get your check-up before we go for your dress fitting. Why are you looking at catalogs?"

"Passing the time of day until you came. Please keep me from a stress filled wedding, Beatrice. If the tornado had swept through and taken everything, we could go to the justice of the peace. I'm not up to much excitement."

"I approve your choice and you must stay right here to

avoid the entanglement of words from others. I hope you hold
no animosity toward your new in-laws."

"I find myself thinking up all kinds of reproaches, and
you're right. I hibernate until the day comes to return to
the Loft."

"Can you remember the kindness and love of Tip and Sarah
Anna? The promise of TeJay shows all the traits of the
smitten one?"

"I guess out of sight, out of mind. You bring the
positive side of remembrances that I must not forget."

"It doesn't take a reason to build a wall of hate and
resentment that hems you within. Cayrolynn, you know what I
tell you, but the emotion that controls a stalker swings like
a needle on a gauge. All the positive factors of agape love
yields kind thoughts, but negative thoughts extinguish truth.
Understand?"

"Makes sense."

*   Twenty-eight   *

"Now what?" Cayrolynn spoke aloud and reached for the
ringing telephone. When she answered, Lexie began to talk.

"My Mother told me you went shopping for the dress
material, Cayrolynn. Are you sure you wouldn't like for me
to purchase a dress for you here?"

"I think not, Lexie. Since you volunteer, I do make a
request. For my hair, I want a headband with no veiling
because the hood of my robe will cover my hair. I want the
headband to be a flat or short tiara."

"I feel needed with your request, Cayrolynn, and do you
think of other ways I might help?"

"I need a medieval belt like a girdle made of golden
rope chain. I might find a picture, if I'm not making .
sense."

"Several rental places for costumes might carry what
you're looking for, I think."

"Lexie, no imposition on your time, please. If it's too

much trouble, then don't."

"I promise, Cayrolynn. I think it shouldn't be any problem. And, you have your flowers?"

"Freesias and white roses with Easter lilies every where. Sarah Anna abhors fake flowers or silk trees, as you know."

"The ceremony, what do you think?"

"I'm not there yet in my thoughts, but very traditional and from your pastor's handbook. I would like for the cousins present to repeat all the words except where the covenant uses our names and becomes personal. Please think about this idea for me and how you could change the words for our verbal repetition. No change in clothes or special clothes for the cousins. I'm planning to focus the attention of wiggle-worms, I hope ."

"Cayrolynn, we need to plan the music and I'll talk to TeJay, too. Think about the music."

"I don't want music, please, Lexie. It's our family gathered before the altar for the covenant. It's not the usual production. We leave the farm together at the same time and go to the church for the covenant, then return home for dessert and coffee or afternoon tea."

"Cayrolynn, I listen and I approve."

After the phone conversation, Cayrolynn picked up the

devotional booklet sent by Lexie for Lent. This meditation
concerned the stone lapis lazuli. Most times, she read fast
which meant skip and skim. These two words caught her
attention, so she opened the dictionary and found the
definition said blue stones.

"In a wedding, you wear something borrowed and something
blue," she self talked. "Could I wear ear rings and a drop
chain necklace with the stone lapis lazuli?" She found
herself making descriptions with words. The color azure
spoke to her with the clearest of sky blue. The word blue
positive or negative? How would blue taste? Blue and blah's
contrast. For my eyes I see, a field of blue violets or
miniature blue daises so small to float in a dish.

Women shop to find a release from sadness or anger and
women eat to get peace. Often when she worked with her
murals in stitches of thread, thoughts drifted by and then
kept returning. Today, she kept seeing lapis lazuli.

Sometimes, when TeJay came, he began conversation as
though he never went away to work or where ever. In the late
afternoon, Cayrolynn leaned her head to the back of the couch
and entered dreamland where she drifted in a blue sky with a
blue blanket and a blue balloon. TeJay's voice kept calling
and the peaceful drift seemed to steer her toward him. She
awoke when the apartment bell rang and TeJay called her name.

He held her warm and close while he asked about her day.

"Do you know the color lapis lazuli? I'm intrigued with the color blue and it dominates my thoughts."

"Have you used it in your work?"

"Not yet. When I was younger, I loved Crayolas because each color's printed on the paper cover. This one violet and another magenta. Colors push around in my senses and blue sounds like a bell ringing for peace and quiet."

"My creative wife-to-be, if I didn't know better, I would question these thoughts without meaning. Want to come to the Condo for a bowl of soup."

"Beatrice works late and attends a meeting after work, so I stay quiet here in my cocoon. You want to return after you feed yourself?"

"Sure. I missed the paper today, so my catch-up reading will keep me company while I eat. Since Beatrice allows you peace and quiet, I'll return in a bit, okay?"

TeJay went to eat and Cayrolynn washed away sleep from her face and put on new make-up. She felt no hunger, so she poured apple juice for herself and took a graham cracker from a package. Next, she turned on the television. Orchestra on the educational channel. Preaching on the Christian channel. Comics with vibrating music. She stayed with the news until it became gory, then changed to Louisiana Cajun cooking. She wanted to work on needlepoint but because her eyes lacked focus, she leafed through a magazine and listened to the cookery.

When he returned, TeJay brought a hamburger with all the trimmings the way he remembered she liked it. After she finished, he found a movie, then sat beside her and held her hand as though they shared a date at the movies.

"So, you worked and tried to figure out colors today? Crayola's in a new box for school, shades of thread for needle work, and paint in a can mixed for hues of color. Do you think a person's personality compares to a color chart?"

"Once TeJay, I remember a discussion with rambling inane questions and comments about what color is God with decisions like 'foolish questions and foolish answers.' Our leader asked again and said, how about clear pure light? This led to a discussion of colors. At the time, I thought God's the color blue that you see in the heavens with no ending."

"What color's love? Is it fuzzy pink?"

"Fuzzy pink leaves out tough love that's a label. If God's pure love, why the label tough?"

"How do you see hate? Does hate get a color?"

"Sure and I think it's green like jealousy. What do you think?"

"I think anger's red hot and I think laughter's

exhausting red, too. When we talk of energy, do you see your energy quotient related to color? Cayrolynn, don't look at me like I have smudges on my chin."

TeJay went to the mirror in the bath to see what she saw.

"You jump to conclusions and why the quick response to correct anything I saw?"

"Because you must see me as perfect without any flaws?"

"Really?"

Words led to laughter before TeJay put on a travelogue of the Mississippi River. At the end, Cayrolynn felt she must inspire a pillow fight. The tangible vibes she felt seemed like those the night she sang and he almost walked out. Her laughter turned to distaste and then to despise. She moved to stand in front of him and saw the disgust in his eyes.

"The red haired wife of one of the attorneys in your office said you marry me because you need a wife before you become a partner. Why do you marry me, TeJay?"

Cayrolynn watched his eyes. For a moment, her words didn't penetrate his thinking. Like the clicking of the computer chip looking for a program, his eyes changed. He stood and placed his farmer's hands on her shoulder joints.

"She told you that? And, you carry this burden, all this time since Thanksgiving?"

"I need to know, TeJay. Please don't cast me away."

"Don't you know, Cayrolynn. Don't you know that two people make one. She's wrong. You know so. I'm the oldest sibling and I cannot remember not being the leader. My Mother whispers when she teaches and her students hear. When I was in first grade, she stuttered. Almost never, does she stutter now. I overheard an older boy copy-cat her speech and I tore into him. That's how I feel now. Somebody's a busybody in my territory."

Cayrolynn watched his eyes melt in tears and felt the bones of his arms when he pulled her into his body with her head under his chin.

"Lexie didn't have a date for her senior prom, so I asked Andy to come home from the university with some orchids and take her. Sam took off because his grade point average couldn't match Tip's. I found him. When Rae didn't make med school with Andy, I feared her crack up and stood in the wayside for her. All my life, my elder brother role didn't allow any love for myself. Now, that I find you, I'll not allow you to go. All my life, I turn away and you see and hear that tonight. Walk away and keep on walking, nope, not this time."

"I started to ask you, but it hurt too much. Please don't marry me so you can be a partner in your firm. Please want me more than job, or lifestyle, TeJay."

Cayrolynn moved her head so that she could look into his eyes while she talked. So, they stood trying to fathom the depth of their souls in their eye contact. When Cayrolynn turned her head back to the ridge of his collarbone, she could hear the beat of his heart. The word you, in I love you, became the strongest beat.

"I tell you, I love you, Cayrolynn. Can you tell me you trust me when you say I love you. When I'm not present, can you ward off words like arrows that come at you? Can you remember that we're one whether I'm holding you?"

"These years with no one but myself didn't make me stronger inside, but left me with my fears never to be the chosen one and never to experience story book caring with the courage of honest love. Strong love is patient love. Can our love be patient and strong until I'm well and beyond? Softness and weakness might be labeled love. Weak men destroy their wives and their wives destroy them with their tongues. I'll try to remember what our lives mean together."

Neither wanted the other to move away, so they stood bonded with an intensity of togetherness and Cayrolynn knew this love meant more than some answer with chic verbal promises.

"When we fight, TeJay, I'll try to fight fair. It's not my personality to bicker and nag. I never want to murder you, nor to walk away never to return. Sand-papering changes us and makes our relationship better, but no screaming nor low-rating you because you're you. Iron sharpens iron. When I fail in trying, TeJay, please give me another chance."

TeJay made no answer, but Cayrolynn knew he heard and on another day he would open the conversation again. His best answer would be roses sent to bless her heart.

*   Twenty-Nine   *

Beatrice came at mid-night.

"Cold, cold rain and like a steady down-pour. You still awake? Cayrolynn, do you need a tablet or hot cocoa?"

"No. My nap at mid-day plus caffeine causes my big eyes, but I'm waiting for you to tell me about your hospital visit."

"My friend needs TLC. Tender-loving-care. And, I wonder who created that acronym. That's what I need, too. I met a family in the hall, wife and children of a man I don't know. They kept asking me questions and I tried to shield them from reasons and consequences of the virus. It seems the patient and doctor keep silent and this family wants to know."

"I can understand, maybe the patient avoids facing his fate, too."

"Your friend TeJay. Did you enjoy his visit tonight?

Have you discussed your thoughts about his mother and father?"

"What would I say? I'm afraid of them? They're too close and nosy? Neither's true. Why am I in hiding? Maybe, TeJay understands the 'clay feet syndrome.' I'm too close to them and they see my foibles, or I begin to see their inadequacies. When I lived in the Loft, I couldn't plan my own wedding. I became co-dependent to my in-law family, and it left me with more feelings of the inferiority complex. If I'm asked about fibromyalgia, then I explain again and they say they think I'm well."

"Some people feel driven to explain themselves. Sickness allows a personhood they never knew. You belong to another group who never talk about problems because of fear to call 'something into being that be not.' Forsure, TeJay doesn't marry a hypochondriac and the more he loves, the faster you heal."

"Where do emotions and feelings come from, Beatrice. Joseph's brothers couldn't look at him with truthful eyes. How will my eyes look at Tip and Sarah Anna?"

"Time for sleep, Cayrolynn. I think your creative sensitive self informs you about becoming a daughter-in-law."

"Goodnight, Beatrice and I hope the cold, cold rain that

I hear stops by seven."

* * *

With a book marker in place, Cayrolynn answered the phone. The background noise and Rae talking to someone in that noise caused Cayrolynn to pause, then answer. "I'm here Rae, and how are you?"

"Oh, Cayrolynn, I'm sure Andy spoke with TeJay, but I wanted to tell you I'm sorry to miss your wedding. Andrew called Andy to propose a professional trip to Japan. Andy gave him our decision for us to live and work together. Andrew showed good manners with nothing negative, then said he planned to go alone. I feel the need to stay here, and you can stop by if your trip brings you this way."

"TeJay didn't say Rae. Please know I'll miss you. Our day becomes so important to us, and I understand. Enjoy where you live and we'll talk soon. Thanks, Rae."

Previous telephone messages reminded Cayrolynn about the tinted shoes ready and her dress completed. She felt the motivation to collect the shoes and dress, but decided to contain her impetus by reading. When Beatrice came at four she told her of this need to do errands. Beatrice decided to tag along.

"Are you expecting TeJay today?"

"No.   He works tonight."

"Where first?"

"The dress and then the mall to collect the tinted shoes, please."

When they came from the mall, Cayrolynn felt a premonition to wait at the door for Beatrice, who seemed to tarry looking in several store-fronts. The way seemed clear to outside parking, so she felt in her pocket for her car keys. She took her key ready to unlock the car door when a person running fast came behind her and reached for her purse. Cayrolynn felt surprise and experienced unbalance with a dizzy head and fell to the asphalt. She heard some one screaming help and the person who pushed left running. For a few minutes, she lay still. Then, Beatrice came with questions about what happened.

"Cayrolynn, I followed you from the mall. Do you need help to sit up?"

The golf cart marked security arrived and Cayrolynn could hear their talking.

"Help me get my friend into the back seat. I work at a clinic and I'll take her there."

"How did this happen?"

Cayrolynn knew she couldn't stand. With the help of

Beatrice and a strong security woman, both lifting her shoulders, they brought her to her knees. Then, they shifted her into the car.

"Did they steal anything? Where's her purse?"

"She lay on her purse with her billfold inside. She bought shoes and they're under the car."

"I need information to file this incident, so before you leave can you make notations and I'll call you later."

"Cayrolynn, please open your eyes and tell me what happened."

"Beatrice, I think I fainted. I felt light-headed and tried to get to the car. I unlocked the door before I was pushed."

"Did you hear someone screaming help?"

"No. Someone in a red sweater helped me open the mall glass doors and seemed to be following me. I thought they wanted to help me." Cayrolynn eyes opened and closed and then she found it too difficult to keep them open.

She heard Beatrice talking to the doctor at her clinic and then talking to TeJay. She kept going in and out of consciousness. She wanted to cry and felt tears escape from her closed eye-lids. Sanity came with short insights.

"Cayrolynn, we need x-rays. We transfer you to the

emergency room at the hospital. Do you understand?" She
remembered saying yes.

When she felt a need for the bathroom, she began to
awaken. TeJay sat beside her bed wearing his kilim sweater.

"TeJay, I need the bath, please."

"Sure, I'll get a nurse."

The woman came and helped her to the bath, then asked
her to drink as much water as possible. When she felt
comfortable again, the nurse left and TeJay returned.

"Why am I here, TeJay? Why am I in the ER?"

"You're here because you're dehydrated. You have
bruises and a new injury to your head. The scar where you
hit against the bell during the tornado has a new bandage."

"When will I go home?"

"Tonight, you can return to Beatrice's. You need a
couple of x-rays. Your doctor sent you here because of your
head injury. The Condo still has painters. They'll be
finished when we come home after our wedding."

                    *   *   *

When Cayrolynn watched TeJay wearing his new sweater,
she found herself thinking of some international sailor she
might have seen in Pensacola. His hair clubbed like a pirate
cut with a razor instead of by scissors. Denim shirt and

tight jeans like some admiral incognito made her feel like a
spy. Or, like a confederate or union spy living in the
hollow and hauling water from the spring on wash day.

* * *

TeJay called seeking lunch plans. "Cayrolynn, if you
avoided breakfast, we'll eat pancakes for lunch."

"Thanks, TeJay, that's what I need. If we can find
some place where people don't stare at my bandaged head. My
Mother hated the rude stranger who looked without a blink."

TeJay remembered a drug store near Vandy and the
hospital with a front counter and back booths that
specialized in omelettes and fried corn flap-jacks all day.

"We park in the back and avoid the front traffic. This
allows some conversation."

Before the waiter came, TeJay began his explanation of a
pre-nuptial agreement for them.

"Before Claude died, he asked Tip to give his share of
the farm to me. Maude agreed, but kept survivor's right as
long as she lived. I doubt that Tip told anyone. Half of
the farm belongs to me, so I want a legal agreement. If my
death comes before yours, then the farm goes to my Dad and
Mom or to their estate. Your share at my death includes the
Condo, any other property we own, and insurance."

"This idea of legal agreements before marriage never entered my thoughts."

They stopped to order and waited for their food. When the meal ended, TeJay said, "You want time to think about these legal agreements?"

"Not really. Love and trust go together in a marriage. Sometimes in life we go back, however the cycle of life goes forward. If you left me, I think I would go home to Florida. The farm offers a place for renewal and healing. My days there gave me solace, but Andy and Rae choose the sounds of the ocean. Without you TeJay, no, in my thoughts I refuse to go there."

"You stay with Beatrice instead of the Loft. Why?"

"My feelings aren't a measure of yes and no decisions. I knew I needed time to think about the wedding and I want to live in town, not at the farm. Please make the legal decisions and bring the papers for me to read and sign. Who'll sign with us as a witness?"

"Can you feel secure and happy about my plans?"

"TeJay, yes, I'm glad my day isn't spent in the hospital."

When they arrived at Beatrice's, Cayrolynn took her key in her hand, but TeJay opened the door. She didn't tarry.

She needed the couch and the cool air of the apartment.

"You feel unsteady, Cayrolynn?"

"It's okay, I know rest equips me to feel good again.
It's noon, so I encourage your going to work, TeJay. I'm
fine. If I need help, I'll call you, but truly no problem."

TeJay took a moment to bring her water and juice from
the frig, then accepted her send off. He locked the door
when he left and Cayrolynn turned on the television so he
could hear if he waited outside the door.

"Are you asleep, Cayrolynn?" Beatrice came at eight and
Cayrolynn admitted she slept all afternoon.

"TeJay took you for lunch or supper?"

"We went to lunch, but no supper and I'm not hungry."

"Good. Then, it's a cup of soup and tell me about
lunch."

"TeJay wants us to sign pre-nuptial agreements."

"Did you say yes? I'm surprised. TeJay doesn't strike
me as the type person to be dishonest."

"These pre-nups seem like living wills. He wants his
parents to be owners of the farm, if he dies."

"Do you want a share of the farm?"

"If something happens, then the situation changes and
I might want to protect my place at the Loft. I've been

thinking about what TeJay said. When you own something,
does it own you, or do you own it? Are there mineral rights
of value connected to the hillsides like coal or gas?"

"Cayrolynn, I can listen and try to be your sounding
board. Your job at the insurance company gave you insights
my job hasn't provided."

"Right now, my plans include reading those legal papers
like an insurance policy and signing. I see protection for
my marriage. I stay in town, otherwise, with my personality,
I might seek approval from the parents for our every move."

"Clam chowder or split pea with some hot cornbread?"

"Chowder and toast, please."

*　　*　　*

Cayrolynn kept thinking of TeJay. He didn't call last
night nor this morning, so she sat holding his photograph
while she watched television. Around three, he called.

"I hope I didn't call at the wrong time. I'm at the
farm, Cayrolynn, and Sarah Anna wants to know if you think
everything settled or is there something she should do?"

"I can't remember, TeJay. Will you come by when you
return to town?"

"Sure. I think about five, if it's okay."

She felt they would eat at the country store. Beatrice

never came before eight, so she left her a note. When TeJay
knocked, she picked up her jacket before she opened the door.

"Cayrolynn, Tip and I spent time walking over the
charred hill trying to decide which trees to plant. Sam
wants to bring his sons this summer for two weeks of work.
They'll help plant the fruit sprouts and we'll decide whether
to broadcast pine seed or use the hill side for Christmas
trees."

"I felt concern that you didn't call."

"My narrow focus, sorry. I talked to Tip and Sarah Anna
about our living wills signed before our marriage. If it's
alright with you, we'll ask Beatrice and Shafe to serve as
witnesses and sign our papers."

"Do you think we'll retire at the farm?"

"I think you must make that decision. New roads and new
houses will bring new neighbors. Change can influence
whether you want us at the farm or some other place."

"You drove in a hurry. I want turnip greens, cornbread,
and berry cobbler."

"It's a mighty good thing I didn't eat with my parents
and came home to feed you. With two big appetites, we need a
country supper."

*   Chapter Thirty   *

"Cayrolynn, the painters finished our Villa and I want us to go there to check for fumes." TeJay called before lunch on Saturday. "If possible, I need you to diagram the place for me while I measure. Our placement of furniture depends on sizes."

"Whenever you come by, I'm ready, TeJay."

Before the painting began, the condominium manager asked her to look at samples. She looked for clean appearance and a background for hanging her works of art. TeJay arrived with his truck loaded with equipment.

"You plan to work all afternoon?"

"Cayrolynn, I brought my tools so you can try out your carpentry skills. You won't disappoint me, I'm sure."

"Don't tease. Why the loaded truck?"

"The utility closet might hold most, so what we need, we own without going to the hardware." TeJay handed her keys before they opened the new condominium door.

"Your password to our Villa, Madame Hillabee."

"These keys don't require a shibboleth, do they?"

"Poor joke and a test to see if you know definitions."

"I remember from crossword puzzles."

"I asked your friend the prior owner, Jo, if she left a hide-away key, and she said, no. I checked the outside covered electrical outlets and found one key. We need to decide on a hide-away. After we explore the place, we can decide."

"When did you schedule movers?"

"Monday, if you could be here some of the hours."

"Will you help with moving?"

"Yes and Shafe, too. Shafe plans to move into our Condo as I move out. Also, his Condo sold within the hour he placed it on the market. Shafe suffers rejection. Vida moved to New York with a promotion and took her parents to the aunt in Virginia. The same aunt who came to live here. After all these years, Shafe finds himself rootless."

"Whether I feel sympathy or empathy, I know I feel turmoil for him."

"Me, too. He plans to take some time to help us move and come to our wedding."

TeJay helped Cayrolynn examine the walls. No fumes from paint nor from insect spray, so they went to lunch.

Together, they examined a diagram Cayrolynn drew for the placement of furniture. Several furniture suggestions from her consignment shop met TeJay's approval.

"I'm feeling too high, TeJay like a train on a track with no brakes. It comes like three Christmas mornings at one time."

"Enough food and enough excitement for one day. Back to your habitat for quietness."

*   *   *

Monday afternoon, TeJay brought a folder with legal papers. "Use the included pasters to write your comments and stick them to the pages, Cayrolynn. With your questions, you may call me so I can implement changes before tomorrow night." Cayrolynn noticed his busy push and encouraged him to be on his way.

Tuesday night, TeJay came to Beatrice's and brought along Shafe. They sat around the small kitchen table and began reading the pre-nup papers.

"Shafe, if you and Beatrice will witness our signatures when we finish. Cayrolynn reviewed legal documents at her job, so she reads with precision."

"Cayrolynn reads with a photographic memory, TeJay, and she'll ask questions, so be prepared," Beatrice said.

TeJay moved his chair so he could hear Cayrolynn when

she read aloud.

"Here it says Claude and Maude gave you their half of the farm when they died, but you return your half to your parents. And?"

"Only, if I die first. If my parents die before us, then I plan to change my will. You'll see I leave an insurance policy and our new Villa to you. Legal and tax restrictions could hamper what my parents plan for their retirement years. My marriage makes change in unexpected ways, and my brothers and sister need their attachments to my parents. The hollow stabilizes our family for now and must be kept intact."

"I see the arrangements for unexpected death, but no plans in case of divorce. Will you cast me aside?"

"I hope no divorce occurs, Cayrolynn. According to court procedures, you'll find protection and I'll not cast you aside. I hope you know me well enough to trust my character to be generous with you."

Cayrolynn remembered a friend with three small children, a divorce, and no legal recourse. Beatrice felt the tension and brought frozen grapes for munching.

"You make reciprocal forms for the two of us, TeJay. Then, you include a living will with the power of attorney naming Tip so if both of us experience an accident, he can act for us."

"And, the durable power of attorney for health care for each of us which means I listen to your wishes and try to carry them out. Do you want your life prolonged, Cayrolynn?"

"If an accident occurs, then decisions must be made. I need time and conversation about my health."

"So, Cayrolynn, if you are in a coma, what do you think?"

"Often when a person's in coma, they awaken and live good lives for an extended time. With a flippant answer, I would say, let me die. I find that answer too simplistic. Have you thought this question through for yourself?"

"When we were teenagers, one of our friends went into a coma from a hunting accident and died. At the time, my parents began a legal file that included their wills and our decisions about death. Claude and Maude executed forms that my Dad held for them, but he never used."

"These go into a safety deposit box?"

"Yes and we'll keep copies. Sometimes, opening a safe deposit box can present legal problems."

"Do healthy people take time to be legally correct, TeJay, or do most people let this slide?"

"Procrastination is the word. It's not easy to face the difficult decisions and then traumatic consequences."

Cayrolynn finished reading and picked up the pen to make her signature on the lines marked. When she began this path to marriage, she held hope and no financial status. She understood she signed from a position of poor health, but with assurances of TeJay's love.

TeJay arranged the papers in folders for the security box and a private safe in the new Villa. He called a notary friend married to a justice of the peace.

"Cayrolynn, we need to finalize these papers with a legal ceremony of marriage. On Saturday, Lexie will ask for our covenant before the Lord and my family. She'll bring a certificate for our wall. Tonight, I ask you to help me make these vows legal."

Beatrice felt surprise and watched Cayrolynn thinking about this proposal.

"I'm not sure I understand, TeJay. Those phrases, 'hidden agenda' or 'clock the action,' with questions."

"My friends'll come and bring a notary stamp to make our signatures legal. The justice of the peace has a license to say we're legally married."

"I agree, TeJay. It's okay with me. It's strange because once my friend feared interference from her Dad so she married legally, then had a church wedding, so no rejection could occur. Do you think someone might object at our wedding on Saturday?"

"No, our family agrees to Saturday's wedding. Tonight, legal arrangements with Beatrice and Shafe, present. I don't keep secrets that might cause objection nor do you, but we cement our lives together."

"These people'll come soon?"

"Absolutely. We need to talk about going to church on Saturday. Shafe and I plan to park at the back door and leave space for your car. Beatrice, if you could bring Shafe back to town. Lexie and the family fill spaces behind the church, too."

"I plan to take the hill road from the crossroads, not the hollow road by the farm, so tell me in minutes what you think," Beatrice asked.

"Sam's children want to play their violins until we take our places, if Cayrolynn approves. Maybe ten after and if you run late I'll give you a cell number to call."

The knock on the apartment door verified TeJay's planning, so their discussion about Saturday waited.

Later Beatrice asked Cayrolynn about her feelings when the legal marriage occurred. "You understood you were being married in Williamson County not Davidson nor Cannon Counties didn't you Cayrolynn?"

"I did understand, Beatrice, and I felt so secure

because TeJay said he loved me. It's proof that if anything happens during these days of change, TeJay made my financial future secure."

"You seem better and how do you feel?"

"Because you're my friend and a nurse, I remember the intruder at the parking lot. I left you and felt unsteady. I looked before I walked to the car. I steadied myself against the car before I felt the push. Part of my trauma came from the surprise of the push."

"Cayrolynn, you need to try to forget some inadequacy you feel. I'm concerned about your facial abrasion and the ceremony on Saturday. TeJay's planning takes care of most problems. I don't subscribe to your being accident prone. Do you feel like sleep or should I make hot milk?"

"So many thoughts tonight, but I'm tired. With the lights out, I think sleep'll come. Thank you, Beatrice."

*　　*　　*

In the morning, Cayrolynn drove to the consignment gallery. She rambled around finding furniture for TeJay's opinion. Looking took time and she forgot to drink water or stop and rest. The first wave of tiredness caused her to sit and drink from the bottle she carried.

Near the front entrance she took a rocker and leaned her head for support, then closed her eyes. Some dream caused

her to think of barefeet and sand between her toes. The
hands of a small child pulled on her skirt. When she looked
a toddler with her pacifier wanted to climb up. Cayrolynn
lifted her and she cuddled and went to sleep. The easy
rocking caused Cayrolynn to doze again. The owner saw this
pose and went for his camera. The Mother worked with a
decorator. She saw the child at peace and continued her
shopping. Warm children sweat, so Cayrolynn awoke with a wet
chest and the soft throbbing of a heart that matched the beat
of her own. The beat of two hearts brought a release to
tension, confusion, and sadness she carried for weeks. She
gazed at tiny eyebrows with eyelashes resting below closed
eyes. The fooler-pacifier reached the child's nose and the
automatic suck kept some-off-beat-time with their heart
beats. The pain and questions about marriage and TeJay, Tip
and Sarah Anna disappeared. She felt freedom. She felt
wholeness with no lingering fears about marriage or
motherhood. How can this be, she thought. The symptoms of
nausea and dizziness seemed caught away and replaced with
joy.

The child awoke and watched Cayrolynn talking to her.
She slide her little feet to the floor and ran to the counter
where her mother looked at books of wall paper and window
treatments. She pulled at her mother and her mother reached

down to place the child on her hip and continued the looking.

Cayrolynn left her place in the rocking chair and thought about cataclysmic change in her emotions. When she reached her car, it felt warm and comfortable not like wintertime coldness.

"If I go the back road maybe I can be at Beatrice's before another attack except I don't think there'll be another," she thought. She walked into the apartment before Beatrice came to lunch. Beatrice found Cayrolynn resting on the floor. She handed Cayrolynn another pillow for her head.

"Do you find the floor stabilizing?"

"I tried looking at some furniture for our new place, but the exertion caused my swift return."

"Want to tell me about it?"

"Nothing new to tell. I'm fine now, but no more shopping today."

"I came home for an apple and a peanut butter cracker. Are you hungry, by chance."

"Not yet, after a nap, I'll eat milk toast."

*   Thirty-One   *

"My treat Cayrolynn," Beatrice said. "I want us to
spend the night at a bed and breakfast near Sewanne. We pack
tonight and eat supper there and breakfast in the morning."

"How come you think of something so foreign to your
usual planning?"

"Lexie called me and she'll meet us there with some
surprises she brought from Houston. Bachelors enjoy a last
night fling and brides can do the same. Please don't say no.
We may talk all night like teenagers on a sleep-over."

"Makes me feel special and I did make a careful list to
be sure in my forgetfulness, I included clothes, make-up, and
essentials. I'll show you my list for your help with
additions and the check-off."

"Fifteen minutes for a ceremony but our party should
make long-time remembrances of friendship."

*   *   *

Lexie sat on the front patio of the bed and breakfast

where willow furniture with chintz cushions looked inviting.

"Do we eat supper and breakfast here, Lexie?"

"And, raid the fridge if we need a snack."

Hugs not words welcomed these friends.

"Drive around back and we enter a private wing so our laughter doesn't disturb the owner."

"I told Beatrice, I feel so special. Did Sarah Anna approve of your leaving the family?"

"My Mother showed joy that I would spend this night welcoming my new sister-in-law."

*   *   *

Saturday noon, Beatrice parked in front of Wayside School waiting for TeJay's call. Cold springtime sunshine called dogwood winter seemed perfect for a country wedding. Early morning frost showed Cayrolynn's wisdom in choice of her dress.

"Did you enjoy our party time with Lexie last night?" Beatrice asked.

"Foolish question and you know the answer. I thank you and Lexie. I hope we have sister parties in the future, and you must come."

The cell phone rang with the que from Shafe to come to Brush Arbor Church. They took the road climbing to the barrens along the hillsides rather than the hollow road.

Cayrolynn felt the need to hide her symptoms from Beatrice. Early morning, she felt the nerves in her feet like Florida smidges playing suicide with unseen needle sharp stings. Her cream seemed best and calmed the nerves, but not the muscles. Now, her bones felt like ax handles with blunt axheads. Her breath widen her nostrils and her lips parted with each spear of pain. She took two tablets from her purse and swallowed without the water she needed.

"Do you feel shy, Cayrolynn?"

"My heart beats in my throat, but I'm not shy. TeJay comes to me like a brother and after today like a husband. Beatrice, someday you'll enjoy such a friendship. I'm glad Shafe will drive you home so you won't experience lonesome let down feelings after the wedding."

"We'll follow you to Sarah Anna and Tip's so you can leave your wedding finery for Lexie to return the items she borrowed for you. I look forward to this lunch including wedding cake and country food for grandchildren."

They drove to the back of the church where Lance took pictures when she left the car. Lexie went first into the church, then Shafe and Beatrice, last TeJay and Cayrolynn who seemed to forget where they were as they presented an entwine pose for Lance's camera.

Cayrolynn knew Lexie followed a traditional wedding for

vows with a repetition of "I plight thee my troth." The
children voiced A-men's and made the service a participation
and drama. At the end they sang with merriment while
circling around, "The Farmer Takes a Wife." Each child chose
a couple: Cayrolynn and TeJay, Sarah Anna and Tip, Beatrice
and Shafe, Sam and Toney, Lexie and Lance, then all danced
out the front door.

Some community friends filled the back of the church so
they extended the line. Cayrolynn and TeJay stood on the
concrete steps with family and friends. Someone called,
"You must throw the flowers," so Cayrolynn threw high, but
Shafe jumped and pulled the flowers down to Beatrice.

TeJay pulled Cayrolynn to his car and they left before
the others. "You may think we missed the bird seed or rice,
but wait until we leave our luncheon. The clanging cans and
shoe polish can't be avoided. My Mother promised she'll make
a way for us and we must depart back to the Interstate by the
barrens not down the hollow."

"All the weddings I ever attended seemed very serious.
Was our wedding too frivolous?"

"Our unforgettable wedding makes for a new life of
happiness."

"Why the parked sheriff's car, TeJay?"

"Tip thinks with our family home and the Easter sunrise

service tomorrow, someone might decide to crash the party. Vodka added to the ice tea punch as a jest could make us sick especially the children."

"Do we change clothes first or more pictures?"

"Change first, and be ready to disappear when My Mom gives her signal. We leave by the front door not the deck."

"TeJay my muscles seem stuck, so I need your help. Too much pain and too much medicine makes me weak."

"Did you tell Beatrice?"

"No, maybe Lexie noticed. I thought as we stood there with all the people, here's the church and here's the people and why couldn't I touch His hem and be healed."

"You will be Cayrolynn, try not to crash and I'll tell my Mother. One bite of cake with a photo by Lance and we're out of here."

Beatrice came to help her dress before she stood with TeJay to cut the cake. The children sang "happy wedding to you" and the camera kept flashing. In the midst of voices and family laughter, they went out the front door and it seemed as though no one noticed.

"Are you hungry at all?" TeJay asked.

"Maybe, a coke, TeJay. I think if we stop at the Interstate, you could help me with my seat." She knew a moment of peace with her meds would bring sleep. So, she slept until they reached the Villa.

"Cayrolynn, when we get you settled, I want to call the gym where Beatrice takes you for massage. If someone's on duty today, maybe they can help with your dizziness and pulled muscles."

"It has been so long since I crashed. I'm not hungry, but thirsty. I'm better and I hope someone can help me."

"You need to tell me what you take and how each affects your system. Thank you for bravery with my family."

"I'm so glad we enjoyed sunshine today. The hollow haunted with mist says hibernate, but sunshine speaks of outside doins."

"We're home and I help you inside. Rest for awhile sweet love."

Cayrolynn buried her head in the pillow and thought, "No one, not my Mother or Dad, ever called me Love or kissed me good night."

Sometime during the night Cayrolynn awoke and felt the warmth of TeJay asleep beside her. She went to the bath and returned, then cuddled to his back without his awakening.

* * *

For a week, TeJay wouldn't talk about a Florida trip.

Cayrolynn lost her pain and muscle tightness.

"I can travel now, TeJay."

"I fear even the thoughts of travel might cause trauma and a relapse."

"I think no problem and I want to show you where I lived."

"On Sunday, we'll take the plane and take our trip. Not a year later, but a week. I think you're at peace for now. We'll enjoy Florida sunshine."

*   *   *

Cayrolynn didn't say, "This plane ride's my first." Either TeJay knew or he showed possessive ownership by holding her hand during take-off and helping position the foam ear plugs into her ears. She looked at the masculine frazzle of hair on his hand and his watch on his bare wrist. Seats on their plane leaving Atlanta filled with Army personnel and other servicemen going to one of the bases near Pensacola. The stop at the airport near Columbus gave an ear pain that hurt and more pain when they landed at the airport in Florida.

"My ears hurt, TeJay."

"Some gum, a coke and cheese crackers." He bought these from machines at the rental car kiosk. She felt tension when they waited for their car. Students on spring break made waiting for the car longer. At the motel in Navarre, they ran into groups of students waiting for room keys.

"This might take longer than expected. We eat supper here, then collect keys before we journey down the beach to watch for a red sunset."

"Sounds extraordinary."

"Few early diners, so we get a table right away and we both need food. How're your ears?"

"They popped like trips up and down Monteagle mountain. TeJay, after the coke and crackers, my hunger diminished."

"Smaller orders."

On her green order pad the waitress wrote and "what to drink?"

"Two bottles of water that we can take with us. One order of fried clams, one french fries, and one onion rings. Small shrimp dinner salads with ranch dressing on the side. Another suggestion, Cayrolynn?"

She nodded no, and enjoyed the insight of TeJay. He reached for a newspaper left on an adjoining table and gave the comics to her.

Before they went to the beach they put on boat shoes made for sand and surf.

The sky to the west bathed the atmosphere in hues of pink and orange. They stood holding hands and enjoying the

392

kaleidoscope of sunset, then walked along the wet rind of
sand with the receding foam and occasional slosh. At dusk,
they reversed and returned to the walkway made of anchored
cross ties above the white sand of Navarrae beach. The sound
of the surf seemed like a symphony of ocean waves with the
oboe call of sea birds.

"You remember your parents, Cayrolynn, and I remember
the stories of my Mom and Dad."

TeJay heard the first hiccup. Please no, he thought.

Cayrolynn tried to hold back her emotional response and
couldn't. She laughed and cried with intensity. TeJay
allowed the burst of tension and memory. No prolonged
explosion this time, but a needed moment before ending.

"Better?"

"Over for now. These days of memory where I lived and
explored as a child may cause more tears. I'm glad I can
hang on to you and not be swept away."

"I hope you'll find laughter with me and these times of
closeness become a bridge and beginning of our new life.
Alone on the white sands of Navarrae Beach and ready to
forget those things of the past. Do you know the word mosey?
Mosey on home, okay?"

                    *   *   *

TeJay bought a map showing all the local roads and

suggested finding a fish house for lunch. Cayrolynn couldn't
remember the road home. Past hurricanes left the roadhouse
where her mother sang, ready to fall into the Gulf.

"Could we drive out to East Bay and try to find my dirt
road near the church and graveyard?"

"Sure. Tell me where."

Cayrolynn looked at the plotted county roads with state
numbers. "I never used a map because I knew we turned where
the road curved with the mail boxes set off to the left."
At a road labeled Boat Ramp Landing, she saw the church,
cemetery, and mailboxes. TeJay parked and they walked
through rolls of sand deposited during flooding by tidal
waves. The cemetery appeared above water marks of some
recent hurricane.

"This is Lavender and this is my Mother."

"Use you camera because you need closure with your
memories." Cement blocks edged terraced grave sites
protecting slabs and markers from shifting sand.

TeJay walked to the church and found the door unlocked.
The paint on the cement floor cracked from water damage.
Behind the piano someone hung frames with the names of the
members past and present, and along the front a kneeling
bench. No plastic flowers, but two pots with growing ferns.

Cayrolynn came and stood beside TeJay.

"Our standing here seems right for me. My memory evokes feelings of security and comfort. The two air-conditioning units set above kept the chapel cool during summer and on a cold blustery day, the gas heater gave warmth better than a furnace."

"I think the door stays locked and we happened along when someone forgot."

"True and I know where Lavender kept the key."

"Strange to compare Victory Tabernacle and Pleasant Rest Cemetery with Brush Arbor Church and cemetery."

After being inside, coming out into the Florida sun caused a moment of blindness.

"I'll check to see if the key stays in its place. Yes. It's here, so we lock the door."

When TeJay drove into the edge of the cemetery, he failed to notice graveled clay parking beside the church. Now, when they returned to the car, they found the tires and body settled into the soft sand.

"Sometimes, we stuck a truck in the field, so Tip kept a shovel behind the seat to dig space under the wheels for us to drive out. I have no shovel and with the sand, no traction."

"I thought someone with a boat might drive by, and they might call a wrecker for us."

"How far down this road to the river and the boat ramp?"

"At least a mile, TeJay. Before the hurricanes, mobile homes lined the ridge. It seems storms took the units and the utilities because I don't see telephone nor electric lines."

"Do you choose to walk with me to the boat ramp or do you want to wait here?"

"I want to walk through the graveyard and if you'll walk with me, then I'll walk to the river with you."

TeJay took her hand and they walked looking at each grave site. When they came to Lavender's grave, Cayrolynn went to the gravel and took some stones that she placed behind the headstone and covered with sand.

"I brought no stones of remembrance but these will serve."

They walked down the row until they reached the granite slab with a lettering that showed death at Christmas for her Mother after Cayrolynn went to the children's home. TeJay place bits of gravel by the headstone. Sand covered the next granite slab and TeJay stopped to clear away the covering. Storms caused harden sand to cover this grave and with time it slid and tilted into the earth. This grave belonged to her Dad. Before the death of her Mother, her Dad took his place here. Lavender died five years later.

"Why did she not write you, Cayrolynn?"

"Because my Mother asked her not to tell me. She wanted
a better way for me and she tried to find that way." She
took some stones of remembrance for her Dad's grave and knelt
to place them beside the sand shifted slab. She felt the
moisture of tears and wiped these away.

TeJay heard the motor of a truck. The driver came from
the river so he stood beside the road. When the truck
stopped, TeJay asked for a wrecker to pull them out.

"My brother-in-law keeps a wrecker and he can come in
about thirty minutes."

The man stopped the loud motor of his truck and came to
stand in front of Cayrolynn.

"My Dad, Jimmy Jemison, preaches in this church and you
look like Ginny Sue Selaco. Are you her daughter?"

"Yes."

"Well, don't you know it. I remember you and Bobby went
to school in the same grade and I'm older. I'm Zeb Jemison.
I remember my Dad looking for you when your folks died, but
Miss Lavender said she didn't keep your address." Cayrolynn
said nothing. "Well, I'll send Oscar over to help you folks
out."

Cayrolynn felt the heat and sweat on her neck.

"We can stand in the shade, TeJay. There by the

building. I didn't ask any questions, but when Oscar or the preacher comes, I want to know about the deaths of my parents."

The wrecker, when it came, turned out to be an old log truck used to snake logs from the cutting site to a loading area. Oscar hooked the front end to the car and pulled it to the road.

"That'll cost you ten dollars, I reckon."

TeJay gave him two fives. "Zeb said Cayrolynn's parents are dead, and how did they die?"

"Ms Ginny Sue had cancer real bad, Jacob ruined his liver with booze, and Ms Lavender died with pneumonia one winter before the storms took all the trailers out. You folks moving back here?"

"No, we're passing through."

"Well, I guess I better be off. They need my truck until dark."

TeJay motioned for Cayrolynn to wait until the air conditioner cooled the car before they took the road back to the beach.

"I think I'm past the grieving, TeJay. Daughters end a family line and so far as I know, I'm the only one for my parents. My Mother's friend who took me to the children's home told me that someday I should go see Mom's family."

"Do you know where they live?"

"I saw their home, after the Alabama River joins the Tombigbee, near a post office named Mount Vernon. My grandmother fills their front porch with pots of hanging begonias. Neighbors enjoy the rockers on their porch where they can come and set a spell. My Mother said she liked to swing and sing."

"Whatever life is or becomes, I find joy in our being together, Cayrolynn. Sure, marriage means family and children. Ours is something better because for as long as we shall live, who we are is bound up in our togetherness."

"Are you happy, TeJay?"

"What a question. I'm happy. Did you want to see the end of boat ramp road?"

"No. I'm hungry."

"Funny. Hungry, huh. We'll take the road from Navarrae. Navarre to Pensacola to Orange Beach and find a fish house before we watch sunset from a fishing dock on the Gulf minus mosquitoes, if we can find such a place."

The End.

NOTES

Chapter 1.   Fibromyalgia...internet various sources.

  Browning, Elizabeth Barrett. Poems, Sonnets from
    the Portuguese #43.

Chapter 2.   Ecclestiastes: King James Version.

Chapter 5.   Coledrige, Samuel Taylor. "The Rime of the
    Ancient Mariner."

Chapter 8.   Child, Lydia Maria. Flowers for Children, Vol. 2.
    1844. "A Boy's Thanksgiving Day." First line "Over
    the river and through the woods."

  Conwell, Russell.   Acres of Diamonds. speech:
    internet copy.

  Christmas Story.   Matthew and Luke (KJV)

  Moore, William Clement.   The night before
    Christmas.

Chapter 13.   Drummond, Henry C. The Greatest Thing in the
    World. speech: internet copy.

Chapter 15.   Menotti, Gian Carlo.   Amal and the night
    visitors. information from internet entry.

Chapter 16.   Carmichael, Amy. Whispers of His Power. Dohnavur
    Fellowship, Fleming H. Revell, 1982.

Chapter 18.   Collins, Ace. Stories behind the great
    traditions of Christmas.

Chapter 20.   Gunther, John. Death Be not proud.

  Lewis, C. S. A Grief Observed.

Chapter 23.   "Knoxville Girl". blue grass public domain.

  "Walk on the Sunny Side". internet listing.

Chapter 26.   Drieser, Theodore. American Tragedy.
    copyright, 1953 by Helen Drieser.

Short Memoir for <u>Katherine</u> <u>Billingsley</u> <u>Duke</u>

I grew up in Prattville Alabama. Two years I studied at Judson College in Marion, Alabama and graduated at the University in Tuscaloosa. My first year of teaching was in Montreat, North Carolina. Next, I became Dean of Women at Virginia Intermont College.

For my master's degree, I went to Columbia University, Teachers College and met my husband, Don Duke(CPA), who was a graduate student in the School of Business. We married in New York, then moved to Dallas and Boise before returning to the South for my husband to teach accounting at Tennesse Tech University. Along the way, I spent a year at Southern Methodist University to obtain a Texas teachers certificate.

When Don went to the University of Georgia for his PhD in Accounting, I taught school and completed my EdS in Counseling. His next professorship was in Nashville where I obtained my PhD at Peabody College at Vanderbilt.

My writing began in high school when I wrote a column for the Prattville Progress. My myriad of interests take time, but writing calls and opens to creativity whenever I put pen to paper or turn on my computer. Gratitude goes to my retired professor husband; our son, Chip, a computer consultant, and to my encourager grandson, Austin.

11546116R0023

Made in the USA
Lexington, KY
12 October 2011